MARK JACOBS

A Handful of Kings

A NOVEL

Simon & Schuster

NEW YORK LONDON TORONTO SYDNEY

SIMON & SCHUSTER
Rockefeller Center
1230 Avenue of the Americas
New York, NY 10020

This book is a work of fiction. Names, characters,
places, and incidents either are products of the
author's imagination or are used fictitiously. Any
resemblance to actual events or locales or persons,
living or dead, is entirely coincidental.

For information about special discounts for bulk purchases,
please contact Simon & Schuster Special Sales:
1-800-456-6798 or business@simonandschuster.com.

Manufactured in the United States of America

1   3   5   7   9   10   8   6   4   2

Library of Congress Cataloging-in-Publication Data
Jacobs, Mark, date.
A handful of kings : a novel / Mark Jacobs.
p. cm.
1. Attempted assassination—Fiction. 2. Conspiracies—Fiction.
3. Ambassadors—Fiction. I. Title.
PS3560.A2549H36 2004
813'.54—dc22   2003065353

ISBN 0-7432-4590-3

The author and publisher gratefully acknowledge permission from the following source
to reprint material in its control:
University of California Press for Robert Creeley, *The Collected Poems of Robert Creeley, 1945–1975*.
Copyright © 1982/The Regents of the University of California.

for Anne
tu ciudad

Mind's Heart

Mind's heart, it must
be that some
truth lies locked
in you.

Or else, lies, all
lies, and no man
true enough to know
the difference.

—Robert Creeley

A Handful
of Kings

1

An American woman of thirty-three, standing on a very old black iron balcony in a very old Spanish village at night, was supposed to get a serenade, not a tirade. Vicky Sorrell got a tirade. The moon was bright. Night-blooming jasmine on a trellis in the garden below shot up sticks of sweet fragrance in her direction. One street away, a restless dog yapped. It was late. Inside the Claustro Cobalto, everybody was asleep. And below her in the cobbled plaza, totally pissed, Wyatt Willis ragged on her in a voice bigger than he was.

"Goddamn it, Vicky, this is your fault," he shouted up at her. He waited a moment, appreciating the echo of the shout he had loosed in the plaza. Then for some reason he repeated his accusation in Spanish. *"Tú tienes la culpa."*

"Shut up, Wyatt. You'll wake up everybody in the neighborhood." She wondered why she was shouting, too, and why shouting felt so good.

The Claustro Cobalto took up the north end of the plaza. Wyatt yelled something outrageous and insightful linking constant love with constant betrayal, and a light was switched on behind a shutter in a low, dark house in the middle of the south end. He went on for a couple of minutes, then stopped and struggled to come up with the Spanish equivalent. It was a paraphrase, but when he got there his string of accusations sounded even better in Spanish, which was known for its iron categories describing sin and guilt and individual responsibility.

A second light went on inside the bedroom of a house on the little plaza's eastern edge. Vicky and Wyatt were making a scene. They were diplomats. Diplomats were not supposed to cut loose in public—being discreet was one of the rules of the profession. Vicky was tired of obeying the rules of her profession. Wyatt wasn't tired of the rules, he was just drunk. And angrier at her than she had believed it was possible for him to be. In the year and a half that they had been together, she had never heard him shout before. She could not help feeling a sense of accomplishment at being the cause of his explosion.

"Victoria Sorrell," he hollered, "You *tricked* me! You *made* me come here!"

"Here" was a bright white town in a cove on the western nub of the Costa de la Luz. Sor Epi was heavy with history. According to legend, for a brief period at the end of the fifteenth century, paving stones bled in the village, gulls became doves, cooking pots sang, horses grew wings, and the hands of women making love with stone-hearted men turned into flames.

But Vicky was not in the mood to carry the load of grief Wyatt was trying to unload on her. "You're drunk." She pointed out the obvious to him, more loudly than was strictly necessary, to get his attention. "You'll say anything as long as it makes me feel bad and you feel good. Go away. I don't want to talk to you anymore, Wyatt, do you hear me?"

How could he not hear her? If he hadn't provoked her, she would not have put so many decibels behind it.

More lights were being turned on around the plaza. She heard sleepy voices muttering and wooden shutters sliding in wooden casements. Drunk as he was, Wyatt noticed, too, that between them they had woken everybody who lived on the Plaza de la Suprema Visión. *"Tú tienes la culpa,"* he hollered again. As long as they were all awake, he wanted people to know it was her fault, Victoria Sorrell's, the cultural attaché from the American embassy in Madrid. Not his.

"Damned drunk Americans." Vicky heard a man pronounce the sentence. He was leaning out of the window in the front room of his house. In the moonlight his white pajamas took on a spectral sheen. He lit a cigarette. After the match flared, smoke hung like small weather above his head, and he coughed his disapproval.

Behind him in the high, narrow window, his wife finished his sentence for him. "Think they own the world."

Two or three doors down from them, somebody amplified what the wife said, adding his own opinion, and everybody within earshot laughed.

Wyatt loved having an audience. He was a born performer. That was one of the reasons he was so good at his job. Consular officers had to connect with the visa applicants they interviewed even while separated from them by bulletproof glass. The good ones understood public relations as well as they understood consular law. Wyatt Willis was one of the good ones, a one-man refutation of the image of the heartless foreign service officer. But he was used to working on a small stage. Having a whole plaza as his theater went to his head.

Ignoring the sleepers he had woken and playing to them at the same time, he backed his way to the center of the plaza, jumped onto the iron bench that went around the stone fountain, then slipped and almost fell into the pool of water. A few people clapped, not because they wanted to see the American diplomat fall and make a fool of himself, but because Sor Epi was a village, after all, and entertainment was entertainment, and a live-wire walk was better than television any day. Even those who didn't care for the show seemed tolerant of the interruption of their sleep.

Wyatt steadied himself and told anybody who wanted to listen, "It's her fault."

"What's her fault?" Someone helped him along.

"She invited me to come with her to Sor Epi just so she could tell me she was tired of me. We live in Madrid. You know, Madrid, *la capitál de España*? Don Quixote slept there. But this one"—he shook his head, aiming an accusatory finger at Vicky on the black balcony—"this one was afraid to tell me the truth in Madrid. The truth is, she's leaving me. Is that fair? Of course it's not fair. Not after . . ." But then he lost his train of thought.

"An intelligent woman," said one man. From the balcony on the second floor of the *pensión*, Vicky couldn't see where he was, but she respected his point of view, his calm analytical perspective on her relationship with Wyatt.

"I'm being abandoned," Wyatt clarified for everyone.

"Why don't you say it straight?" said a woman. "She dumped you." She sounded like a person who knew all about being dumped.

"It's time for everybody to sleep," another woman decided, less charitable than her neighbors, or less curious. "Even the drunks. Even American drunks."

But Wyatt wasn't willing to give up either his audience or his rear-guard action to keep Vicky from leaving him. Jumping down from the bench he wobbled a little, then made a slow, crazy-legs circuit around the plaza like a dancer who didn't know much about choreography; he had the moves, but nowhere to put them. As he circled he went on ragging. He must have realized it didn't matter much if most of what he said to her came out in English. His Spanish was unraveling, but no one had any difficulty following his end of the story.

Vicky's Spanish, by contrast, stayed impeccable under stress. Even the difficult tenses came out correctly, and she had all the vocabulary the situation called for. She knew she had to play her part in Wyatt's public spectacle with conviction or everyone would be disappointed. And if they were disappointed she would lose their sympathy. As it was, it seemed to her that the population around the Plaza of the Supreme Vision—they were all awake by now, including little children—had roughly divided their sympathy between jilter and jilted. It was impossible to say for sure, but there seemed to be no gender bias in the breakdown. Some of the men were clearly taking Vicky's side, while a handful of the women made clucking noises of solidarity every time Wyatt stopped to breathe.

Vicky wasn't sure why she cared to have their sympathy, except that Wyatt had made it a contest, and she didn't like to lose contests.

"I'm coming up," he warned her when the play began to lose its appeal to the villagers. Wyatt had a phenomenal feel for people's reactions to him. That was partly why he was so good at his job. Even drunk, even desperate, he knew when it was time to stop performing.

"Don't come up," she told him in Spanish. "It's over, Wyatt. *Se acabó.*"

It came out peremptory and cruel. The force of her words made him stagger to the bench by the fountain, where he collapsed. His shoulders sagged. His weeping was the real thing. But even the women who sympathized with the handsome young American diplomat remembered that they were tired, and that morning came early along the Costa de la Luz, and that the drama they were watching belonged, after all, to somebody else. After a few moments, before Vicky left the balcony and went inside the room she had shared with Wyatt, he was crying without an audience.

Wyatt was right. Vicky had lured him to Sor Epi to tell him it was over. In retrospect she realized it was a stupid way to go about doing what she had decided to do. The village was too small. They couldn't get away from each other in Sor Epi. They were the only English speakers within a radius of ten kilometers. But she had worried about telling him in Madrid, where Wyatt had too many friends. He would have enlisted them to help fight her decision, which he would go on believing was a whim that could be undone with the right word, if only he could find it, say it, make her hear it. He would have sent envoys to her apartment to persuade her to try again. And Vicky, notwithstanding her enjoyment of the scene in the plaza, was a person who preferred to conduct her private life out of sight of the rest of the world. Inside the embassy community, she and Wyatt were tagged. They were an item. Even Ambassador Duffey made something of a deal out of inviting them both to official dinners.

So she talked Wyatt into a long weekend away from the embassy and told him in a sherry bar, "I'm leaving."

Her decisiveness cut like the real thing. It sliced him in two, coming out of her mouth like hardness of heart. She had overcompensated. All she wanted was for him to acknowledge that she was serious, but she hit her target and then some.

Wyatt, being Wyatt, needed to hear the specifics. "Do you mean leaving the bar? Leaving Sor Epi? Are you trying to tell me you're leaving *me*, Vicky?"

"I'm leaving the foreign service." If he didn't get it, he didn't want to get it. That much, at least, was not her fault.

Half a small glass of sherry was percolating through his system. His laugh was a nervous bark. The snapping sound caused the wall-eyed bartender in La Viñalesca to look harder in the other direction, scrupulously away from their messy domestic comedy, the sort of stormy relationship you saw in the imported television series that people in the village watched every week.

La Viñalesca was maybe the only sherry bar in Spain that had not been written up in the guidebooks. The wood of the tables and chairs, the wood of the bar and the casks behind it, the dry, smooth wood of the floorboards had outlasted political change and fashion shifts and intergenerational strife. Even the grime on the posters commemorating thirty years of sherry festivals in Andalusia had the appearance of an artifact preserved.

When Vicky saw that Wyatt was unwilling to take in what she was telling him, she pushed, forcing him to hear the details that proved she was serious about breaking up. "When we get back to Madrid, I'm sending the papers to Washington. I filled them out last weekend. It's happening, Wyatt. My foreign service career is over."

"You can't." He was shaking his head slowly as though even considering the prospect made it ache. "You're the only patriot in the foreign service, Vicky."

He tried to hang on to normalcy, passed her the crockery plate of olives before taking one himself. For the moment he was calm, almost detached, as though they were discussing the quality of the sherry he poured from the dark bottle into her light glass. Then he rocked back on the hind legs of his round-shouldered chair, brought it to rest on the floor again, and drummed the fingers of both hands on the surface of the wooden table like a honky-tonk piano man. She saw understanding go through him like a shudder.

"This isn't about my patriotism," she said. "It's about—"

But he wouldn't let her finish. "Now is exactly not the time to leave the service. Now is when they need people like you. You know what I mean—I'm talking about the terrorist thing, Vicky."

"What do terrorists have to do with my leaving?"

"If people like you leave, all we'll have left in the embassies are the bureaucrats and the action junkies. Spooks, drug busters, visa-fraud hounds. And people who fill out forms. They'll get the terrorists all right, sooner or later, but there's a cost."

"What's the cost?"

He frowned at his *fino* glass, as if the fault lay in the sherry, not in the woman whose love he was trying to hold on to. "People think Americans are one-dimensional. You're living proof that we're better than they know."

"I think you should stop pretending," she told him quietly.

He flared. "Who's pretending? You're the best thing the embassy has to show to the world, bar none. What? You think we ought to give up and let the hard-boiled guys like Marc Karulevich run everything? I'm sorry, I didn't sign up to hunker inside Fortress America, I signed up to represent the country."

She thought keeping it simple was an act of kindness. "I'm sorry it didn't work for us, Wyatt, I really am."

"Goddamn it, Vicky." His hands flung air toward the walls of the bar. He pushed back his chair, and she was left sitting at the table.

Under the bartender's nonjudgmental eye she waited for a while, expecting Wyatt to return, which was the reasonable thing to do. Wyatt was a reasonable man. She drank a little more *fino*, but eventually she realized he was not coming back.

Leaving La Viñalesca, she walked toward the central square, which was dominated by the church named after Sister Epifanía, the wandering woman whose religious visions gave the village its name and identity and its footnote in the Spanish history books.

Vicky wasn't looking for him, but that was where she found Wyatt, hands folded on a bench installed to permit contemplation. The sky was purple, mottled dark with clouds whose rims still reflected the sun's last light.

In the air above the cobbled plaza and the big church, bats whizzed through the quiet night air. A large boy of twelve or so, wearing short pants and a pressed white shirt that somehow suggested the enforced conformity of the Franco era, watched his ice cream cone melt and drip onto the ground as though he couldn't imagine how to stop it. From a second-story window in a building down an alley of whitewashed walls, six or eight measures of a Strauss waltz were offered and then withdrawn, like a clever idea announced at an inconvenient time. Somewhere else, a woman laughed self-consciously, then stopped. A breeze from the beach picked up and strewed sea smells across the town.

"Nice night," Vicky tried.

"Somebody ought to teach that kid how you eat ice cream." Wyatt pointed. "Look at that getup."

"It's the return of the repressed," she explained. "Under Franco all the kids had to dress like that. It was like a loyalty oath."

The child threw his ruined ice cream cone on the ground and lumbered off, unchildlike and unhappily massive. Vicky watched him move reluctantly as though summoned by the warning whistle of a tyrant father. She imagined an anachronism of a man who wore scented oil in his dark hair and a wide belt he was ready to take off at the least provocation to remind his disappointing son what discipline felt like. Vicky sat next to Wyatt on his bench.

"It's me, isn't it? I mean that's why you're quitting."

"It's everything," she said. "I'm tired of being official. Of being on all the time, like some kind of human cable channel. I'm tired of smiling on command, and pretending that boring people are interesting. I want to say what I think whenever I think it, without editing every last comment for foreign consumption. I'm tired of catering to ambassadors. Mostly, I think, I'm really tired of life inside the bureaucracy. I'm changing my life."

"That's a cliché."

"So I'm a cliché. I never said I was going to stay in the foreign service forever."

Saying it, she imagined for the first time what it was going to feel like to surrender her black passport, which advised anyone who cared to read it that the bearer was abroad on a diplomatic assignment for the United States government. She was giving up her guild identity. A sensation of loss washed over her, leaving a residue of maudlin feeling that Wyatt would call her patriotism. She believed in service to one's country, and in not talking about service to one's country.

"What about me?" he wanted to know.

"You're where you should be. You love the work. It gives you satisfaction. There's not enough of you to go around. At high levels of the State Department there's serious talk of cloning Wyatt Willis."

"Now who's avoiding the hard stuff?"

"Okay," she agreed. "No avoidance. Here it is straight on, Wyatt. I'm not ready to live the rest of my life with you."

He nodded as if that were a just and reasonable conclusion to eighteen interesting months of trying each other on for size. Then he stood quickly and left her a second time. It was too easy. She should have known he wasn't going to give up without a fight, but she pretended for a few minutes that the hard part was over, that it was just a question of direct communication, and she had done her difficult duty. She didn't get up from the bench in the plaza until the dark thickened around her. She felt bruised, the quick blowback from telling Wyatt she was leaving Spain and the service and him, too, and the darkness comforted her as if she were a child swaddled in infinite folds. She traced her way slowly along narrow streets that were fronted on either side by whitewashed high walls to El Claustro Cobalto, two stones' throw from the beach.

In the room she had been sharing with Wyatt, she took off her shoes, her jeans, her blouse, and lay on her back on the bed. The room was small, exactly what you'd expect a cell to be like. Until the last habited nun was taken out in a wheelchair to another level of contemplative isolation, the hotel had been a convent for an order of religious women who took the vow of silence. Past ten at night, if you knew what you were listening for, sometimes you heard the hard rubber wheels of the poor palsied sister's chair going over gravel to an undisclosed location. Trading on atmosphere, the owner of the place had left the nuns' austere crucifixes affixed to the otherwise bare white walls of the rooms he rented out.

The mattress on the bed was a lump, like Spanish mattresses from the Inquisition right up through the Franco era. The theory underlying the mattresses was to affect sleepers' dreams, recognized since Plato as incubators of political dissent. But Vicky's mind was not on politics. Having told Wyatt it was over, now she wanted to make love with him. They both deserved it, they needed it. She was sure they both wanted it.

The sherry made her doze. When the sound of gravel against the window woke her, she got up to find Wyatt drunk in the plaza below, spoiling for a fight and an audience and a way back into the castle keep of her affections.

He was quieter when he came into the room, almost calm, but the fight was not yet taken out of him. He stabbed the air once, impaled an invisible attacker. She admired his resolve. He wasn't giving up. He smelled of sweat and Scotch whiskey.

"This room is half mine," he challenged her.

"Wyatt," she began.

"Shut up, Vicky. Just shut up. You've said fucking enough already."

In the cozy blur of the green-shaded lamp on the bedside table she watched him undress. His manner was formal and deliberate. He was a private exhibitionist. Wyatt had the body of a Spanish bullfighter who didn't need to work out, a strawberry blond *torero* with gray-ice English eyes. The hair on his chest was closer to blond than brown, a tight-weave carpet on which she was accustomed to rest.

He made love with freedom and a spirit of play to make it plain to her exactly what she was giving up. As if she didn't know. She tried to give back as good as she got, which was good indeed. She licked the sweat from his skin, memorized the taste of it, let herself be licked through an unhurried buildup of sensation too powerful to be called feeling. Feeling was reconstruction, how you thought about it afterward.

"Don't do this to me, Vicky," he said once. "Please."

"Can I tell you something important?"

"You changed your mind. You *do* want to stay with me forever. I knew it. That whole thing about leaving the service was just a fantasy. You were just thinking out loud. Right?"

He wasn't straining for a bad joke, he believed what he was saying. She felt culpable, almost treasonous, for having made a smart, sensitive man go blind and stupid. If he was a little pathetic now, if he was afraid to face the one hard fact she held up to him, it really was her fault. She was lashed to her lover with thick cords of responsibility, and all she could think about was cutting free.

She told him, "My father was a spy."

"My mother was a bareback rider in the circus."

"I'm serious," she told him, but he thought she was only constructing an analogy, an obscure way of explaining her selfish decision to abandon the foreign service and bliss with him.

"It's not about whether I love you, Wyatt."

He sat up, excited on the way to angry again. "Yes, it is, Vicky. That's the thing, you just don't get it."

"What don't I get?"

"It's always about love. It's only about love. All the rest is just . . . politics."

In the cavernous dark in the nun's cell, he turned toward her in the bed. With a hand that owned nothing, not even the touch it took, he felt down her back. It felt good, it felt to her like the one sensation she could not live without, as necessary as oxygen, but more reassuring.

Wyatt was wrong about one thing. She got it. She knew.

Always and only. It was about love.

2

Sprawled on his back next to her in the uncomfortable bed, Wyatt was snoring like any old drunk, inhaling air in big, irregular gulps and forcing it out in a compressed stream that made him sound like an exhaust pipe with a hole in it. Vicky got out of bed carefully so he wouldn't wake. Standing, she felt a little of Wyatt's semen leak down the inside of her left thigh and wished she had not made love with him. He knew what he was doing: trapping her with passion, making it harder to get away. And she *had* to get away, before the artificial gravity of embassy life weighed her down for good. That was what she was most afraid of. Moving around the world, she would become a cliché, an FSO with war stories, a facility in several languages, and a highly developed ability not to feel.

She had been in the service long enough to be able to picture in vivid detail what would happen if she stayed on. Her life would disappear, subdivided into three-year tours of duty, while she and Wyatt juggled their competitive careers inside a succession of American embassy compounds around the world. She saw them facing one another in government-issue wing-backed chairs, drinks in hand, trading gossip about people they disliked. She saw them skillfully humoring ambassadors who had little humor of their own, escorting congressional delegations on shopping junkets, shaking hands with strangers in a thousand reception lines. She imagined them attending insular dinner parties where the conversation was so predictably dull that it made her want to cry, or shoot a spitball at the minister-counselor for political affairs, or fall off her chair, pretending she was choking on a chicken bone, so she could ride in a foreign ambulance away, away, anywhere away.

Sitting at the defunct sister's severely plain wooden desk, she lifted the screen of her laptop and waited for the machine to boot. The air was cool and dry. The village was quiet. It was too late for the dogs, too early for the roosters. The compliant hum of the CPU and the artificial glow of the screen were out of place in Sor Epi, in the bedroom of a nun whose life had been devoted to prayer and abnegation of the hungry self, but Vicky had to read her mother's message again. Twenty times wasn't enough.

This is like opening my mouth and finding another voice coming out of it. If you weren't in Spain, I would never have bothered with email. The reason I'm writing now is to tell you something about your blood father. You ought to know, your line of work being what it is. I think he was a spy. I don't mean he was lying about being an agronomist. There was something about Mr. William Tipton, the way he was outdoors and around animals, that he had no reason to fake. Anyway why shouldn't the CIA sign up a farmer?

Bill and I got married in a rush. All I remember is lilacs and magnolias and no Tiptons. Your father said his people were peculiar, which was easy to believe because we never heard from them once. When USAID sent him to Vietnam I was all wrapped up learning how to be mother to a baby girl by the name of Victoria, so I made it easy on him. I remember telling him not to stand close to anyone in pajamas because loose-fitting clothes made it easy to conceal a weapon. Anyway here is the long and the short of it: after eleven months I received word that he had been killed in the line of duty. They sent someone out in person to tell me. He left me a letter explaining everything. Then two weeks later another letter showed up. The information in the second letter contradicted the first letter. I called the man who signed the first letter.

The next two people they sent out to see me could not have been more apologetic, but they couldn't explain the contradictions between their letters. They should have picked one version and stuck with it. I would have swallowed that, but I guess I needed a project. I took you with me on the bus to Red Flats, Iowa, which is where Bill Tipton claimed to be from, and lo and behold, there were no Tiptons to be had. When I got back, the secretary I called at USAID put me on hold and came back with a story that sounded like she was practicing from notes.

I was angry. I blamed everybody, LBJ, Robert McNamara, the generals and the spymasters and the arms makers. Also, don't ask me why, Dan Rather. Most of all I blamed William Tipton. I could understand living a lie in the service of your country. But not under your own roof, in your own bed. Enough, agreed? I've surprised you. I surprised myself, too. I thought I had stopped being angry. Maybe knowing your father was a spy changes everything, maybe it changes nothing. Things are different for you. It's a different kind of danger, isn't it? I try not to worry about terrorists. I know it's a big world, and you can't just quit living and hide, and I believe that people in your embassy must know how to protect their people.

Twenty-one times was enough. Vicky deleted the message and powered down the computer. She thought of her mother in Leesburg, Virginia, unwilling to forgive a man who had been dead almost as long as Vicky had been alive. But learning about her father's master lie made Vicky feel resentful more than angry. She had been cheated. She had been told an uplifting story about her father, the Iowa farmer, who gave his life in the service not just of his country but of people trapped inside a nightmare war who didn't have enough to eat.

When she thought about William Tipton she always imagined him on the muddy edge of a rice paddy, talking production technique in passable Vietnamese with a shy, barefoot peasant farmer while naked children ran around their father's legs and aggressive black chickens foraged in sparkling grass. Mr. Tipton had something to offer to the shy man, he had something worthwhile to share, politics be damned. He knew practical things about growing rice and improving drainage and doctoring sick hogs. That was what he was doing, sharing what he knew, when an anonymous assassin—a Viet Cong soldier or just a sympathizer, it didn't make any difference— shot him from behind. Mr. Tipton fell forward into the arms of the barefoot rice farmer. There was a kind of nobility in the way he went, wrapped in an intimate bloody embrace with the man whose life he had gone to Southeast Asia to improve.

Vicky didn't mind learning late that her father had worked for the CIA. It wasn't even the lie so much, as it had been for her mother; as it still was for Edna Sorrell in Leesburg. What bothered Vicky was losing the story she had believed in for so long.

Reacting to Bill Tipton's betrayal, Vicky realized now, her mother had married his opposite. Dan Sorrell was a CPA, a Rotarian who followed the Baltimore Orioles, win or lose, who calculated and recorded the mileage he got with every tank of gas he had bought since he was sixteen. Dan was not the kind of man to travel undercover anywhere, let alone Vietnam. Adopting Vicky was a happy chapter in the one and only life story he had any interest in, which was not a fabrication but a solid construction, built brick by solid brick and with a brass number plate on the door.

Dan treated Vicky well. He gave her his name and called her his daughter. His expectations were minimal and sensible. She was good with people. He thought she might study to become a social worker. But Vicky had no interest in social work or any of the other careers that people were always suggesting she investigate. There was powerful romance in the story of the Iowa agronomist murdered in Vietnam, and enough vagueness in the details that she was able to fill them in with colors from her private palette. Dan strongly opposed her joining the foreign service. The work, like the locations where it went on, lay outside the boundaries of his imagination, which was rooted in Leesburg. Her mother didn't mind Vicky's leaving home so much, and she admired her independence the way another parent might admire a child's skill on ice skates. But Edna's priority was preserving the link of feeling that kept her daughter and her second husband banded together in a family unit that was anything but a lie. If Vicky joined what Dan called the foreign legion, he might interpret the decision as a lack of gratitude.

But Vicky persisted. She aced the difficult entrance exam and went to Washington and learned languages and became a diplomat. Unaware of what she wanted to achieve until she got there, she realized, eventually, that she had made herself a character in William Tipton's exotic family legend. She was what happened next.

It got old. Madrid was her fourth overseas assignment. It was time to leave when she found herself fantasizing shooting spitballs at a dinner party. She had made up her mind to quit, and to leave Wyatt. And then her mother sent an email informing her that her biological father was a fraud. The story that William Tipton had started, the one she had taken over for herself, was a kind of cheat. Without it, she thought, she was back to nowhere. She had to start over.

What scared her was not having any words.

3

It was J. J. Baines's fault that Vicky didn't leave Madrid. She held that against the American writer, whose overinflated personality got in the way when he tried to make nice with her. Baines didn't seem to know how to behave the way normal human beings behaved with one another. When he opened his mouth to speak he put the emphasis on the wrong emotional syllable, creating a strangely dissonant language of his own that was hard to listen to, and harder still to interpret. She wondered whether the defect came from being a writer or the writer came from the defect.

The ride back to the city from Sor Epi was long, boring, and lonesome. Vicky and Wyatt had driven down to the coast in his car, a high-performance dark green Opel that he loved. But he refused to make the return trip in the same vehicle with her. After they checked out of the Claustro Cobalto, standing in the plaza in which he had entertained the villagers a few hours earlier, he handed her the keys to the Opel with a flourish of surrender.

"Can't do it," he said.

"You can't do what?"

"Not me, you. You can't make me drive with you back to Madrid. It's cruel and unusual, and I don't have to do it."

"That's stupid, Wyatt."

"Nope," he corrected her. "Stupid is walking away from love when it's as good as it is between you and me. That's what stupid is, Vicky."

Wearing traditional mourning black, a small, shriveled woman who looked a hundred years old was sweeping the stones in front of her door on the far side of the Plaza of the Supreme Vision. When Wyatt raised his voice she lifted her broom, shaded her eyes, and stared in their direction. She appeared to want more of whatever it was the Americans were providing, but the show was almost over.

Wyatt shouldered his backpack and trudged downhill toward the bus station. At the far edge of the plaza he stopped and turned back to look at Vicky. The sweeping woman was still waiting, maybe hoping he would speak in Spanish as he had done during his exhibition the night before.

But he didn't. "I know you, Victoria Sorrell," he called.

Vicky wasn't going to give him any help, not in public, anyway. She waited to see what would happen. It was Sunday. Dressed for mass in a white frock and yellow hair ribbons, a girl of about ten had joined the old woman in *luto*—widow's weeds. She clutched her grandmother's black skirt and stared at the two foreigners whose conversation was like a long-distance phone call being played out by actors.

"You think there's something better out there somewhere, don't you, Vicky. Better than me. Well, there's not. I'm as good as it gets. All I ask is you do me one small favor, later on. Before we're both dead."

"What do you want me to do, Wyatt?"

"Let me know when you figure that out."

"Please don't take the bus, Wyatt," she asked him again, but he was already moving downhill on the dark cobbles, which were still wet with dew. The girl in the white frock ran to watch him go. The old woman in black went back to her sweeping.

Nothing about Jack Baines added up. Probably that was why Vicky said yes to him when he called her at the embassy on Monday morning. He let the name dangle a little to be sure it registered. It registered all right—it dropped into the slot exactly as he intended it to drop.

"This is Jack Baines," he told her. "I'd like to talk to the cultural attaché."

His voice made a reasonable request sound like a donation to the needy. In two short sentences he established his superior vantage. The way he spoke gave the impression that anywhere he looked was downhill from where Jack Baines happened to be standing. His impatience was accomplished, probably an acquired skill. She already knew she didn't like him.

"I'm Victoria Sorrell," she admitted.

But she caught herself. What was wrong with being Vicky Sorrell? What was wrong with being the American cultural affairs officer in the U.S. embassy in Madrid? She was not going to be put so easily on the defensive by an offensive telephone caller with a famous name and a blinking neon attitude.

"So what's your gig, Victoria?"

"I don't think I understand."

"I mean are you a poet? A painter? Underwater basket weaver? How does a person get to be cultural attaché in Spain?"

"I'm a foreign service officer."

Waiting to hear what he wanted from her, she couldn't help sizing herself up as a character in a J. J. Baines story. She was not about to tell him that she owned hardcover first editions of all his books, or that his fiction had figured in her decision to join the foreign service. Baines's writing converted the world outside American walls into a mystery whose center a person just might penetrate, if she went about trying the right way. The women in his stories were generally more appealing than the men. There was more depth to their dimensions, more play in their intellect, more healthy fiber in their emotional diet. She wondered how much of that was literary calculation and how much was authentic.

"I'm catching you at a bad time," he told her. "I'm sorry."

She was sure he didn't know how to be sorry. "That's okay," she said. "I have a few minutes."

"I mean a bad time for the official culture business. It's been a downhill slide since Duke Ellington crossed the Soviet Union in a club car to combat communism, no? My theory is the Politburo knew the music was subversive, but they just couldn't say no."

"Is this an interview or an editorial? I'm not sure where you're going with this, Mr. Baines."

"Jeez, you talk like a diplomat. Do they send you to school to learn how to put the starch in it? Jack, call me Jack. We're both plain old Americans. Listen, I'm not going anywhere, I'm here to stay. Believe it or not, pretty soon you'll come to like me."

"I doubt it."

"That's the spirit. A little candor from government officials is always refreshing. Will you answer a question for me?"

"I don't think I like you."

This was new. New was good. Before she made the decision to leave the foreign service, Vicky would never have spoken so bluntly. She would have muzzled herself and sent Baines a mixed message. She would have kept taking it until he got tired of dishing it out. She felt a small sensation of liberation that was definitely worth repeating.

"That's okay," Baines told her. He seemed genuinely to want to reassure her. "Very few people like me. They love my books, but they don't have a kind word to say about the man who wrote them. Rourke likes me. Levy likes me. But they're writers, and they're both assholes. Compared to those guys I'm a prince, and they know it."

"I have to go. I'm on my way to a meeting."

"That's a pretty thin lie, Victoria."

"Then tell me what you want from me."

"For now, just a little civilized conversation. This will all make sense eventually. By the way, subsidizing Allen Ginsberg to go around the world banging his big queer drum was smart, very smart. Those were the days. You're too young to remember, I can tell by your voice."

"You called to ask me how old I am?"

"Now you've got CNN, you've got twenty-four-hour global Disney, you've got universal McCulture. And everybody hates us. They hate the shit out of us."

"What's your point, Jack?"

"Guess there's not much the official culture mavens can do, is there? I mean against all that heavily armed hostility."

"We do what we can. That's my job. Talking about America."

"I'd like to help."

"Why don't I believe you?"

"You don't believe me because you're having the same negative reaction to me that most people do. But I really want to think you can get past it, Vicky. Are you willing to try?"

When he asked her to host a reception for him, she assumed the reason he gave her was a lie but couldn't guess his real intention. J. J. Baines was entering the reaping phase of his career. Everything that happened came out as harvest, as triumph, as confirmation of his mighty voice. On the strength of earlier books, his last collection of short stories had won grand prizes. He told her he had been in Barcelona to talk about the Spanish edition of another book, a Baines reader with critical essays by half a dozen name-brand Europeans. It was true that the serious publishing action was in Catalonia, and he might well want to have a look at the first Baines reader in Spanish. But why would he make a side trip to the capital to talk about his fiction with whatever group of culture vultures Vicky was able to put together?

"You don't buy it," he said. "I can tell by your voice."

"I don't buy it."

"But you'll do it anyway?"

She resisted, just as a Baines character would instinctively hesitate before diving down into the murk.

"It takes time to put something like that together," she pointed out. "The important *madrileños* you'd want to have are hard to get on short notice. If you come back to Spain, give us a call ahead of time and we can do it the right way."

She didn't bother to tell him that if he came back to Madrid she'd be gone. He didn't need to know she was quitting. If she told him, he would start asking prying questions. She would refuse to answer them. Both their time would be wasted.

But he told her, "Forget important people. Important people bore me, Victoria. Concentrate on interesting."

He didn't need the modest puffery any crowd she could assemble might offer up. Maybe he was after a pretext to spend some time in Madrid for a personal reason. A woman? A man? She didn't know whether he was married. In any event he was not likely to take this much trouble to concoct an alibi. He gave her the impression of being a man who did not play by many rules. J. J. Baines didn't wait in lines, or ask anybody's permission to live his life. He didn't punch anybody else's clock.

"I don't have a representational apartment," she warned him.

"What in hell is a representational apartment?"

"A place that's big enough and fancy enough to do serious entertaining in."

"Your guests will be charmed by your unassuming style," he assured her.

She hated being lied to; it seemed like insulting her intelligence. Like a J. J. Baines character, she said yes, finally, because her attraction to what she didn't understand overcame her distrust. It would take awhile for the paperwork to be processed so she could leave Spain. Even though she didn't like Baines, she thought she wouldn't mind meeting the writer in person.

On the Friday morning of the reception, getting her apartment ready for the reception before she went to the embassy, Vicky considered hiding her Baines books. She moved them to her bedroom, but before she left for work she put them back in place in plain view on the bookshelf in the living room where she normally kept them.

Jack Baines respected certain forms. He showed up ten minutes before her cultural crowd did with a bird of paradise flower under one arm and a breezy demeanor. He was fifty, he was writerly slick, he was psychically dangerous. He wore his dark hair long. His shirt was purple, his jeans were pressed, his shoes were expensive, the kind of shoes Eric Clapton might wear because the money wasn't really the point.

"I really appreciate your doing this," he told her as he surrendered the flowers in her foyer. "Even if you don't like me. Even if you consider me untrustworthy before we've even met. I'm working on my people skills, Vicky. In the second half of my life I'm going to be known as a decent guy."

"Decent guys talk straight," she said, then wished she hadn't. Baines was not the kind of person to let an opportunity to hit back get past him.

"Whoa," he held up a hand. "Let's not go overboard. You don't strike me as a puritan. I bet you have excellent cornering instincts. Did you ever drive a race car?"

When the doorbell rang she was relieved not to have to bat heavy pleasantries back and forth with him any longer. She wasn't sure but thought he might be the sort of man who couldn't hold a conversation with a woman, any woman, and not try to make it a conquest. She had no interest in becoming a notch on whatever stick of wood he recorded his kills.

The party was proof, if she needed any, of the anesthetizing power of diplomatic service. The internal switch was flipped, and she was on. She smiled appropriately. She moved around her apartment as though it were a playing field and she was coaching both teams. She shook hands, listened attentively to punch lines, offered snippets of commentary on subjects that mattered to her guests in a rhythm that felt like cutting and pasting on the computer. She knew exactly where to insert the right text. This was the part of her that Wyatt admired, it was why he thought she was good at her job. And probably she was. Her bosses were convinced she was. She had been promoted through the ranks as fast as the regulations permitted. With every posting she was given increasing responsibility. A career glittered in front of her.

But not a life. She felt herself shrinking to fit the part she played. The better she became at her job, the more efficient, the less she liked it. It was not so much that the work owned her, or took up her time. It was the silting-up she could feel going on. There was a river. Sometimes she thought she was the river, sometimes just that she was riding it. But with every assignment, every command performance for an imperious ambassador, every airless, overlong meeting she sat through, she became aware that the bottom of the river was filling up. If she didn't do something drastic, if she just waited, kept on doing what she had been doing, sooner or later silt would stop the river's flow. She wasn't going to wait. She wasn't going to drown in silt.

Her apartment was on the seventh floor of a building near the Bilbao roundabout. There was no wind. Dry June heat hung on through the evening, but she had turned off the air conditioner. She threw open all her windows as well as the door to the tiny terrace overlooking the bepigeoned plaza, where people seeking relief from summer posed for an urban postcard, the kind of view her friends at home assumed her life was about.

She watched Baines cruising the reception like a shark in a school of slow fish. She took a glass of *fino* from the Moroccan waiter she had hired to serve her guests, who drank alcohol and ate finger food at a prodigious rate. The waiter, new to Spain, rushed morosely to keep up with the crowd she had assembled. Someone noticed a Mercedes Sosa album on a shelf and shoved the CD into Vicky's player. She was buffeted by surges of animated conversation, then dropped in a temporary trough. A Bolivian from Cochabamba took her arm and asked her whether she had ever chewed coca leaves; it was a shame that the North Americans failed to respect the jurisdiction of local gods. A Paraguayan told her a bad joke about Argentines. A woman from Paramaribo with low-watt black eyes and canary-colored high heels rehearsed her proposition about the superiority of coastal cultures over those of the mountains.

But the Latin Americans on Vicky's guest list stood out uncomfortably from the casual Spaniards in her apartment. She had seen people like them before, Bolivians and Colombians and Uruguayans who appeared surreptitious and suspicious at the same time. They didn't trust their luck. A stint in the glittery ordered chaos of Madrid was a reward for services rendered, or a providential dispensation.

Despúes de Madrid, el cielo, the *madrileños* said. After Madrid, heaven. The Latinos who washed up there wanted to believe it. But they couldn't get past their ambivalence about the colonizing motherland, and they assumed the Spaniards were lying when they told them that anti-Latino discrimination was a thing of the past, all Franco's fault and Franco was dead, thank God.

"It's a hit," Baines took time out from cruising to tell Vicky in the trough. "You're a hit, Victoria Sorrell. I'm grateful."

Vicky disliked the shine in his eyes, and his larcenous cocktail stalk, and his high-priced casual shoes. She disliked his presumption that he understood more of what was going on in her living room than anyone else did, including her.

She shook her head. "This doesn't make sense to me."

"Did it ever occur to you I might just feel lonely, being in Spain on my own? Not everything has to be complicated."

"You were lonely, so you decided a cocktail party with a bunch of strangers you'll never see again would make you feel better?"

The yellow-heeled woman from Paramaribo was waiting for Baines to notice her slink, her style, her wondrous beige complexion. It was clear that he preferred talking with Vicky, but she shook free, pretending she thought he wanted to go flirt with the Venezuelan.

The reception was a flop, from Vicky's point of view. The handful of Madrid people who showed up kept to themselves, uncertain why they had been tapped to keep company with a writer of the stature of J. J. Baines. They didn't mix much with the Latin American crowd, who asked the writer deferential questions and seemed to be trying to memorize his answers, which he offered the practiced way the Moroccan offered roasted pepper strips wrapped around nuggets of Manchego cheese. Baines's Spanish was clear and comfortable. He wore the language as though it were a decoration, the Order of the Tongue, First Class, using a screen of friendly accessibility to condescend to everyone in the room. J. J. Baines, Vicky decided, would be impossible to live with.

She was relieved when it was over. She hoped Baines would leave with the guests, but he hung back to perform his thanks.

"I assume you didn't buy the books in honor of the occasion," he said, pointing to her shelf. "You don't strike me as that type of person."

She shook her head.

"I'll sign them if you like."

"That's okay."

"Good," he nodded.

Without trying, she had come up with a response he respected.

"How come you joined the foreign service?" he wanted to know, as though being a writer gave him the right to inquire and get an answer.

"Do you want another drink before the waiter leaves?" she asked him reluctantly. "I joined the service for the same reason a sailor goes to sea."

"To see the world," he nodded. "To see the other side. I get it. Yes, please, I'll have a glass of water."

She escaped to the kitchen to tell Hasan they wanted two glasses of mineral water with a slice of lemon and to pay the man. She had learned that it was proper to tuck the money into an envelope, as if disguising the nature of the transaction were basic good manners even a coarse American could learn. The waiter was wiping sweat from his face with the dish towel her mother had sent her at Christmas, a sprightly yellow print. Hasan looked at her as though she were responsible for the contemporary Spanish social order, inside which he found himself trapped with insufficient cash to cover his reasonable aspirations. His smile cracked, and she felt bad for him. She wished she had something to say to him besides, "Thank you very much, Hasan. It went well, I think. May I call you again?"

The Moroccan nodded severely, and she went back to Baines.

"It was a great party, Victoria," the writer tried to convince her.

"But?"

"I was a little surprised you didn't invite any of your embassy friends. Aren't they supposed to come out and show the flag at this kind of thing?"

It was an exchange of small-arms fire. Vicky shot one back at him.

"You want me to believe you're disappointed I didn't include the embassy crowd? That's stretching it, Jack."

"I'm just a little surprised. I was looking forward to talking with them. I'd like to know what makes diplomats tick. Who wouldn't? That's okay, there will be another occasion."

She changed her mind. Telling him would make her decision seem real. "Not hosted by me there won't be. I'm leaving Spain."

"Is this a way of avoiding me? You can admit it, if it is. My feelings don't get hurt anymore. I'm used to people looking for ways to steer clear of me. They don't usually leave the country when I show up, but who knows?"

He shrugged and played distractedly with his empty glass. He looked at her to make sure she knew he was communicating something difficult, or sincere, or else that the conversation was code for something more serious that she would definitely care to learn. She wanted to believe he was capable of being honest, but didn't think now was the time.

She shook her head. "It's a long story."

"I like long stories. To be able to tell good stories, you have to listen to lots of them."

"How long will you be in Madrid?" she asked.

He knew she meant, when are you leaving? But he did not take offense.

"I'm here for a while, I guess. I was seventy pages into a new manuscript before I realized the walls in my apartment in New York were hostile to it. That can be devastating, especially toward the beginning of a book. It kills your forward motion."

"And the walls of your hotel room here are more sympathetic to your plot?"

"A willing suspension of disbelief, that's all I ask from the space where I write."

"It still doesn't make a lot of sense to me."

"Do you want everything in your life to make sense?"

"Not necessarily. But I would like to know what you're after."

He shrugged again, dismissing all of her assumptions about everything.

"I'm after what writers are always after, a new book. I write all day, but then I crave a little human contact. I want to get to know you. You'll be around for a while, right? I mean you're not leaving tomorrow morning."

Not tomorrow morning, she admitted. When he left the apartment, she picked up her copy of *Mario Moving*. She had read the novel while she studied Spanish in Washington before she went to Honduras, her first post. The story had stayed with her. Jack's Bolivian hero Mario Mamani was as real to her as realpolitik, and more compelling. While she was in the kitchen with Hasan, Baines had autographed the book. *For Vicky, the cultural attaché, with gratitude, Jack Baines.*

It didn't add up. Like any Baines character, she liked the challenge of working on a problem of faulty math. At that point she still thought she wasn't going to be around to figure it out.

4

When he left Vicky Sorrell's apartment, Jack Baines was afraid to go back to his hotel. He walked a hundred yards to the traffic roundabout and stood on the edge of the circle waiting for a taxi. But as the driver of a yellow Peugeot slowed to pick him up, Jack waved him off, and the man gestured at him with what the American assumed was the Spanish equivalent of the finger.

"Fuck you," he waved back.

He didn't normally curse taxi drivers. On certain days, if the wrong person provoked him, he could be an unpleasant person. He admitted that, but he was not an asshole the way some writers he knew were full-time, major-league assholes. These were special circumstances. His nerves were worse than frayed. If there was somebody keeping track of his sins, he ought to be forgiven this one. He couldn't just go docilely back to the luxurious isolation of the Palace Hotel and wait like a sheep until they decided whether to keep squeezing him or to kill him.

"Fuck you," he called to the driver of the Peugeot again. Then he changed his mind. He called, "Hey, I'm sorry," but the taxi was gone.

On one edge of the Bilbao roundabout there was a small park. No greenery, but there were benches and pigeons and a handful of people civilizing the city space with gossip and flirtation and slow cups of coffee. He walked over and sat on an empty bench. Across from the seat he chose, a teenage girl in jeans and a skimpy T-shirt giggled and moved closer into the warm orbit of her boyfriend, an androgynous-looking long-haired kid who offered her a hit from his cigarette and hunkered low as though embarrassed, for some reason, to be seen with her.

Vicky Sorrell's party had drained him. Parties always sucked the life out of Jack, especially when they were held in his honor. Worse, she knew that something was wrong. She hadn't believed a word he said. He was used to telling stories, not lies.

He realized he should have gone to the FBI for help in the beginning. Now it was too late. How did you get your government to help when you were overseas? Was he supposed to call up the local CIA station and tell them that his nephew Benjamin Burke had been kidnapped by Colombian terrorists? If he called them now, this far into it, they would assume he was part of the plan, not its victim.

He had done the right thing. He didn't always do the right thing, but this time there had been no alternative. The Colombians had instructed him to travel to Madrid. He bought a ticket and went as ordered, immediately. They had told him to make contact with people at the American embassy. The cultural attaché was the logical person for an American writer to speak with, and Jack had talked her into hosting a reception for him in her apartment. So far he had done exactly what Ben's kidnappers told him to do, and done it as quickly as he could. But he knew that the Colombians would require more of him, and the next thing they asked for would be harder to deliver. Whatever this was about, it was not about Victoria Sorrell. Vicky was only their entry point into the embassy. She was only involved because Jack had involved her.

He had begun the trip to Spain afraid for Ben. Now he was afraid for himself.

More than anything, he wished he hadn't made the trip to South America in the first place, which had been a disaster from the beginning. Jack hated the Spanish title they glued to the translation of *White Sand*. They never asked. They were supposed to ask. Writers with less to say than J. J. Baines did were consulted about translation titles. This one should have been simple: *Arena Blanca*. He had snapped and snarled when they explained the marketing rationale they came up with to justify misnaming his book—*The Singular Adventure of a Tall Man in a White Hat*—but the damage was done.

Buenos Aires was tedious. The questions from his audience were all condescensions, tossed casually like pocket change from the hand of a distracted rich man. On top of that, the hand-holder his publisher assigned to him went out of her way to let him know the American novel was like American society—in decline—notwithstanding the glitzy stir it provoked. Her sympathy for his fiction was tainted.

After Argentina, Chile sapped him. The problem was too much idyllic sunshine wherever he looked, making the Andes scenery look like a geographical affectation: so much natural splendor in a single country, and a photogenic coastline, too. No fallible people, and certainly not a people who had produced the likes of General Pinochet, deserved such a homeland.

It got worse. Lima was an ambush. He left a lunch in his honor before the brandy, took an unscheduled break in a small park in Miraflores. Sat. Under a gritty gray sky he watched a woman with swift brown birdlike fingers coax a landscape onto paper with a stubby charcoal pencil. No one had ever beheld a landscape like the one that emerged on her paper. For the first time since leaving New York, Jack Baines felt a little ease lapping at his private shore. Then a highlands Indian with a burnt face and mutilated fingers came up to his bench to accuse him of making off with the mineral wealth of the Andes. Suddenly he was a crook. He was predatory capitalism's last running dog, America the Bootyfull's mumble-mouthed spokesman.

"Dynamite?" he quizzed the man, who must have been a miner. "Were you in an accident?"

No response. The Indian waited to be asked to elaborate on his silence, but Jack turned away. The landscape painter was gone from the park. Maybe she hadn't been there in the first place. There was a telltale tinkling in the air, as if things around him were dissolving.

Venezuela. Caracas was worse than nothing. Everybody they introduced him to seemed to be reading from cue cards. They were nervous, surreptitious, going through stiff motions. They loved his book. They didn't love him. He fled to Bogotá, Colombia.

Where there was a misunderstanding. His friend Juan Cruz never lied. When he said Gabriel Garcia Márquez had told him to his face that *Mario Moving* was splendid, Jack had to believe him. Juan Cruz didn't lie, but he was a serial embellisher, just as he had embellished his immigrant English grandmother. He made her an aristocrat, a ferocious Edwardian character with silver-knobbed canes and an aviary of polyglot parrots and a brindle mastiff that obeyed only her. Cruz claimed her as the source of his legendary literary sensibility; he was the continent's top talent spotter. Juan Cruz had told Jack that Garcia Márquez wanted to have dinner with him when he came to Colombia.

At the tavern in Puente Perdido, Cruz couldn't quite explain away the absence of the great Colombian writer, who was definitely in Colombia on a visit. Gabo had been unaccountably delayed. Jack was aware of the same tinkling in the thick tavern air, which smelled of bloody beef and tobacco. The noise was infernal.

"Fuck your English grandmother, John Cross," Jack told the editor, who wanted to eat and drink and talk literary gossip and go on pretending Garcia Márquez was going to show up any minute.

"Ten paciencia," Juan Cruz told him, tapping his arm as if he had earned the right to be close. *"Pónte cómodo."* He pulled out his cell phone and dialed, but if Garcia Márquez was home he didn't pick up.

Jack didn't want to make himself comfortable, nor was he about to be patient. His emotional overreaction to the disappointment went some of the distance to explaining why they were able to take him by surprise on the street outside the tavern when he left, frustrated, ashamed of the intensity with which he had wanted to spend an evening with the author of *A Hundred Years of Solitude.*

The mackerel-colored Mercedes slowed, didn't quite come to a stop. The rear door on the street side was swung open, and a man in a leather jacket with mint-and-onion breath shoved him into the backseat of the rolling vehicle, which accelerated before he sat up.

"You've got the wrong guy," he explained at the first corner they came to. He was sure that was it, a case of mistaken identity.

When he sat up, the man in the leather jacket, now riding shotgun, shoved him back down.

"Stay down or I'll knock you in the head with this."

He didn't bother to show Jack what *this* was. Anyway, it was dark. The man's face was in shadow. The street lights in the Puente Perdido neighborhood were erratic. Safe to take it on faith that whatever weapon he threatened to knock Jack on the head with was sufficiently heavy to get his attention.

"You're looking for a businessman, I guess that was it." Jack was willing to forgive them a dishonest mistake as long as they let him out of their car at a convenient spot downtown. "I hate to tell you this, *caballeros*, but I'm not the businessman they told you to pick up."

"Shut up."

"Of course, I'm shutting up right now. I'm staying downtown at El Potrerito Hotel. Are you going near there? What is he supposed to look like, this businessman you were supposed to kidnap? I assume you weren't looking for a gringo diplomat? There's no percentage in that, is there? I mean it wouldn't be worth the aggravation to stir up the CIA. Those guys have no sense of humor. We have an expression in English, the long arm of the law. Does that translate? Does it make any kind of sense to you?"

"*Cállate.*"

"Is he a tall guy? As tall as I am? Any distinguishing marks or scars? There was a tall American in the tavern. In the dark it would have been easy to mistake me for the guy you wanted. All Anglo Yankees of a certain age look alike to foreigners, I've been told."

He observed the driver, who lacked a leather jacket but had a butterball paunch that called for one, look back at him in the rearview mirror and blink, as though to convey a friendly but useless warning. The right arm of the man riding shotgun moved so quickly that Jack was unable to identify the weapon with which he knocked him out.

They must have pacified him with an injection. No blow to the head, however excruciating, was likely to keep him out for as long as he had been gone when he returned to consciousness.

He had a hard time focusing. His head throbbed. Pain gathered above the left ear where he had been hit because he refused to shut up and be abducted. That was it, as close as he was likely to come to demonstrating courage. From there on out he was going to be Mister Cooperation. It had only been nerves anyway, a fast stutter of fear moving his mouth. With the ball of his index finger he traced the outline of the lump on his scalp. Dried blood had matted the hair. Feeling it brought on a motion of panic like tumbling.

"Where are we going?" he asked his captors, because that was what you were supposed to do, talk to them so they knew you were an individual being, not just a handy example of the species they wanted to exterminate. But it was as though he had spoken in Urdu. Nothing registered.

He remembered a book by a newspaper reporter from Peru. Investigating government corruption, the reporter had been jailed on a trumped-up libel charge, and tortured. When they let him out of prison, he fled to France and wrote a book about his experience behind bars. He divided his fears into categories. They were noble and base, mortal and venial, petty and primary. In the book, what seemed to bother the reporter the most was having to make those distinctions. Now, Jack began to understand why.

Lifting his arm, moving his body even slightly, made him queasy. He was sweating cold. The soles of his feet ached.

"Mind if I sit up?"

No response. He sat up.

It was past noon. They were in the country, already a long way from Bogotá. The gravel road they were traveling wrapped itself like a scarf around the side of a hill that might be a mountain. The dust the car stirred hung white behind them as they climbed. Overhead, the sky had the kind of sealed surface you couldn't score with a knife. The sunlight coming through was encouraging, on the way to fierce. On the worrisome side of the road, the hill fell away down a sheer face of rock toward double-canopy woods whose drowsy green head concealed all kinds of rural unpleasantness.

Under pressure, his mind usually tended to riff. The riffs tended to be absurd. He had controlled the impulse in his fiction; he kept the writing clean. He did less well in real life. *This is the first time in my life that I've ever had to be scared,* he admitted to himself.

"What about turning down the music?" he tried. His voice cracked like a teenager's.

But at least he got an answer. "What about it?"

"Will you turn it down, please? My head aches."

"You'll want the music in a minute," the shotgun told him. "Here, put this on. Tie it tight or I'll tie it for you."

Jack didn't ask why he might want the music. He tied the black handkerchief around his own eyes. He didn't mind losing sight of the road. He didn't want to know where they were taking him. Presumably it was safer not to know. He wondered how rich they believed he was. The problem was, no one could get at his money to wire some down, because that was the point: it was *his* money. Complete independence, he had thought, was the one thing he could not live without. The tedious logistics of moving money ballooned in his foggy consciousness. He couldn't make it come out right. He had to convince the guys in the front seat, or their bosses, that he was less than they thought. It was too much to contemplate.

"Lie down," the driver told him. "It's not healthy."

"What's not healthy, being abducted?"

"If they saw you with a blindfold on," the other one explained. "This is disputed territory. There would be a misunderstanding, guaranteed."

"Guaranteed," agreed the driver, shaking his head, which was prematurely jowly.

"It's better for you this way, it's better for us."

Jack lay down gingerly. The movement made the pain lap inside his body, waves of snarled sensation spreading across a queasy sea. The accordion music didn't sound any better to him after he was blindfolded. He fell asleep again as the two men in the front seat argued about automobiles. The driver didn't care for Mercedes. His partner had a little German blood on his father's side. He wouldn't drive anything but a Mercedes, if he drove. But he didn't drive; his job was to keep the peace and do the clubbing.

They didn't stop moving until early evening, after they had come down out of the white mountain and into a valley where it had rained through the afternoon. The fresh scent of clean overpowered the American writer. Only curiosity kept him from sobbing.

At the entrance to the village, the road ended abruptly. The driver parked the Mercedes sideways, the blindfold was lifted, and Jack was pushed out to walk the muddy path.

"There's nowhere to go," they explained. "Don't even think about running anywhere. This is where you have to be, understand? Don't even think. The blue house on the left, up there where the houses stop and the fields start in again. That's where you're going. They're waiting for you."

"Blue," said Jack. He wanted to be cooperative, but his voice was fragile, not quite there.

"*Sí*, the blue house."

"My feet hurt," he established for the record. He felt the way he had felt as a kid in school when the teacher didn't believe his complaint even when he was legitimately sick and ought to be sent home where it was quiet and his mother understood how things stood better than other people did.

"Don't even think about running," they told him again, but their attention had shifted to a pair of collapsible chairs and a wicker picnic basket they pulled from the trunk of the car. There were bottles and glasses, and the driver rummaged until he found a yellow-handled corkscrew, which he stuck in the breast pocket of his shirt. He was humming a Colombian fight song, the tune they sung for his favorite soccer team.

"Where are we?" Jack asked them. He wasn't trying to be obstinate. He thought he had earned the right to know. "What's the name of this place?"

"This place?" the driver said absently.

"Be careful," the shotgun chided his partner. "You're going to drop the whole basket."

They were off duty, ready to kick back after work on their one day away from city stresses: the blasting noise, the frantic traffic, the inflation and the smutty air. West of the valley, the setting sun rested briefly on the rim of the visible, but the air was going to stay warm. It was heavy enough to float words on.

"I'm not dropping anything. This place"—he glanced up at Jack as if only then hearing the question that had been put to them— "this place is noplace."

Run out of questions, Jack went slowly up the muddy path. Noplace might be a pleasant spot to live. The adobe houses he passed were painted in pastels. Most of the roofs were of orange tile, but the thatch on the humbler houses was watertight, thick and perfect. It must be a market town, the local center where farmers traded and the Saturday night dance bands played on acoustical instruments and people's secrets were common knowledge. There were half a dozen commercial establishments that would have been hard to tell from the houses if it weren't for a Coca-Cola sign on a metal pole, or a stack of crates in the back patio, or a hand-lettered announcement on a street-side wall: A. BUENDIA & SONS—DRY GOODS & PERISHABLES. Peaceful in a verdant valley, it would be a tolerable place to live a certain kind of traditional life.

Except that there were no people. A pickup squad of runty chickens with muddy wings followed him up the path, expecting to be fed. Two brown dogs with black legs and big dangling ears stopped harassing a bristle-backed sow to stare at him suspiciously. They bared their teeth in his direction, and a concealed rooster crowed as if to get somebody's attention. But no people.

Until a man in sterile fatigues and mirror-polished army boots waved at him with his rifle from the small porch of the blue house on the high edge of the village. The house was set far enough back from the street to warrant a garden in which the tomato plants were neatly staked and the pepper plants were weeded. Jack wished he knew what kind of rifle the man on the porch was wielding to signal his arrival. Probably it was a Kalashnikov. Kalashnikov suggested Sandinistas and bitter ideological conflict and other extinct romances.

The man leaned his rifle against the porch railing, cupped his hands, and called, *"Bienvenido, Escritor."*

Welcome, Writer. Jack had been called that before. In Central America, on his first book tour, an obsequious man of letters had once inclined his upper body in Jack's direction and breathed the word *poeta,* signifying respect and a secure social identity that the American couldn't help warming to.

"Go right on in." The man on the porch ushered him forward. From the practiced way he stepped out of harm's way, it was clear he was a born underling, a man with a sense of entitlement to the low perch in the natural order that he occupied. A toothpick jutted from between his flat front teeth, poisoning his smile. "The boss is waiting for you."

Waiting, it turned out, behind a screen. It was like going to confession, had Jack been Catholic. Halloween-colored light spilled from a kerosene lantern hanging from a bent wire that dangled from a rafter. All of the furniture and the homey furnishings had been stripped from the room except for a square wooden table on ungainly high legs, along with a single chair. In one corner, beyond the reach of lantern light, a bare wood screen with lattice work like a garden trellis blocked a triangle of secure space. Cigar smoke made a smooth cloud above the triangle.

"Sit, please."

Jack was getting used to following simple orders: sit, stand, cover your eyes, walk to the blue house. He sat.

"You must be hungry."

"I'm kidnapped is what I must be."

"Food is being prepared for you, cooked fresh. You will find nothing contaminated with preservatives, nothing from a tin can. You're not a vegetarian, are you?"

"I'm not a vegetarian."

"That's good. I understand many North Americans with a strong social conscience won't touch animal flesh. That suggests some sort of compulsive reaction."

"A reaction to what?"

It didn't seem likely that a man chatting with him about the root cause of vegetarianism in the United States would shoot him, at least not before he finished the conversation he had started. Relax wasn't the word for what Jack's body wanted to do. A person didn't relax in such circumstances, he adjusted the angle of his discomfort.

"So much fat," the man behind the screen mused. "That's what makes them unhappy. Vegetables and rice, now that's a reaction."

"Will you tell me what you want from me?"

"You must be thirsty, too." He clapped his hands together, and a boy in fatigues with bad teeth and worse acne came through a door Jack hadn't noticed. "Bring him water. And beer."

"No beer," Jack told him. "How did you know I was in Bogotá?"

"We'll also want a bottle of whiskey at some point," the Colombian told the boy. "You're an internationally renowned figure, Mr. Baines, a celebrity. When a man like you travels south, it's big news."

Jack didn't realize he was parched until he drank a quart of cool water, which tamped down the pain in his head but made him sleepy again. The boy with the bad teeth brought in a plate of scrambled eggs slopping over onto a pinkish slab of roast beef. On another plate there were fresh tomatoes and half a loaf of crusty bread.

It irked Jack to have someone watch him eat; the man smoking his cigar behind the screen seemed to be studying him as he put away the food. There had been something about that in the Peruvian prisoner's book, too. Continual observation was another form of battering, subtler than what they did to a person's body but plenty injurious. In English the technical term was mind-fuck. But he was hungry, and he cleaned the plate quickly, wiping the dregs of the eggs with a hunk of bread.

"Okay," he said when the table had been cleared by the boy, who left two bottles of whiskey and two glasses, one of each on the table and the other behind the screen.

"Okay," the Colombian agreed.

"So what do you want from me," Jack asked him, "if it's not money?"

"I'm curious. I'd like to know how you came to write a book I read last year, a novel. In Spanish, of course. My English won't stand up to literature. I would tackle a political tract in English, if anyone in the Anglo-Saxon world produced such a thing anymore, which they don't. They've substituted anxiety about their individual identity for what used to be a serious left wing. But a work of serious fiction? My English would betray me in the first paragraph."

The voice was like meditation. It was the sound the fishes heard when they dived down low to the river's deep bottom and listened to the water going through the bed, making its secret commotion, sealing its private pact with the earth. It was impossible to guess, from the voice, how old the speaker was.

"What was the name of the book you read last year?"

"Mario Moving."

If it wasn't like going to church, it was like coming across the right interviewer, finally finding the one you'd assumed wasn't there to ask the questions you wanted to answer, the ones nobody ever came up with. In the gathering dark in a noplace village, in a rinsed and scented green valley, observed through lattice strips by a man who liked one of his books enough to abduct him and ask pointed questions about where the damn thing came from, a bottle of Johnny Walker Black Label at hand, Jack Baines found it easier to talk than he normally did.

"I guess you're not coming out from behind that screen."

"The screen protects both of us."

"I didn't plan on being a writer."

"One would not."

"When I was a teenager, I thought I was going to be a minister, an Episcopalian. That was the religion of my mother's family. A very high-toned denomination, as I was led to understand. Theoretically. Samantha, who preferred to be called by her given name, didn't take her children to church much. The sermons upset her. She thought the minister was singling out her sins. But she liked to tell people she was an Episcopalian, so my sister and I were, too."

"But not your father, I gather. What religion did your father profess?"

"My father was an Alaskan snow worshiper."

"You suffered a crisis of faith."

"I won't go into the details."

"I won't ask you to."

"I drifted for a while." He thought about describing his job repossessing cars from angry deadbeats and hard-luck Harolds but wasn't sure his Spanish would do it justice. "I went to work for DISC because they believed what I told them I believed."

"Which was?"

"That I was a committed leftist, as dedicated to the struggle for global justice as the people on the committee who interviewed me were. My God, they were grim."

"The Democratic Initiative for Social Change. Years ago they had an office in Cali. They didn't last in Colombia. That was their mistake."

"Opening an office in Cali?"

"Thinking they could bring justice to the world by the force of their opinions. They thought outrage was a real weapon, like a machine gun."

"You saw through that right away, though. You never made that mistake in your career."

"This conversation isn't about me, it's about the source of your inspiration. Tell me about Mario. I assume that wasn't his name? The only way you could make him real was by changing his name?"

"DISC sent me to Bolivia, to Sucre. Make it local, they told me, make it real. Make it count."

"Link the practice with the theory. I think there is a word in English for how all that sounds these days." He mispronounced it but got the idea right: quaint. DISC and its theology of social change were as quaint as men in spats pedaling high-wheeled bicycles.

"There's not another place in the Western Hemisphere as beautiful as the valleys of Chuquisaca," Jack remembered. "Or one that holds as much human misery."

"It will take so much longer than the romantics thought it was going to take," said the Colombian. "More time, more toughness, more planning. More guns, more intelligence, more organization. More of everything. More willingness to take casualties. And to inflict them. More patience."

Jack understood, by then, that he was not supposed to respond to what the other man said. His job was to tell his own story.

"I was supposed to manage a large gardens project. By DISC's standards it was a major investment. They had to raise consciousness on the cheap. Their theory was, the more vitamins and minerals you packed into the diet of oppressed Bolivians, the quicker they would throw off the chains of dependency."

"Quaint."

"When I had been working for six months, a young man came into my office in Sucre. He had walked there from the poorest, most miserable valley in Chuquisaca."

"Let's call him Mario."

"He was a force of nature."

"And he had a story of his own."

"I quit working. I started writing. It started out as kind of a translation. Of his story. I didn't know it was a novel, I didn't care. Not in the beginning. I wrote ten, twelve, sometimes fourteen hours a day. Lived on cigarettes and bread and raw vegetables and red wine. It took the DISC people a long time to realize I'd stopped working for them. They kept paying me. They kept expecting progress reports."

"But all you cared about was putting Mario on paper."

"I'm glad I burned the drafts. No one had the right to see them."

Jack's passion surprised him. He realized that he had been protecting his privacy long before he knew it might be threatened.

"How many drafts did you compose?"

"Twenty, maybe. What if I said a hundred? They didn't stop paying me until a year later. When they figured it out, they sent someone down to call me to account."

"But you weren't there."

"In Sucre I didn't spend half of the little bit of money they gave me to live on. What was left over bought me another nine or ten months in La Paz."

"So you escaped to compose more drafts about this man Mario."

"Something like that."

"You were irresponsible. You abandoned your work, you accepted their salary, you holed up and made yourself a writer. You applied DISC's scarce resources to your own selfish project."

"How come there are no people in this village?"

"Paramilitary forces came through last week. They pretended to believe that the residents were sympathetic to the other side."

"To your side."

"Tomorrow morning when there is light you might want to stroll around and see the bloodstains."

"I get it."

"Congratulations. Inoculate yourself with another slug of that Johnny Walker, why don't you?"

"You blame the North American government."

"Your government."

"For what happened here last week."

"What happens in Colombia is for Colombians to decide. In any case your government chose the wrong side, the side of reaction. Now, if we ask them to leave, they won't go. They have to be persuaded."

"Doesn't this place have a name?"

Jack wondered why he was pushing so hard to know, as though knowing improved his chances. When he got no answer, he figured it out. He wanted to think that they were going to release him, after they stripped him of whatever it was he had of value to them. If they weren't going to release him, they wouldn't care whether he knew the name of the village in which a massacre of rural civilians took place that wasn't going to make the papers anywhere. The reason he kept asking was reassurance. He wanted the Colombian not to tell him the name he was asking for. As long as he didn't know, he could stay alive.

He got up from the chair, spring driven as if by an idea. He crossed the bare room, listening to whispers. Through the front window he looked into the darkness, which had come down hard while he listened to the meditative voice of the Colombian who had been moved by *Mario Moving*. There was a texture to the dark that you only felt in Latin America, and only out in the country. Like a fabric but too fine to be silk. You wanted to run your fingers through it. It was an erotic sensation, but without an object.

Impossible to make out more than shapes, but Jack was pretty sure the underling with the poison smile was sitting on the porch steps, his back to the front door. If he was, his rifle was either cradled in his lap or leaned against the railing within reach. For a split instant, the writer imagined diving through the window, grabbing the gun, then hijacking the Mercedes from the picnicking thugs who had picked him up in the city. Only an instant. Somewhere near by, within hailing range, there would be more guerrillas standing guard. His ineptness, huge as his helplessness, staggered him.

"Blame," said the man behind the screen, drawing him back with the force of his voice. "An old-fashioned word for an old-fashioned idea. It's the kind of word you expect from the mouth of a hot-blooded Latino, no?"

"Then how do you explain what happened here in the village?" Jack pushed him.

"Alliances. Everybody has to choose a side. Neutrality is not realistic. The paramilitary chose to support the government in Bogotá. They are the military's disreputable cousin, capable of hideous atrocities but still a member of the family, when all is said and done. *Your* government—"

"It's not *my* government."

"They made the same choice. They may turn up their nose at some of the abuses of the paramilitary, but hey, boys will be boys. If people learned of the massacre that happened here last week, your embassy would be the first to condemn it as a senseless act of violence. They have a dozen such phrases. What they say."

"What do they say?"

"For public consumption: that they have sided with the government because of the drugs."

"You don't buy it."

Behind the screen Jack heard wooden chair legs scrape the brick floor, and the shifting of the speaker's body, as if words were not adequate to express his disgust, which was physical and complete. The disgust that Jack felt was different. He had been nabbed by thugs outside a tavern in Bogotá because his government had dirty hands, it had impure thoughts, global reach, multiple-theater capabilities, big rockets, and spy satellites that eavesdropped on anything that sounded politically salacious.

"What your embassy mouthpiece spouts doesn't matter. What those people believe in their top-secret brains doesn't matter, either. What counts is the choice they made. Their death song."

"Death song?"

"It's not only the Arabs who hate what your government has done in the world. The siege is only just beginning. Sooner or later, they'll be brought down."

"That's what you brought me out here to explain?"

Better if he had stayed behind the screen. He was the ugliest man Jack had ever seen. Like his philosophy-and-melted-butter voice, his appearance obscured his age. He could be thirty-five, but more likely he was fifty. Stooping and tall, he was meatier, redder, bulkier than Jack expected a guerrilla to be.

His jaw spread half again as broad as the rest of his face, as though it had been wrenched and then squashed in the last critical moments of birth. He wasn't heavy, but the flesh on his face drooped. It was the face of the survivor of an ordeal, famine or fire or some scarifying disease. The eye sockets were deeply recessed, the skin dark as a mask. He reminded Jack of an animal he couldn't name. He wore baggy military camouflage pants and a blue T-shirt. On one bony bicep an illegible hieroglyph was tattooed in red and black. The cigar between his fence-row teeth had burned down and gone out.

"I brought you here," he said, shaking his head as if rejecting

Jack's question even though he was going to answer it, "because I need your help."

Allowing himself to be seen was like pronouncing a death sentence, it seemed to Jack, like telling him the name of the village because it didn't matter, he wasn't going to be alive to tell anybody where to look for the guerrillas. The Colombian poured whisky from Jack's bottle into Jack's glass, drank it off like a double dose of medicine to counteract the unpleasantness of delivering hard truths to an obtuse North American.

"The problem," he explained, "is you're a writer."

"I'm a writer," Jack agreed. "That's a problem."

"There's a defect in the design."

"In the design of a writer?"

He shook his head impatiently. He was probably more accustomed to giving orders than carrying on a conversation. His ugly face frowned, ominous and beastlike. "There is no such thing as an uninvolved observer. Maybe it works in a story. In the real world, everyone is involved."

"Whatever it is you want me to do, I won't do it. It's not my war."

He shook his head again. "You're tired. The trip from Bogotá was a strain, and it gets dark early out here in the country. We'll finish our conversation in the morning."

Jack slept in a camp cot of army-green canvas in an empty bedroom of the blue house. He slept in his clothes, shoes on, as though to be ready for a chance to escape. He woke during the night's slow dead middle. The dark air was no longer a cape, it was coarser, wrapped tighter around his sweaty body like burlap meant to wrap a victim in. A rooster crowed irritably, and he thought about Bolivia, where he had first learned that cocks didn't necessarily crow at dawn. He needed a locus for his fear, a place to put it. He chose the palm of his left hand, let it collect there, heavier, hotter, until it acquired enough mass and density to be able to cup and throw it. He cupped, threw. It landed in his other hand.

In the morning, no one stopped him from going out onto the porch when patrolling guards brought a prisoner in, hands tied behind his back, bare feet bleeding, the buttons torn from his shirt. In another place he would have been a boy, new folding money and the unfamiliar smell of a woman and maybe a silver-studded saddle for a tall black horse the only things on his mind. Encircled by guerrillas with guns, he shivered, moaned, cracked. Next came breaking in half.

To the extent that Jack was able to follow the fast, angry Spanish, the case against the prisoner seemed strong but circumstantial. He was found with cash in his pocket. Under questioning, he admitted to having a cousin in one of the region's paramilitary units known as the Black Mustangs. He could not explain what he was doing in the woods outside the village. His political vision was blurry. Additional facts and circumstances piled up like a mountain the poor kid couldn't begin to climb. When the ugly man made a sidelong gesture of dismissal with one hand, the prisoner was taken away. Jack watched him move, escorted, back behind the blue house, across a serene pasture of tall grass, then into a stand of trees into which the early sunlight did not penetrate. The shots sounded close. The noise intensified Jack's sensation of helplessness, and he rebuked himself bitterly for having agreed to do the *White Sand* tour.

"His ignorance, that's what no one could correct," the ugly man explained his decision to Jack. He shook his head ponderously and rubbed his big, flat, brown hands together. He spat from the side of his mouth into the garden. Spittle string hit a tomato plant stake and dripped. The disoriented chickens of the day before had been drawn by the human stir. They were hopeful, no memory of yesterday's failure having survived the night. "The boy was foolhardy. He did several stupid things."

It was the opening to a conversation that Jack was too unsteady to keep up with. He was weak. He lacked mental focus. His body leaked sweat. He was more confused than the prowling pea-brained chickens. His head ached harder than it had the day before.

"Circumstances force a person to come to a decision," the ugly man insisted.

"Is there any aspirin in this place?"

"One either plays the game or he doesn't. I decided long ago that I was going to play, play hard, play with everything I've got, even though the game will probably kill me. But you see, there's a problem."

"What problem?"

"Your side holds all the aces."

It didn't seem like poker to Jack. In fact it didn't seem like a game at all. "It's not my side, for God's sake. You keep saying that, but I'm not on anybody's side. I'm not playing this game."

The ugly man ignored Jack's feeble objection. "Keep an open mind. You're about to make a significant contribution. You're going to play your own little part in convincing the government of North America to get the fuck out of my country."

"I'm not getting involved in your war."

The Colombian guerrilla shook his head. "Did you think I was going to ask you to pick up a rifle and go into combat?"

"I'm not thinking anything at all. My head hurts too much to think."

"There are direct flights from Bogotá to Madrid. Don't go back home. There's no time for that."

It sounded like a non sequitur.

"You can kill me," Jack told him, his back up. That was the way he inevitably responded when somebody threatened his independence. He needed complete and unrestricted freedom to be able to do his work. And next to the work, nothing else mattered. "You can kill me if that's what you decide you have to do, but you can't make me get on an airplane if I don't want to."

"You plan on swimming? Your mission is in Spain."

"The hell with Spain. I'm not going."

"You will talk to a few people there, you will build up a relationship with them."

"Which people?"

"People who work in your embassy. Then, after you talk to them, you talk to us. You keep your conversations with us confidential. What could be simpler?"

"I won't do it."

"We have a friend in Bogotá. He's on the right side, so he is sympathetic to what we are trying to do for Colombia. He's a member in good standing of the oligarchy, but he has a conscience. And by an odd coincidence, he happens to be friends with Mr. Juan Cruz. Cruz is a friend of yours, too, am I right? Our friend had a chat with the editor, who likes to brag about the literary lions he has tamed. He's also something of a gossip. How close are you to your sister and her family? There's a nephew, according to Cruz. Benjamin Burke. Is Benjamin your only nephew?"

"You prick," Jack told him in English. "You fucking prick."

He heard shouting from the stand of trees where the prisoner had been executed. There was a disagreement. The guerrillas had been in a hurry to shoot him. No one thought to order him to dig his own grave, or maybe they pitied him because he was ignorant and doomed and he was going to die more boy than man. They couldn't help thinking about some of the specifics they were depriving him of: a line of sweat drying down his back after he made accidental love to a woman in a field at night when both of them were supposed to be elsewhere; that was just one. Now no one wanted to bury the body.

"I do what I have to do to even the odds," the Colombian said.

"You bloody goddamn bastard."

"A fair game, that's what I'm out to play. It's not easy when your side holds all the aces. The best I can hope for is to draw a handful of kings."

In the early charred morning a ragged cheer went up from the stand of trees. Someone must have come up with a workable solution to the problem of the recent corpse. The ugly commander sat heavily on the porch steps, grunting out one chopped syllable as his butt landed on the rough-sanded plank. Standing in the sandy track, Jack kicked a chicken for the pleasure of watching it bolt in fleeting terror.

"I won't go to Spain," he told the Colombian again.

✤   ✤   ✤

But he did. And he had scrupulously obeyed the orders he was given. It would have been better had Vicky Sorrell invited a few Americans from the embassy to her party. He had assumed she would. But he had enough of a relationship established with her that they could go on talking, if that was what the Colombians wanted from him. That was what Jack hoped, that all they wanted from him was talk. But he didn't believe it would stop at that.

He stood up suddenly from the bench. He was jumpy. He knew he must look a little crazy. The teenage couple across from him pulled closer to each other as though they expected him to attack.

"Relax," he told them. His smile hurt his mouth. "I'm sane. I'm late is all, I'm really late."

He walked back to the traffic circle and flagged another taxi down. He wondered whether the Colombians were watching him now. If they were, what were they looking for? Did they want proof that he had made contact with the embassy? In the backseat of the cab he slouched as though a low profile might protect him. He wished again that he had gone to the FBI.

When he came into his room at the Palace, the phone was ringing. He thought it was going to be the Colombians. If they had been trailing him, they would know he had been to the cultural attaché's, and they would want a read-out on Vicky Sorrell's party. What would he say? She was smart, she was extremely attractive? The combination of dark hair and light eyes was deadly?

He picked up the receiver. It was worse than talking to the guerrillas.

"You're dog shit, Jack. I've always known you were. The first time I met you I told your sister, your genius artist brother is a contemptible piece of dog shit."

"I'm sorry, Philip. Christ, am I sorry. It's a major screw-up, I admit it, it's a nightmare. But it's not my fault. That's why I'm in Madrid, I'm trying to straighten it out. I called Eavy but she wasn't home. I left my number. I'm not trying to hide, I'm trying to fix this problem."

"I don't know who these people are, or what the fuck you did to piss them off, and I don't care. All I care about is getting my kid back safe. So I'm telling you—and you better understand this the way normal people understand things, not like a genius writer—figure out what it is they want from you and give it to them."

"Let me talk to Eavy."

"Eavy's got nothing to say to you."

"Maybe we should call the police."

"I spent seven years as a prosecutor, Jack. I know cops. They'll make things worse. This is my decision, not yours. He's my son. You don't have a son. You're not qualified to have an opinion. The cops . . ."

Philip didn't finish the sentence, which meant Eavy was in the room with him.

"Philip?"

There was a pause, the flat kind you could skip a stone across. Philip wasn't going to cry. That was one good thing about having Jack to blame. Anger kept the man on his feet. But he wobbled.

"Talk to them, will you?"

He was begging. It embarrassed Jack to be a witness to his brother-in-law's humiliation. As lawyers went, Philip was located at the arrogant end of the spectrum.

"We can work out a swap," Philip went on. "They can take me in trade. Ben's the most innocent damn kid in New York State. He's an idealist. They don't even make kids like Ben anymore. Ever since he was little and I could see he didn't know how to defend himself, I pulled my hair out worrying about him. I can't live without him. If it's money they want, I can lay my hands on a lot. Fast. Overnight."

"It's not money."

"Talk to them."

"Let me talk to Eavy."

"You can talk to your sister after you fix this."

"I'll fix it, Philip. I'm going to fix it."

"Call me."

"I'll call."

When Philip hung up, Jack crossed the room and looked out the window at the traffic moving in the street below, the pedestrians on the sidewalks. The orderly bustle appealed to him. Madrid was a stylish city. In the Spanish capital, people knew how to walk, how to look, how to eat and drink, how to live a proper city life. For a moment he forgot why he was there. Only for a moment. Then he repeated slowly and distinctly, as though to someone who might absolve him, "It's not my fault."

5

Ben knew from the beginning, somehow, that his drawings would either save him or get him killed. He believed that if he drew the right pictures, at the right time, the two men who had kidnapped him would be unable to kill him. Now they were looking at the drawing he had done, on a piece of cheap photocopier paper with a stubby pencil, of the thin one's black pistol and the Buffalo Yellow Pages on which it rested. They were clearly impressed by his skill, which encouraged him to try to explain the situation to them again. The first time, he had failed completely to make himself understood.

"My name is Benjamin Burke." This time he spoke slowly, his voice under control. "The marijuana that you're looking for does not belong to me. But I know where it is. And I'll tell you. If you'll listen to me."

"*No es mi droga,*" he added. It's not my drug. He had to make them believe it. Besides, it was the truth.

He wondered whether they were Mexicans, or Bolivians, or maybe Colombians, as though knowing their nationality might make some sort of difference to him. But he felt self-conscious putting together even a simple sentence in Spanish, which he had studied in high school, as though he were trying to show off.

Maybe he should draw them a picture of the dope he had stashed, as a gesture of his good faith, or at least so that they realized he knew what was going on.

At his parents' house in the upscale neighborhood near the zoo there were twelve cardboard cartons, each one packed with high-test marijuana wrapped in Ziploc plastic bags. Ben had only been able to stash three of them in his room. The other nine cartons he stowed in the attic, where nobody ever went because none of the Burkes ever made time for existential reflection. Dusty trunks of memorabilia—a coonskin cap, a letter sweater, a wooden box from India with a secret compartment hiding the picture of an old lover—all that and more was going to waste up there. Fearless Fly's marijuana was more secure in Counselor Burke's neglected attic than it would be anywhere else in Buffalo.

In a dive of an upstairs apartment in a neighborhood of new immigrants, the two South Americans ignored Ben's attempt to speak with them in pigeon Spanish. When they spoke to each other, he could not pick up a single word. A phrase from a high-school reading assignment came into his head: *laguna de comunicación*. That seemed about right. He was separated from these two foreigners by a language lagoon.

Five minutes after they picked him up on Main Street across from the U.B. campus, he had already named the thin, supercilious one. He was Don Quixote, because his beard came to a bristling point. It seemed important to give the guy some kind of an identity. He looked like a born malcontent, the kind of man who saw himself as an aristocrat-in-waiting. Inside the drug-running organization that paid his salary, Quixote was frequently given responsibility, but not the deference he believed he was due.

"Mi nombre es Benjamin Burke," Ben began a third time to explain, laboriously speaking in Spanish.

But he changed his mind. These guys had to know English if they were operating in the U.S., which put more criminals behind bars than some countries had free citizens. They refused to respond to anything he said only to aggravate him. The harder they rattled him, the faster they could get to the bottom of the case of the missing marijuana.

The round, plump one with soft, olive skin should have been Sancho Panza, but he wasn't. For no reason that he could discover, the name that occurred to Ben for the second kidnapper was Chick.

"I can tell you where the marijuana is."

He was enunciating too intensely, the way his father had once done on the beach in the Dominican Republic, causing his family to wince. I see, Eavy needled her husband, nodding with her head to one side the way she did, you figure they'll understand English if you raise your voice. But Philip had the hide of a rhinoceros, and his wife's words didn't penetrate it. Although that couldn't be true, or not completely. Every morning of the vacation in the D.R. his parents had emerged from their room flushed and looking happy with each other. Ben didn't want to be unfair to his father, who had a partly deserved reputation for reading poetry for pleasure.

"The marijuana belongs to a person named Fearless Fly," he explained doggedly, even though he could not be sure that Chick and Quixote were paying attention.

Quixote picked up the drawing of the pistol and the phone book and inspected it as though looking for flaws.

No one was ever going to believe him, but the marijuana really did belong to his friend Fearless Fly, who only sold the stuff. Fearless was a businessman. He never lit up.

They had met last winter in a bar downtown called the Filibuster Sunset that was supposed to be a multicultural gathering place, a local defense of diversity. There were no video machines in the Sunset, no screens. The music was live. Sometimes it was good. The bartender was named Evo. His ponytail reached his waist. Fearless Fly, an athletic black man in a sweatsuit with a shaved head and one severe earring, had admired the drawing Ben was doing of Evo's arms. The skill lay in suggesting the tattoos.

Quixote said something about the sketch of the pistol that Ben didn't understand. Chick shook his head, then wandered into the kitchen and began cooking. Ben heard a spoon scrape the bottom of a pan. Something liquid glugged. A chopping knife thunked against wood, releasing the smell of onions. It was a small apartment, the kind of place where they never gave you back your security deposit no matter how careful you were.

Quixote took a seat on the low-sprung purple couch. In front of him on a flimsy maple coffee table, the gun still rested on the phone book. He compared Ben's sketch to the actual objects, his dark eyes going back and forth between them several times. Then he crumpled the paper into a ball and threw it on the floor. He shook his head and laughed to himself as if Ben weren't there to see him.

The living room opened onto a railinged porch that ran across the front of the house. The door was open, the summer evening spilling in like sand. Kids in the street shouted at each other, their voices raspy. Looking out level with the tops of the trees made the apartment into a tree house, a place where adventures happened. This was not the kind of adventure Ben had wanted to lose himself in.

Fearless Fly had not asked Ben to hold the dope for him. Ben volunteered when he realized that doing him the favor would simplify his new friend's life, which was cluttered with people trying to work him. Fearless admitted that he had a hard time saying no to friends. A flood of regret overwhelmed Ben. If he hadn't made the offer to stash the marijuana for a week, one single week, he would not have been kidnapped. It was the closest he had come, so far, to crying.

Chick was whistling when he brought a bowl of beans in hot sauce with sautéed onions from the kitchen and handed it to Ben with half a dozen slices of doughy white bread, the kind of crap Eavy would never have in the house. Ben wished that the tune was an aria from an obscure work by a neglected Italian composer, which he recognized because his parents had taken him to the opera since the day he turned twelve. But the sound Chick made was more like notes escaping under pressure, hardly a tune at all. And the Burkes were not opera fans.

Dark was coming down, but the kids were still out running on the streets. Inside the apartment, all three of them scooped their beans with tablespoons. Nobody spoke. Ben was tired and hungry. The white bread didn't taste too bad, and the food steadied him a little.

When they finished eating, Chick collected the bowls and the spoons and the leftover bread and carried them to the kitchen. Ben heard water running in the sink as he rinsed the dishes. When the tap was turned off, Quixote picked up the pistol from the phone book and motioned with it for Ben to go into the kitchen. Then to sit at the table, over which a broken light fixture dangled.

Ben felt the way he always felt in school just before the test began. He wasn't ready. He knew a lot, but they were all the wrong things. His father liked to tell people the story of how Ben had failed skipping in kindergarten. When the report card came home, Philip hauled his son by the hand out to the sidewalk in front of the house to practice. Eavy distracted his big brother, Darrell. Darrell had passed skipping with flying colors. In fact, he had gone directly from skipping to flying a fighter plane. *This is how you do it, buddy*, Philip had said, trying to make it easy on him, make it a joke between the two of them. But it wasn't easy, and afterward Darrell's silent smirk was worse than being laughed at out loud.

From the cupboard next to the sink, Chick took a small cassette tape recorder. He placed the recorder on the table in front of Ben.

While Chick did a microphone test with the recorder, Quixote grabbed Ben's right hand and laid it flat on the kitchen table, palm down. Ben removed his hand, put it back in his lap. The trembling infuriated him. But the recorder was ready now. With a show of patience, Quixote took Ben's hand again and flattened it against the table. Then, very quickly he brought the butt of the pistol down on the back of the hand before Ben had time to remove it again.

He wanted to scream but stopped himself by crying. The crying shamed him. This was not the way you were supposed to react to danger and pain. Chick pushed an unlined index card across the table at him. On the card, written in English in a childish hand, it said *Talk to your mother and father.*

Chick hit the RECORD button on the machine and moved it closer to Ben.

"My parents don't know anything about the marijuana," Ben explained. "They don't even know it's in the house. The marijuana belongs to someone else. It belongs to a man named Fearless Fly. He's the person you need to talk to."

Quixote pointed to the index card. What they wanted was his voice on tape, which they would play into the receiver in a pay phone in another part of the city. But how could they even think his parents were in on the dope deal? His father was a lawyer. His mother served on the board of the Erie County Medical Center.

The irony was, Ben's parents would not have called the police. Not yet. They expected him to disappear periodically, ever since he took a bus to Memphis at age fourteen because he liked the way the word looked printed on the schedule hanging in the station.

Eavesdropping once, he had overheard his father grumble to his mother as they played a game of gin rummy at the dining room table. Somewhere else in the house a girl from Ipanema went walking, which normally put Philip in a better mood. *That's him, that's my boy, the amazing vanishing Benjamin Burke. Catch his act before he's gone again.*

Quixote and Chick were both speaking to him at the same time. Ben had the impression that they were saying exactly the same words, although he couldn't be sure. He understood he was being ordered to tell Señor y Señora Burke that his hand hurt, that several of the small bones in it were broken. But he wasn't going to start the conversation with his hurt hand.

"I'm in Buffalo," he said deliberately into the mike, trying to make it sound like *hello, I'm fine,* "in a fifth-floor apartment off Hertel somewhere, I think."

That was one way to prove they knew English. Quixote clipped him suddenly on the side of the head, hard but not as hard as he might have hit him. Chick shook his head and clucked in Spanish. He reached across the table and rewound the cassette in the machine, not so much put out by the delay as distracted by the mechanics of getting the right words in the right voice down on tape.

They knew it was not necessary to break Ben's other hand to get him to cooperate, so they didn't. Ben wondered whether it was the custom in Latin America for married men to carry family photos in their wallets. Probably not. Maybe they didn't even use wallets. But if Quixote and Chick were married, and if they were carrying pictures of their wives and kids, Ben wanted, for some reason, to see them.

He began again as soon as he could be sure the quaver in his voice was under control.

"Hi, Mom," he told the recorder.

To his own ear he sounded totally upbeat. That was not quite right. He downshifted. "Hello, Philip. I know you're not going to believe me, but this whole thing is not what you think it is."

It never was, that was the first thing Eavy would think when she heard his voice. The only reason Ben was crying now was the pain in his hand, which had already begun to swell and discolor. What happened if you didn't set the bones? He saw himself in old age with a twisted claw, unable to perform any of the simple daily functions that required two hands. The marijuana, he wanted to be sure everybody understood, did not belong to him.

6

Carlos Infante had been collecting intelligence for the Americans for long enough that it seemed like a career. Sometimes, on the good days, it had been almost like having a calling. He had his reasons for doing the work. They were not the reasons his American handlers through the years had assumed they were. In fact the money they paid Carlos was only a minor incentive. He insisted on the money because it kept his transactions with the Yankee establishment clean and simple. He preferred an exchange without ambiguity. But his reasons were his alone, not subject to market forces or the prodding and probing of CIA case officers.

Marc Karulevich, his current handler, thought he had Carlos scoped out. He never came out and said it in so many words, but from comments Marc let drop it was clear that the American operative had worked up his own theory of Carlos Infante. According to Karulevich's theory, Carlos collected intelligence on Latin American guerrillas and terrorists in order to channel his deep, long-running rage at the failure of the Left to achieve utopia when they had had the chance. Carlos didn't bother correcting him. It was easier to manage the relationship with a couple of solid touchstones; they didn't have to correspond with reality.

It was not that Carlos underestimated the capacity of the American intelligence machine. In fact it had a certain ruthless efficiency, like a monstrous vacuum cleaner that sucked up everything, garbage and gold alike, then tried to sort it out. But money aside, motives aside, the occasional professional satisfactions aside, he had come to despise the system in which he played a steady, modest part. He was ready to get out. Getting out meant getting clean. To do justice to Mercedes's love, he needed to feel clean.

In simple fairness, however, he was not going to sever his relationship with the Americans until he had passed on to Marc the tidbit he got from Paco Pacheco. You couldn't call it sympathy, exactly. The feeling that went through Carlos when he heard about the Colombians' plan was different, it was more like an enlarged capacity to imagine the Americans' terrible vulnerability. He was not moralistic about their dilemma. He had no urge to quote from the Bible about sowing and reaping, nor did he long to see people suffer. To shape the shadows in the world in which he worked, he had been scrupulously faithful to an ideal of duty. He was paid to collect useful information. This was the most useful information he had ever come across, and the most explosive. He owed it to the Americans to pass it on.

The only problem was the source. Paco Pacheco was not reliable. He was scared witless, or he was pretending to be scared witless. Either way, the transplanted house painter from Medellín was out to dramatize the risk he ran by agreeing to meet him. The way Paco saw things, more risk called for more reward.

Not exactly nervous himself but appropriately alert, Carlos closed his antiques shop in El Rastro early and took the Metro under Madrid to a bar with a pocked facade and grimy elbows in Moncloa, near the university. The bar was called El Pequeño Paradiso.

Stepping through the doorway of The Little Paradise, Carlos was distracted by a vision of Mercedes Antón, widow of Garay. His lover smelled of anise and starch and gardenias. She was faithful to the memory of her dead husband. But she loved and respected him, Carlos Infante. She was without guile. It was the force of Mercedes's love that had decided him: he was getting out of the spy business.

The noisy bar got on his nerves. Apart from a handful of students, it was a working-class crowd, in the first flush of realizing that work was done for the day. There was a sacred quality to the cigarette smoke rising to form a cloud of pollution overhead, as though the workmen were lighting tiny fires to commemorate their freedom.

Pacheco had taken over the one digital slot machine. On a table between his glass of red wine and the ashtray he had half filled with dirty butts, a stack of one-hundred-peseta coins was getting shorter.

"I can't breathe this filthy air," Carlos complained. Better to start Pacheco off on the defensive. The painter was impressionable; he took directions if a person spoke with authority. "Let's take a walk."

But Paco wouldn't look at him until he was sure the machine had eaten another hundred pesetas. There was paint in his black hair, although he had changed out of his work clothes into jeans and a T-shirt that said, in English, FREE SPIRIT WHACK OUT! NOW?? If he let it grow any longer, his mustache was going to eclipse the lower half of his face. The only perfect feature about the man was the obsidian eyes, which contributed to an expression of integrity he did not deserve. Paco wasn't that deep.

Pacheco was instinctively political, but his instincts betrayed him. He believed that the conspiracy to keep Latin America poor and downtrodden was simpler than it was. More than of any political adversary, he was afraid of turning thirty. To Paco, thirty seemed like the end of possibility, the end of time, almost the end of life itself. He claimed to be twenty-nine, but Carlos had a hunch he had already crossed the chasm and was unable to acknowledge it even to himself.

"A walk? Are you out of your mind?" he wanted to know. "If they knew what I had for you, I'm . . . extinct. Buy me a glass of wine, man. I'm losing bad. I'm not happy. I have needs, Carlos. Even poor people have needs."

"You can't beat a machine, Paco."

"Not if you don't believe you can, you can't."

Carlos made his way through the crowd to get a glass of red wine for each of them. He would stop at one. Too much wine and the pleasure of Mercedes's company would be soured for him. His body would protest, threatening a shutdown of the pleasure functions. And he wanted to make love with Mercedes more than he wanted peace or prosperity or perfection. His desire for the woman frightened him sometimes. He understood calculation; he was not accustomed to a passion that did not measure itself out in countable units or give receipts or adjust for inflation. Now that he knew what it was like, he believed he would die without it.

Pacheco sucked down the wine. "Lend me five thousand pesetas, will you?"

"You'll only pour it into that machine."

"So what? It's my money."

"No, it's not, not yet anyway." Carlos handed over five one-thousand notes, which the painter accepted as if for services previously rendered.

The little two-step they were dancing together was intended by Pacheco to signal the importance of the information he had to pass along. Huge, he was trying to let Carlos know, this one belonged in the category of extra large intelligence, it was so big. They talked about money as though it were an abstract concept like fidelity, or perseverance. The conversation irritated Carlos more than it normally would. That was the effect of his vision, the smell of anise, the likelihood of love on clean sheets dispensed without haggling. *La vida es demasiado corta para medirla.* Life's too short to measure. It was his first aphorism ever, one for the memoirs he wasn't ever going to write.

"It's about the North Americans," Pacheco said suddenly, staring at the LED images of luck on the screen.

"What about the North Americans?"

"*Jodidos americanos,*" said the house painter, blaming the loss of another hundred pesetas on the world's only hyperpower.

"What about the Yankees?" Carlos insisted.

"These people I'm involved with scare the shit out of me, Carlos. I'm in over my head. The only reason I'm staying in is I need the money. I want to go back to Colombia. I told them that. Soon. That's what they said, I can go back home soon. If you're not born here, Spain is no place to live. I'm supposed to be a logistics guy, nothing big time. Cars, some guns, that's all."

"But you have ears, don't you? And your ears are connected to your brain."

"I'm political, don't get me wrong. I have a point of view. I know who the good guys are. And I know the Americans have fucked over Colombia."

"What is it you want to tell me, Paco?"

It took two more glasses of red wine and the disappearance of another stack of coins—while Carlos was there Pacheco beat the machine only once—before the painter steadied himself enough to tell him, in a few coherent sentences, what he had to say.

Carlos left El Pequeño Paradiso feeling more vulnerable than he had when he went in, and more certain than before that he was getting out of the intelligence business. All the ghosts are laid, he told himself; I can walk away. But he didn't believe it. He wouldn't believe it until it was truly over.

He had to talk to Marc Karulevich. A telephone conversation wouldn't do. He stopped at a pay phone and called the American's apartment but there was no answer, and no machine. Karulevich's cell phone was switched off, which meant he was with a woman. Karulevich prided himself on his invisibility, on how well he blended into Madrid society, but even an invisible man left tracks a careful observer could pick up. Carlos was a careful observer. He should have left a message on the cell phone for the American intelligence officer to call him at Mercedes's. He didn't.

One thing he refused to do was connect Mercedes with the part of his life that she could not imagine he had. Besides, he could play out word for word the conversation Karulevich would drag him through: *This is all you have? This is a highly interesting premise you've got here, Carlos, but where are the legs? It's not going to walk if you don't give it legs.* The thing to do was find a leg and attach it to the body. Then he would call Karulevich.

The early evening was an oasis, a protected space inside which tired people could draw in fresh breath and rest. Carlos walked a few blocks to the Moncloa Metro stop. He took a yellow line train, then transferred to the green line toward Rubén Dario, wondering what Mercedes would be wearing. The woman's sense of touch was her great gift. Before Mercedes, he never knew what it felt like to be touched by a lover, all he knew about sex was the transaction costs a person paid.

Mercedes Antón viuda de Garay had dropped into his workshop in El Rastro looking for shrine pieces. An acquaintance had told her the antiques dealer was displaying furniture from the same village in Castile in which her late husband, Aurelio Garay, grew up and nurtured his genius. She was matronly, her body thickened into middle age. She had let her hair go gray rather than pretend, unusual among the women who patronized Carlos's *taller*. Her face was round in an un-Spanish way, and her black eyes looked Persian. The sexuality was there, if you didn't mistake it for a kind of physical carelessness. She rested the heel of one hand on an oak sideboard that might well have originated in Moriencia, the artist's home village in Castile. He considered telling her it had, decided not to lie.

"Have you been to see it?" she wanted to know. She assumed everyone would find a pilgrimage to the birthplace of Garay worth his while.

"Moriencia?" he echoed stupidly. He had a hard time understanding how he could feel this instant attraction to a woman who lived in a different dimension from the one he inhabited.

"Perhaps you know that the countryside in that part of Castile has the most amazing sunflowers, enormous long fields of nothing but sunflowers. You can see how."

"See how what?"

"How an artist with a sensibility like Garay's would be affected by the vision."

"The vision of sunflowers."

"I believe, Mr. Infante," she assured him—he noticed the tensile strength in her fingers, for some reason, along with the way her breasts pressed against her blouse front—"I believe we just might be able to do some business together."

Climbing the stairs from the Metro at the Rubén Dario round-about, Carlos worried about the wrong things: the rate at which his blood was thickening; the rate at which electricity usage in his apartment was being metered; the rate of interest his money was earning in the bank. He recognized all his tiny anxieties as displace-ments of an affliction that went back to Bolivia. It had to do with his reason to spy, which was his alone. A man like Marc Karulevich, a mere professional after all, was incapable of comprehending such fixity of purpose. He would call it obsession, and he would be wrong.

Carlos crossed the street against traffic and walked toward Calle Miguel Angel, off which Mercedes lived in an apartment in which, she had been pleased to learn, Salvador Dalí once simulated a ner-vous breakdown. Turning up the short, wide *callejón* on which Mer-cedes's building sat, he felt the anxiety suddenly drain away, replaced by a powerful sense of well-being. The sun had fallen low enough to leave the tranquil city street in shadow. The eye's objects thickened in the shade, swelling with self-importance: a lidless trash can, an iron bench, a yellow convertible with the top down. There was a pleasant smell of hot asphalt. Behind him on Miguel Angel, a tribe of teenagers made exuberant noises that sounded like celebra-tion, as though they had just won the only war that counted. That did it.

He stopped. He didn't know why, but hearing the teenagers' noisy jubilation brought him to the decision he must have been turning over without realizing. Second-source corroboration, that's what Marc Karulevich would demand when he heard the load that Paco Pacheco had sold Carlos. Silent alarm bells would start ringing around the world, and the Americans would cast their nets very wide looking for confirmation of Pacheco's news. But there were holes in some of those nets, holes big enough to allow fish of a cer-tain size to slip through. Karulevich knew that. *Help me plug the hole, Carlos,* he would say. *You're into this thing too deep to climb out. The only option you've got is to help me plug the goddamn hole.*

Mercedes would forgive him when he didn't show up. If she

knew, she would say *Of course you'll do whatever it is that must be done to help the Americans.* She was unlike most of the Spaniards Carlos knew. She did not resent the Americans. It was not that she was apolitical, she was simply more generous of spirit than other people he dealt with. As the sole heir of Garay's genius and the guardian of his reputation, she had no time for geopolitical envy.

Carlos knew of two people in Madrid who might be in a position to confirm the plan against the Americans, maybe three. Getting to them would be a logistical challenge, but only that. The difficult part lay in causing the correct questions to be asked in such a way that he obtained the information without raising suspicion. To his credit, Marc Karulevich recognized the level of Carlos's artistic accomplishment. But that was neither here nor there. Carlos knew where to get what Karulevich needed, and that's where he was going.

This was the last time, though. After this one, he would stick to the antiques business, which provided a very different sense of satisfaction, tactile and predictable and somehow more distinctly human than the muddy transactions of the spy business, where someone was always being shortchanged. Threats to the Americans would go on as long as their dominion held.

The feeling of unusual peace he had felt approaching Mercedes's apartment continued. He even looked forward, a little, to making one last contribution to the cause. Never mind that his cause was not the same as the Americans'. He turned and walked quickly back to the Metro stop.

7

If the man possessed the slightest sense of propriety, he'd marry the wretched girl and that would be the end of it. Although I suppose that how a thing looks in society doesn't even enter into Señor Karulevich's calculations. Our Don Marcos is an American, when all is said and done. And the Americans are famous for spitting on tradition. Iconoclasm is part of the national character."

The door to the patio was open. From where he sat on the wide flagstone terrace looking north, out of the city, Marc Karulevich could hear the duke fulminating in his study. For a man in the late winter of his life, Fabio Farrón, the duque de Tolvas y Escaleras, had a powerful voice. He boomed, filling up the domestic air. In a lower voice, soothing but authoritative, Doña Inés tried to persuade him to tone it down.

"I don't see why I shouldn't express an honest opinion under my own roof," the old man protested.

In a wrought-iron chair with ungainly legs, like the legs of a woman who would never dance, Marc drank his Campari and soda slowly. He ignored the plate of sardines in oil on the table next to him. In the distance he could see the pale green of early summer extending its soft inroads across the brown earth, which dissolved in haze toward an illusory horizon. The idea of looking at landscape that contained no people appealed to him. He liked things, vistas included, to be clean.

His attention drifted. He only half listened to Inés as she worked to pacify the duke. In his Spanish life there were moments, like this one, when nothing Marc saw had anything to do with a factory in Dearborn, Michigan, which was a good place not to be from.

Waiting for Lupe to finish dressing, Marc pictured a scene in Dearborn. He used his hometown as a starting point from which to gauge distance, like the kilometer 0 marker in the pavement at the Plaza del Sol in downtown Madrid, extending from which all Spanish distance was computed. Dearborn was this: twenty feet overhead on a yellow-and-black-striped catwalk alongside the hot wash tank; fumes from the chemical soup eating away the blades in the fans turning slowly in the ceiling of Building 41 at Chisholm-Walker, a nonunion plating and grinding shop; Billy T. A. (The Asshole) Burf.

White socks falling down over the knobs of his ankles, one boot on the lower rail of the walk, both elbows on the upper, the foreman coughed at the man below him. He dragged on his cigarette, hitched up his shop overall, wagged a finger stub. Burf needed a shave. Burf always needed a shave; he looked like a constipated bulldog. Coughing his way every eleven seconds through a ten-hour shift was the foreman's objective correlative for what ailed him. *You're a piece a shit, Karulevich. You're the sticky part I can't scrape out of my ass when I take my morning dump. Fuck up another grinder and I'm writing you up. That's what you want, right? You want to go on unemployment and then welfare when that runs out. Right? You're as bad as the niggers. You want to make a contribution to the nation put a gun to your ugly mug and pull the trigger. You're a piece a shit, you're the sticky part . . .*

Then Gregorio was there on the terrace. The valet glanced briefly at the splendid view off the terrace, just long enough to let his employer's foreign guest know he appreciated Marc's appreciation of it, which was available to a privileged few. Quite a trick to convey deference without seeming obsequious. Doing it instinctively guaranteed the guy his job. Short, broad-butted, balding at twenty-five, Gregorio was going to waddle by thirty. He was going to know more about the history of the family he worked for than anybody in the family knew.

"Don Fabio is asking for you, Señor Karulevich."

Gregorio was new. Watching him establish his place in the household was part of the process for Marc. The process had several names, depending on his mood, and his attitude toward his mood: assimilation, transformation, disintegration, reconstruction. The idea was to be in Spain, deeply in, but not of it. The idea was to bury oneself alive, and send back dispatches. The idea was to be credible.

The idea behind the idea was to nail terrorists.

Doña Inés stepped onto the terrace behind the valet, her elegant thinness roped in gold, and Gregorio understood that his orders had been countermanded. Without being told, he knew his job was to inform the duke that, although the American had not yet arrived, he was expected at any moment. He inclined his way back into the big house at an angle that stopped just short of a bow.

"I'm sorry you had to hear that," Inés apologized. The long fingers of her bony hand encircled his wrist. Her hard, leathery face came closer to his than he cared for it to come; her breath smelled of licorice. "My husband went through a wretched night, Marcos. He wants to see you. But if you go in with him right now, he will want to talk politics."

"He always wants to talk politics, Inés."

"Of course he does. Still, the excitement of doing that, the pleasure of your company notwithstanding, would not be good for him. I've been speaking with the doctor. Besides, I bear a message from my daughter. She wishes to inform you that she is very close to being ready."

"I'm looking forward to this, Inés. A whole day off."

She sniffed. Doña Inés's sniffs were multifunctional. This one disparaged the concepts of speed and competition, American impositions both and equally offensive to her sense of propriety and Spanish style. Fast food was no food at all, she liked to point out to him, it was automated barbarism, the picture of unhealth. And the kind of unbridled competition that the Americans practiced was tantamount to rape, a violation of Spain and other civilized countries as savage as anything that may have started in 1492, going the other direction. But what really mattered was the inconvenience. Having forgotten decades earlier anything she might have known about the world of work and its imperatives, she was irritated by the regularity with which other people's work got in the way of the entertainment she enjoyed scheduling.

"I suppose your overseers in the embassy must begrudge you a free day," she complained. "I think they'll wind up damaging your health, Marcos."

"Washington's appetite for insightful reporting is never satisfied."

"What good does it do you to analyze every last inch of this country, if they're not going to pay attention to you? My husband is right about one thing."

"He's right about a lot of things."

"The American government doesn't have the faintest notion of how to lead the world. I feel bad for them. It hurts to learn they are vulnerable just like the rest of us. Still . . ."

"It's because of all the fast food. Poor nutrition and too much grease are clouding the policy makers' judgment."

She sniffed again, but there was Lupe. Taller, not as unreasonably thin as her mother, more moderate in the use of gold jewelry, she was wearing a white dress he associated with sex because of the ease with which it peeled from her.

She pecked her mother's cheek distractedly. "Fede is being picked up by a friend's mother, Mother. Someone from school. You don't know them. You won't like them but you don't have to go to the door. He'll be gone all day. You don't have to worry about him."

But Inés had already turned away to rearrange the chairs on her terrace. If she had had to work, she liked to tell people, she would have been a decorator, because a person either had an eye or she didn't, and one's civic duty obliged her to ameliorate the awful, which predominated everywhere. The most one could accomplish was the creation of small oases of taste in the endless desert of dreadful; she supposed even that little was worth doing. She didn't hear what she didn't care to hear. Lupe's son, Federico, was inconvenient. A ten-year-old with a hoarse voice and sharp elbows, he was a glaring link to an inconvenient past. Poor Fede knew he was not sufficiently loved. Back before he could remember, he had committed a terrible sin, something so horrible he was glad he could not recall it even though he continued to pay for it.

Growing up sturdy and loud, the boy was testimony to his mother's inferior judgment, which she confirmed for the clan when she walked away from the annulment of her marriage disaster that Inés's brother Fausto worked so deftly to arrange. Federico's father was a Greek from Piraeus. What Lupe could not have been expected to know was that the man she fell for was unable to survive long periods away from the sea. Inland Madrid was intolerable. He fled. He was tried, convicted, and executed in absentia. Lupe didn't wait for the verdict. She took her baby and a nanny on a slow boat to the Gulf Coast of Florida, where she practiced Kundalini yoga and studied English and took high-quality color photographs of alligators in their natural surroundings.

"Marcos has just promised me that if his awful cellular telephone rings today while he is out with you, he won't answer it," Inés reported to her daughter.

"If you don't say hello to Father, Marc," Lupe began, thinking about something else.

"Just keep it short, dear. I need to get through the morning without an earthquake."

In his study, where all the books on the teak shelves had similar leather covers, Fabio was explaining the course of the Civil War to Gregorio, who would read alone in his room at night in order to come up with worthy questions for the next session the old man put him through. Along the glass protecting a gilt-framed map of Spain, a trembling index finger located the flash points where, during the Civil War, patriotism had stood up to treachery and prevailed.

Gregorio had decked the old man out for a banner summer day. Don Fabio wore an English double-breasted blazer. A silk ascot, a gift from his Hong Kong tailor, camouflaged his wattled neck. Tasseled Italian loafers over sweatshop-spun socks contributed a sporty touch. In the duke's close vicinity hung just a hint of French scent. Underneath, in all probability, he was wearing American underwear. The most provincial nobleman in contemporary Spain was a triumph of cosmopolitan style.

As a field commander, the duque de Tolvas y Escaleras had been known for the risks he took. His left arm, his right thigh, the small of his back carried scars from Republican bullets that other generals would not have put themselves in the way of. Outside of Valencia in Ranas Muertas, two days after they extracted the bullet from his back, he returned to the field hospital to donate blood for enlisted soldiers. That was how you gave, you opened up your veins and bled out your life for them. That was what people wanted, not a token vote in a sham system of government that was effective only at generating chaos and unreasonable expectations among classes of citizens who required protection.

"Your ambassador," he groused to Marc, waving a weak arm. The duke engaged in a highly stylized form of whining. His sense of outrage would not be placated.

Gregorio removed the heavy map from Don Fabio's lap, and the duke folded his hands there so they wouldn't shake. Marc understood that one purpose of his antiquated political passion was to distract himself from considering his death, which had begun to sleep in the same bed with him.

"Sir?"

"You know what I'm talking about. Don't tell me you didn't read what Ambassador Duffey announced to the press yesterday. This is how you treat your friends."

"Papá, Marcos and I are going out for the day. He's on holiday from work. He's going to take me out to the country. We're going on a picnic." Lupe's simulation of childish innocence was only convincing because the old man allowed it to be.

"Democrat or Republican, it makes no difference. This one is just like the last one." The old man shook his head gingerly, as though it were a flower too heavy for its stalk, in danger of snapping off. "He's been bamboozled by the Socialists and their sugary rhetoric. Blast and damn his 'normal and customary contact with the opposition.' The Left has taken your man in completely and nobody the wiser. You see what's going on, why don't you make an appointment with Mister Ambassador and explain the facts to him? He'll thank you for it, trust me."

He coughed, his face reddened instantly, and Gregorio's back stiffened.

"Ambassador Duffey has a whole staff of people in the embassy giving him information on everything under the sun, Don Fabio."

"A staff?" he snorted. "A staff? He should toss them out on their ear. They're fools, to a man. You're too young to remember Eisenhower—"

"Federico will spend the day with a friend, Papá," Lupe interrupted him gently. It was a form of daughterly aggression. It was a large home. Federico existed on another plane, one that seldom intersected with the old man's secure space.

"As soon as I feel better," he warned Marc, "I'll ask you to set up an interview with Duffey. He can come here. We'll have a civilized lunch. That's how one conducts business, face to face across a table."

"I'm not very high up in the embassy hierarchy, Don Fabio, but I'll convey the invitation."

In Fabio's mind that didn't track, either. If one worked in the embassy, one didn't go around trumpeting one's lowly status.

"Please," pleaded Lupe, "no politics today."

The duke coughed hard. Gregorio intervened to steady him, and Marc and Lupe escaped.

In the car, a boxy, mud-colored Spanish SEAT sedan that confirmed for Marc that he was living in elsewhere-not-Michigan, Lupe put her hand on his leg as he moved into traffic. "Love first, entertainment afterward, okay?"

"Love first," he agreed.

"And you're going to turn off your telephone." She angled the rearview mirror so that she could inspect her face. She was unhappy with her lipstick. She removed it and started again. He smelled her smell, which was unique the way a person's fingerprints were unique, not an odor that could be replicated. Somewhere else in Spain, or in the Gambia, or in Sri Lanka, there might be a woman who gave off a similar scent, but Marc would know the difference in the dark.

At the reception in the Reina Sofia Museum, he knew he had seen her before. The museum was kicking off a retrospective exhibition of pictures by an American artist who had gone to his death criminally underrated in the U.S. If you asked a Spaniard, the Americans failed to appreciate Monk because the artist's sensibility was European. His irony was arch, his sense of play cerebral, his awareness of history as tight as an early Christian's grip on original sin. Even Monk's nuances had nuances. It was up to Europe to canonize the painter, and the Reina Sofia Museum was kicking off the campaign. Maria Guadalupe Farrón Echevarría arrived late and alone. For the length of the reception, which was a scripted event beginning with wine and ending with caustic judgments of Yankee indifference to greatness, she stayed off center. She created the impression of looking for someone who wasn't there and left in the first wave.

The next day Marc went to the Prado to be sure. He found her in a Velázquez, off center to the left of the painting's principal action, which was royal and domestic and self-assured. Philip the Fourth's favorite painter had caught a commanding group of high-strung individuals intensely conscious of their position of privilege. Born to orbit, the woman on their left with a book that bored her would never escape the gravitational pull of the court.

Lupe humming a song he couldn't place, he drove toward his apartment in Lavapiés. The morning rush of commuters into the city center was over, but traffic still clogged the narrow streets.

"I need my mirror," he told her.

"No, you don't."

He had an urge to goad her a little. "I liked Madrid before we were born better. Donkeys in the streets, shopkeepers walking home behind their shadow to sleep the siesta, flamenco singers in dingy bars. Men in hats with knives in their boots and vengeance in their hearts. You remember all that, don't you, Lupe? I mean the way it used to be? This . . ." He waved at the traffic, the high-rise clusters, the web work of high-speed roads. "This is Euro-World. They've made Madrid into a theme park. And you don't much care, do you?"

A different sort of woman would have asked him what the theme of the park was, so he could tell her it was prosperity, prosperity and oblivion. Despite the duke's accusations, the Spanish Left was de-fanged, neutered, housebroken. The real Right lived on the far edge of relevance, like a provincial schoolteacher with fiery opinions who didn't dare say anything that might jeopardize his pension. But Marc was awed by the resoluteness with which Lupe refused to engage him on anything that wasn't there, wasn't now, wasn't something she could touch or taste or smell. He still tried, once in a while, to smoke her out, but she never told him any of the things she might conceivably believe. If she had any opinions about the way things worked in the country of her birth, she kept them hidden.

She looked at him coolly. Humoring her American lover was as tiresome as humoring her father, but just as necessary. She would not be crowded. Her long white face never tanned. Her oval eyes made him think of lighthouse lights. They were beacons. She had a classic fat-free Spanish body, the parts in perfect proportion as if built to order by a connoisseur of shape. He glanced at her kneecaps. Before Lupe, it would not have occurred to him that kneecaps were an important source of erotic inspiration.

"When I was in Florida," she remembered, "I left Fede with the girl one day and took myself to a swamp." When she answered him in English it meant what he was saying fatigued her. It was Marc's job to know when he fell short. "There was a long *acera de madera* that went into the swamp deep. What do you call that?"

"A boardwalk."

"Yes. And I watched an alligator two meters long swim under-neath the boardwalk and come out on the other side. How large was the largest alligator you ever saw, Marc?"

"Five meters, seven meters."

"*Siete metros.*"

"Do you believe me?"

She gave him back his mirror.

She walked through the front door of his apartment on the third floor of a building that lacked character the way she might go into a hotel room where she didn't expect to spend much time. She went to the kitchen and opened the refrigerator door. She refused to drink tap water, so he had begun to stock her brand of bottled water. The more time they spent together, the longer his list of chores got. She unbuttoned and unbuckled him with her left hand, a bottle of water in the right. The white dress peeled, then her thin white underwear, the straps of the brassiere sliding down her shoulder blades as if they wanted to. She sat in a kitchen chair, closed her eyes, rested her head against his belly. It was unusually quiet. He felt her breath jet warm against his skin, imagined the scar it would make.

"*Esto,*" she said quietly. "This."

After a few minutes she carried cushions from the sofa in the living room, spread them in a row on the kitchen floor, pulled him down there as if that had been the plan all along, the place where they had agreed to meet.

"Your telephones."

"My telephones."

"Off."

He got up from the sofa cushions, lifted the receiver from the land line, hunted for the cellular in the pocket of his jacket and switched it off.

"This," she said again. "*Esto.*"

"It's my anniversary," he told her.

"Your anniversary of what?"

"Three years in Spain."

"Then you'll be leaving."

"What do you care?"

"They want you to marry me. They think that will solve the problem of Guadalupe and her inconvenient son."

"What do you want, Lupe?"

It was a test, and she knew it. If she said it, if she said *I love you, Marc, take me with you when you go,* it would be enough. That was all he wanted from her. But he wasn't going to get it.

They made the slowest love ever. Lupe was always deliberate and unhurried. From the beginning she had taught him how to slow down. By force of will she had shamed him, almost, into an act of surrender he had been too stupid to feel. After a while, giving up began to feel like getting. She made love the way people loved before the invention of clocks and obligations, before punctuality became a virtue. This time it was slower still, producing the sort of pleasure that linguists felt the first time they spoke in a strange new language. Afterward, as she dozed on the cushions he realized that the fireworks love was her anniversary gift, the only thing she could think to give him. It came without a card.

He switched the cell phone back on but lowered the ringer to the minimum alarm. Lupe lay on her side with her back to him, breathing lightly. When she got up from the cushions she would be hungry. She would expect him to have a plan to feed and entertain her. He nestled next to her, rested one arm along her side where the sweat was drying. There was no place to go; they had already arrived. He felt a slight vibration just before the telephone rang in his right hand.

"The items you ordered," he heard a voice inform him in cadenced South American Spanish, the sort of voice that convinced you to try a product you didn't want to try.

Then a pause. The pause was a flag for petulance. Carlos Infante was always waving a flag. Marc waited for the man to get past his sense of being wronged.

"I've been calling you for an hour, Marco," he griped. "You said call you anytime. You said feel free. If it was important. That's what I did, and then you didn't answer."

"No jodas." Marc drew him out. Faster that way. He needed to hear the rest of the sentence; otherwise, it was just Carlos waving one more flag to provoke him.

Lupe stirred, sat up. She looked at the telephone as if the instrument itself were responsible for the interruption, not the caller.

"How do you say that in English?" Carlos wanted to know. *"No jodas."*

"Don't fuck with me."

Carlos finally got it together to say his sentence. "I called to tell you that the items you ordered have arrived safely."

Marc pressed the red button to kill the call. "You're not going to like this," he told Lupe.

"You have to go to work."

"I wouldn't go if it wasn't important."

She shook her head. "Not today. Not now. Not this time."

"Wait here. It won't take long. I'll be back in an hour."

"I won't be here in an hour."

"I'm not rich, Lupe. I have to work. This is part of my work. Give me an hour. An hour and a half *máximo.*"

"I'll go home in a taxi."

"Do you want to marry me, Lupe? Would you still love me if they sent me to Ouagadougou?"

She understood that it was not a proposal, or not exactly, it was a request for clarification of status.

But she deflected the question, ventilating her resentment unconvincingly. "They wouldn't be so keen for me to marry an American, especially an embassy person, if it weren't for Federico. I'm damaged merchandise. They need to get me off their hands while I'm still young enough to attract a buyer."

"I'm not talking about them, I'm talking about you."

"Your government is not going to send you to Ouagadougou."

"For Christ's sake, Lupe. What's it going to take to get you to tell me what you want?"

The coldness of her kiss as he left the apartment wasn't revenge, it was a hint, as close as she could come to saying what was on her mind. He wondered why such cool contact gave him an erection.

As Marc stepped inside Carlos Infante's workshop, the cherub with broken wings averted its one good eye. Before Spain, he had not known that a piece of carved and painted wood from a seventeenth-century church outside Pamplona could change its expression every time he looked at it, as if wood had moods. *She's yours for the asking,* Carlos prodded him every month or so, since for some reason the statue didn't sell. *I picked her up for next to nothing. So you needn't worry, I'm not trying to suborn you. That's your job, no? But I'm like you, I want to keep the lines between us clean. It's only a damn statue. Take it, it's yours.*

But the cherub continued to sit unclaimed on a fluted wooden pedestal salvaged from an Andalusian church that had been burned in an anticlerical outburst in the 1890s. Pedestal and cherub gathered dust in a back corner of the shop in the shadow of a massive oak hutch that Carlos had plundered from a farmhouse in the Basque Country and rebuilt to appeal to apartment dwellers with nostalgic notions about rustic life.

Carlos Infante would have led a less conflicted existence if he had stuck to antiques. His shop in the Rastro, Madrid's upscale antiques alley, was welcoming warm. The saints and angels he rescued from oblivion radiated good cheer as if their rebirth as decoration really did prefigure a second coming. Carlos's tidy workshop-with-showroom drew customers even on the slow days when his neighbors' places stood empty.

"I'll be with you in just a moment, sir." Carlos lifted his voice half an octave for Marc.

Close to a sale, he stood at precisely the right distance from a German couple in matching sandals and baggy white pants who were debating in furious undertones. Evidently they had settled on the same piece, so the source of their disagreement was not apparent. Carlos listened to the German going back and forth with the same respectful intensity he would have demonstrated if he had understood their language. They left without buying.

"So what was that all about, Carlos?"

"Art for art's sake."

"This is your meeting. It better be good. This is my day off."

"Don't tell me you're unionized now. Tell me a little about your benefits package, I'm all ears."

It was going to be a longer conversation than Marc was in the mood to put up with. Maybe Lupe was bluffing, and she'd be there when he got back to the apartment, and he would peel her white dress again, and she would finally tell him she wanted to live and die with him. And he would say yes. No way; she wouldn't wait.

"Okay, tell me what's wrong with your life, Carlos. That's what you want to talk about, so that's what I want to hear."

"One would not expect an *anticuario* to suffer what I suffer from, Marco."

"What do you suffer from?"

"One would expect that sustained physical contact with the past would lead a person to believe that all will be well in the fullness of God's time."

"But that's not the case with you."

"I worry that the sun will burn out faster than the scientists predict it must, and our earth will be sucked into a black hole. That a meteor the size of Buenos Aires will wipe us out while we're asleep. I worry that I left a burner lit on the stove in my apartment."

"You should consult a doctor."

"I'm convinced my bank is making a computer error as we speak, and the next time I go to withdraw some cash, the teller will inform me I have no money, my account has been canceled due to lack of funds."

"You're not alone. There are case studies written about people like you. It's what they used to call melancholy. It's an honorable disease, Carlos. Dante suffered from it. It used to drive Beatrice nuts. A doctor can prescribe pills for your problem."

Carlos shook his head. He didn't believe in quick fixes. He pulled down the shade and locked the front door, and Marc followed him into the workshop behind the showroom, where he heated water for tea on a gas ring. With an artisan's focused concentration he sliced lemons, rummaged for the honey pot, set out cups and spoons for two. He was a domestic bear, hairy and lumbering; there was more girth than was good for him. He was fifty-something and folds of flesh hung on his face.

Carlos Infante was from Venezuela. Or Colombia. Or Peru. Perhaps Bolivia. His country of origin changed every time he told his story, which also changed, making previous versions obsolete. But the details of his history were just colored flecks decorating the essential one-act drama. As a young man, he had taken seriously the rhetoric of revolution. He gave up a career in one of the respectable professions, gave up the woman who was his soul mate because she was unwilling to make a commitment to the only cause worth committing to. He went underground alone to make his contribution.

And he was a quick study. He mastered difficult practical lessons having to do with weapons and propaganda, organizational discipline and infiltration and the analysis of intelligence. He looked with hard eyes at the prospect of a life inside the struggle: the huge personal costs, the small satisfactions, the odds of failure, the emotional isolation. He accepted what was because it was. Then he was sold out.

Not just him. A person he trusted betrayed him, and the unit to which he belonged, and the cause to which they were connected. For money, one presumed, or out of fear. Or else because the impulse to betray was as strong in some people as the sex drive was in others. Nothing was perfectly clear. He worked to come to terms with the betrayal. While he was working, more treachery came to light. The weak link was not just one backslider. Digging judiciously, he became aware of interlocking circles of deception and corruption. After a certain point it was impossible to say where treachery stopped and the cause began. He reacted. Over fifty, he was still reacting. He had enjoyed a productive and mutually profitable relationship with the Americans for a long time.

They drank their tea. When Carlos finished a cupful, his bearish tongue scoured the bottom of the upturned cup for sweet residue. He had settled into an overstuffed chair whose stiff brocade was worn shiny. "Sometimes," he told Marc, "thinking about how many disasters could happen keeps me awake at night. But then again, that's one of the reasons I'm so successful at what I do, no?"

"Pills," Marc suggested again. "You want to think what's eating you is cosmic, or metaphysical, but it's chemical. It can be fixed."

The ex-revolutionary ignored his suggestion. "I was up all night last night."

"Is that what you called to tell me?"

"At two, two-thirty, I turned on the television. Spanish *tele* is god-awful. Anyway I caught the second half of one of those childish North American space epics. You know the one I'm talking about—half the characters have fur instead of skin."

"*Star Wars.*"

He nodded, poured more tea for both of them. Marc envisioned Lupe making herself comfortable in his bare apartment, lounging on the sofa reading *La Conquista del Aire.* He had picked up the novel for her because she met Belén Gopegui, the author, at a party once. Lupe managed time alone poorly. She didn't have the temperament for solitude. She suffered it as pure waste, like time spent in a doctor's office.

"A revelation," Carlos said.

For an instant Marc thought he meant his mental picture of Lupe in her expensive flimsy white underwear on his sofa drinking bottled water. The American placed an envelope with dollar cash in it between two fat, old, leather-bound books on Infante's desk. When Crocker left Spain, he had warned Marc that, despite his years of service, Infante preferred to receive his compensation discreetly, not drawing attention to the nature of the relationship. It cost nothing to respect the sensibility, although it would have been more efficient to set up a bank account for him somewhere.

"Even though you have been attacked on your home ground by people who want nothing more than to exterminate your nation, it's still difficult for North Americans to accept," Carlos was lecturing him. "Not for you, of course. You're cosmopolitan."

"What's difficult to accept?"

"The fact that you are the evil empire. Because Americans, for reasons I don't grasp, still identify with the plucky rebels. What is that American word?"

"Underdog."

"That's it. The movie illuminates your place in the world better than any hostile foreign indictment could. The United States is the enemy of the underdog."

"Bullshit."

"Is it? Think about it. Your grand ship of state is the Death Star. And there is no escaping. Close the door on the Americans and they come through a window. Your arsenal is awesome. You've even managed to convert fast food into a weapon in the international culture war. I'm not justifying terror, mind you, I'm only illustrating a point about perception."

"If you were a woman I wanted to sleep with, Carlos, this would be the longest act of foreplay in the history of fucking."

"You're no different, Marc. You see yourself as a lone rebel scout blasting off in his cruiser to plant mines before the Death Star lands. But the fact is, for most people in the world, you're on the wrong side."

"We agreed, Carlos, that if you had something important, you would call me on the cell phone and say the sentence. You called, you said the sentence, I came."

Infante nodded. It was time to talk, finally. "This is something out of Colombia. Something strange."

"How strange?"

"It has to do with the Badger."

"Maximiliano Paredes. The ugliest man in Colombia. Founder of the Justice Concept."

"So they say. You've heard of the writer J. J. Baines."

"He's the guy who wrote *Mario Moving*."

"Until recently, Mr. Baines was on tour in Latin America promoting one of his books. When he came through Bogotá, Max Paredes had him picked up and taken out of the capital to meet with him. He kept him sequestered for a couple days. Then he let him loose."

"And Baines never reported anything to the police."

"Don't you find that odd?"

"Is that all you have? It's odd, I admit it. It interests me. But it's pretty thin."

"I have a long-distance line in to a driver with direct connections to the Badger himself. The line goes through a man I trust. That's all you need to know about him. In fact this driver was the one they assigned to pick up the American writer and drive him to the rendezvous outside Bogotá. He has great difficulty managing money."

"So he's open to suggestions for supplementing his driver's salary."

"If and when useful suggestions are put to him properly, he responds rationally. You've never expressed any reservations about the quality of my tradecraft, not that I remember."

"What does the driver say?"

"That picking up Baines was a small part of a large and ambitious undertaking that the Badger is trying to pull off."

"How large? How ambitious?"

"This driver isn't the only person my contact talks to, Marc. I can say this much definitively: whatever Max Paredes contemplates doing is connected to American interests in Spain."

Carlos knew more than he had said so far. He was like a stripper who enjoyed the slow tease of revealing her secrets by provocative degrees. When Crocker handed him over to Marc three years earlier he had warned him, Infante will drive you crazy he's so slow sometimes. But his work was as close to faultless as anything Marc had come across.

"Why don't you boil some more water?" the American suggested. "I wouldn't mind another cup of tea."

"I hate to keep the front door closed for long," Infante objected. "Bad for business."

"Talking to me is your business, Carlos. It's been your business for a long time. Selling antiques is a front, remember?"

"What if I told you I was getting out of the intelligence business?"

"I'd say you were lying. I'd say you wanted something out of me that you didn't think I'd be willing to give you."

Carlos nodded his fleshy face slowly, as though that was what he'd expected to hear. He turned away to put the kettle on the gas ring.

"Let's talk about Max Paredes for a while," Marc suggested. "Let's speculate about what sort of event a Colombian nationalist like the Badger might be able to pull off in Spain, so far from home."

"You're approaching this backward." Infante turned it back on him. "To get to where you want to go, you have to take small steps, one at a time. Like this one: Ask yourself what in the world the Badger would want from a man like J. J Baines?"

It was a long conversation. When it was over, Marc walked through El Rastro until he found an empty alley; he disliked using his cell phone in public. Before he dialed the station chief, he thought again about Lupe. There was no way she was going to wait all day at the apartment until he showed up. When he said he'd be gone an hour and a half max, he meant it. Things changed, he couldn't help that. But Lupe wouldn't see it that way, she would see it as desertion.

He wasn't sure what would happen if she did, but he still wanted her to say it: *Te amo, Marc. I'll go with you even if they send you to Ouagadougou. I'll stay with you in the heart of Africa because I love you. Let's make a life out of this, you and me and Federico. Because te amo.*

Pure fantasy. Maybe there was a way to get his lover to commit herself—the one right question to ask, an unexpected act of love, a perfectly aimed stab to the heart—but he couldn't find it.

Marc caught the station chief at home. He picked up on the first ring.

"Nice day, Ray. Great sunshine, all that. I love Spain in the summertime. You enjoying yourself?"

"Why do I have the feeling that it's not going to stay nice, Marc?"

"I thought maybe you'd want to meet me for a cup of coffee."

"The usual place you invite me for coffee?"

"Half an hour?"

"It really was a nice day, Marc."

"Until I called."

"Half an hour."

Walking out of the Rastro to catch a cab, Marc wound up behind the German couple who had failed to buy the piece they liked at Carlos's shop. As they walked, window-shopping hand in hand in their immaculate white outfits, they continued to discuss something with heated intensity. It must be nice, Marc thought as he coasted in their wake for a moment, really nice, to care that much about furniture.

8

Watching her walk into Sergio's, Marc recognized the territorial instinct. It showed in her walk, and he approved. Even permanent expatriates had to belong someplace, which also meant the place belonged to them. And it was obvious that for the length of her tour in Madrid, Vicky Sorrell was going to own her Bilbao neighborhood. He knew how it was, because he owned Lavapiés the same way. Every morning on the way to breakfast, she took an inventory of the twittering pigeons and the shifty flower sellers and the prosperous apartment dwellers, the mannerly beggars and the schoolchildren in clean uniforms. When they were all accounted for, she could begin her day. That was the cool thing about living someplace you weren't born, you could own it without a mortgage.

He gave her fifteen minutes alone in Sergio's, a narrow café shaped like a railroad car, which had been squeezed into the side of a long brick building fronting the plaza. It was time enough to drink a slow cup of coffee and read the newspaper before she reported to the embassy. The café, Marc suspected, was more intimately Vicky's than her apartment.

It started badly. She was offended when he asked to sit down at her table. Yes, she minded. But he had already taken the chair across from her. He was already being himself.

"I was just leaving, Marc," she advised him.

"It couldn't be something I said, because I haven't said anything yet."

"I'm supposed to be at a meeting in the embassy in a few minutes. Harris is big on meetings."

Marc knew Harris. Vicky's boss had dog-paddled through Latin American backwaters for years until they gave him the chance to swim in Madrid. He believed that anything anybody on his staff did somehow reflected on him. He was wrong, of course. He didn't look well, either. The man was dying of incurable bureaucracy.

"You're not big on meetings, are you, Vicky?"

"Was there something in particular you wanted from me?"

"As a matter of fact, there is. I want to talk to you about J. J. Baines."

"So you're onto Jack Baines," she said.

"What do you mean, I'm onto him?"

"When he came to my apartment, he admitted he voted Socialist. Once. I think it was in 1976, and he couldn't bring himself to endorse Jimmy Carter. Then last year he sent a check for a hundred dollars to Greenpeace. He's also opposed to IMF conditionality, and sweatshop conditions in the *maquiladora* plants in Mexico, and he thinks dolphins speak some sort of proto-Greek, so catching them in tuna nets is a mortal sin. Isn't there a place you can lock up dangerous people like him?"

Marc had been hoping for a slug. Harder to work with a dull creature of the bureaucracy, in some ways, but safer because they were more predictable. Wherever she came from, Vicky Sorrell had not evolved from the proto-slugs of prehistory. There were foxes in her background, and hawks, and night-vision owls. He didn't care to contend with what he sensed in the woman: a quick political intelligence, a need to ask hard questions and challenge the answers she got. He could not avoid, just then, comparing her with Lupe. The comparison hurt. With his right hand he massaged the back of his left hand, where he felt the pain of it.

Vicky was also more attractive than seemed warranted, or fair if fairness entered in. Thirty-five at most, she had the body of a speed skater, compact and flexible, her limbs molded like advertisements for arms and legs. Her face was a stage, structured space for the play of thought and feelings that inhabited her. The light green eyes made the sort of visual sense you didn't expect with the black hair, which was the same shade exactly as Lupe's but shorter, with a widow's peak defining the forehead in symmetric halves.

"Congratulations," he told her. "You've managed to make cultural clichés out of Baines and me both in less than two minutes."

"If you're interested in Baines, maybe you should read his books," she suggested.

"I have. Even us intelligence goons read books, when they make us."

"He's staying at the Palace. Call him and ask him where he gets his ideas from. If that's what you want to know."

"This isn't the way I wanted our first one-on-one to start out," Marc admitted to her. "I didn't think you were going to be this combative."

"Sorry. It's this meeting I was telling you about," she told him. She looked at her wrist; there was no watch. "Harris has a thing about people walking in late. He thinks it's unprofessional. Actually he thinks he's being dissed, which isn't true but it's not something I'm going to take on."

The waiter, a slant-shouldered country boy who probably considered himself lucky to have a low-stress job, had picked up on his favorite customer's distress. "Do you need something, Victoria?" he leaned confidentially close to ask her. His breath smelled of fresh cloves.

"Not right now, Dionisio." She shook her head, and the boy retreated to the bar, where he stood with a clean white towel folded on his left arm in the event direct intervention was required.

"You don't really strike me as a meeting kind of person," Marc prodded her a little. "You strike me more as the kind of person who can't wait until the meeting is over."

"If I said fuck off, would you go away?" she wanted to know.

"You haven't heard what I have to tell you. Are you the kind of FSO who despises intelligence people on principle?"

"Go ahead and tell me, then you can go away."

"You were in Central America during the bad old days, right? Do you remember hearing them talk about *tontos útiles*?"

"It's what Tomás Borge called the sandalistas who showed up to cheer on the revolution in Nicaragua. Useful fools."

"J. J. Baines is a useful fool."

"Useful to whom?"

When he hesitated, she told him not to play games.

"Okay, no games. I'm talking about a Colombian, a man known as El Tejón."

"The Badger."

"Because he looks like one. He's ugly as a fence post. His name is Maximiliano Paredes. He's an ideological purist. They threw him out of the FARC for his extremist point of view. He wouldn't deal with the drug traffickers. So he went out and formed his own liberation organization. It's called the Justice Concept. His preferred financing mechanism is kidnapping businessmen for seven-figure ransoms. Max Paredes is the ultimate long-ball hitter. He has mastered the art of delayed gratification. His magnum opus is a thoughtful piece of propaganda called the Blue Book."

"Revolutionary used car prices."

"The Justice Concept has never printed the thing. It's circulating on disk. I read an unauthorized review. There's a chapter on protecting the nation-state as a hedge against the globalists. There's a chapter on why using cocaine money is a fatal wrong turn on the road to revolution. There's a whole chapter on being patient. That's the poetic part of the book."

"What does this have to do with Jack Baines?"

"Did Baines tell you he was just in Bogotá?"

She nodded. "On a reading tour for one of his books."

"Paredes had him picked up and taken to see him. Evidently the two of them hit it off."

"And now he wants Baines to do the English translation of the Blue Book."

"Did you ever come across any of the interviews Baines gave to magazines?"

"I don't read many interviews," she told him. "I'm waiting for the one with Blake, what he really knew about tigers' eyes."

"I know Blake. Second baseman. He hit .357 for the Cubs in 1949. Listen, I made some copies for you." He passed her an over-stuffed manila envelope. "Not all this stuff is on the Web. When you have a few minutes, how 'bout you take a gander?"

"I assume he has lots to say about smashing the capitalist world order, and how alienation makes all of us fellow sufferers. And the tyranny of the image in late-capitalist society."

"I think you're getting this wrong," Marc told her. "I don't give a shit what kind of political crap Baines believes. The reason I want you to look at this is so you have an idea how a guy like him might possibly wind up being impressed by the Badger. I want you to have an open mind on the subject of J. J. Baines's susceptibility, that's all."

"Whatever he said in these interviews"—she tapped the envelope with a thumbnail remarkable for its perfect shape, as though a nail like hers were the only conceivable way to finish a finger—"Jack Baines is what the Spaniards call an intellectual. Around here that's not a knock, it's a valid occupation. It's one more way Spain is not like the U.S."

"Being an intellectual doesn't mean the guy can't be stupid."

"Baines's radicalism is all in his mind," she insisted. "It's an aesthetic choice, a way of organizing reality that energizes him. Some of the great artists did their best work while they were Marxists. John Lennon wrote 'Power to the People' driving around in his Rolls. You're being too literal."

"And you're pigeonholing me. You think I'm some kind of true believer."

"I don't know you well enough to pigeonhole you."

"Okay, I'm from Dearborn, first generation of the family to get a college degree. My people work in factories, mostly. But biography bores me. One cool thing about me, however, is how I admire your style. You belong here. There's something about the way you walked inside."

"You've been surveilling me?"

"Belonging is an acquired skill, but not everybody acquires it. I got here early. I wanted to give you time to have your coffee before I bothered you."

"Are you after some sort of report of what Baines talked about when he came to my apartment? Is that what this is all about?"

"I'd be surprised if he said anything, except maybe thank you kindly, ma'am, for arranging this lovely shindig for me on such short notice."

"Then what do you want from me?"

"A little help."

"Sorry." She shook her head. "I'm a short-timer. I'm in the process of resigning from the service."

"How come?"

"That's not relevant to anything you have to say to me."

"Okay, I'll be honest. I already knew you put in your termination papers. Last Friday."

The notion that he could know about her paperwork without her permission was repugnant to her. Unauthorized access was anti-American. Her indignation heartened him. It was the reaffirmation of a basic belief in how things were supposed to work. She was one of the good guys. That was the side Marc was on, too, although she probably wouldn't admit it.

"That makes me angry," she said.

"I can see that."

"What's the point of telling me?"

He noticed that neither one was using the other's name. She wasn't ready to grant him full personhood, and he was willing to mark the time by her clock. Talking with her reminded him that he still had the most interesting job in the world.

"It takes awhile to process the papers," he told her.

"Is that a threat?"

"It's the sad bureaucratic reality of the State Department. Let me tell you what's going on. I should have started out with that, but I got sidetracked. I made a mistake. Sorry. It doesn't happen very often. Among my own kind, I'm known for my superb judgment."

"I'm still angry. And I know what you tell me won't be the whole story, because you station people never say what you know."

"But you'll hear me out anyway."

"The idea of Jack Baines collaborating with somebody like the Badger is so far-fetched I want to see how you put it together."

"We believe the Justice Concept is planning some kind of operation against American interests. Probably here in Spain, although we're not ruling out other places in Europe. There's a lot of static on the communication circuits. Some of it is white noise. Some of it might be deliberate disinformation. Don't ask me to be more specific. I have to take a polygraph next month, and I want to pass. If I don't pass, I lose my job. I love my work, Vicky. Couldn't live without it."

"Fair enough. What does Paredes want?"

"Think local. He wants the U.S. out of Colombia. He knows the government in Bogotá wouldn't stand a chance without American backing. I'm not convinced they can hold off the FARC and hold back the paramilitary units and deal with the drug traffickers and the splinter groups even with our help, let alone put their economy back together. The Yankee embrace can sometimes smother those it would protect. It's funny."

"Nothing you've said so far is very funny."

"Colombia is coming apart in a civil war, and nobody notices."

"I guess you wouldn't rather spend your time picking the right IPO so you could retire rich."

"I have a diseased imagination. I'd rather think about what Paredes's end game is. And I'd rather stop the bad guys from winning."

"We're coming up on the Fourth of July reception."

"It's the obvious time to try and pull something off. High-concept, low technology. It's pretty goddamn brazen. *Un puñado de reyes.*"

"A handful of kings."

"That's the code name his operation goes by. I had to get specific permission to tell you that, by the way. I thought the detail might spark your imagination, and you'd be more willing to cooperate."

She shook her head. "And you think Jack Baines is going to earn his revolutionary spurs by walking into the embassy with C-4 strapped to his body? Give me a break. Baines is too intelligent not to see he's being used."

"It's not his intellect that's driving him, it's the hate he feels for the American empire, which must be some weird variation on the theme of self-loathing."

She held up her hand. "No psychobabble."

"Okay." He nodded. "Assertion withdrawn. But you believe me. And there's another funny thing."

"What's that?"

"How Baines manages to keep the hate from spoiling what he writes."

"His self-preservation instinct is acute. I think he has a guardian editor inside him looking out for his literary interests. The editor tells him when to stop, and Baines listens. He cares about his reputation as a writer more than he cares about politics."

"He's a piece of work, isn't he?"

"So you want me to help you spy on an American citizen. I thought that kind of thing was against the law."

"Under certain circumstances," he tried to explain, but she held up her hand.

"Bureaucracy and secrecy. Put them together and—"

"And what you get is automatic evil? Come on, my business isn't that simple, and neither are the people in it."

"This discussion doesn't interest me."

"Sure it does. It interests the hell out of you. Besides, I'm being straight with you. Why don't you be straight back?"

"What do you want me to do?"

"Call Baines, engage him. Invite him to lunch. Go to a museum together. Take a walk in the park. Play your lute for him, I don't care. But draw him out. He's going to be angling for something specific from you. Now you know enough to see it coming. What you probably don't see is how extraordinary all of this is."

"Ruining my breakfast?"

"Me asking you for help."

"Is that supposed to make me feel flattered?"

"Nope. I'm just giving you a little historical context. I haven't run into many foreign service officers I'd feel comfortable working like this with."

"Let's make a deal," she said.

"What kind of deal?"

"My father was killed in Vietnam. He told my mother he was working for USAID, but she believes he was in intelligence. She only told me that a few days ago. I'd like to know for sure. I'd like to know what really happened to him. Can you find out for me?"

"That kind of thing is complicated," he tried to explain.

But she held up her hand again. She was used to leading the conversation. So was he. "Yes or no."

"Yes," he decided. "I'll try."

"His name was William Tipton. I think I have the right to know how he died, and what his work was."

"Do you want to have dinner tomorrow night?"

"On your expense account?"

"On me. No business."

"I don't think so."

"Maybe you'll change your mind. But there's one more thing."

"What's that?"

"We don't have a lot of time. Be aggressive. Don't spook Mr. Baines—you'll know when to stop pushing, I can tell that about you after one conversation—but you have to get something out of him. Here's my numbers. You can always get me on the cell phone, just don't get specific. The technology isn't on our side. Meantime read what John Jacob Baines told the *Paris Review* about the use of force in a noble cause."

Marc left Sergio's propelled by a cold blast of disapproval from the waiter with the towel on his arm. If she asked him, Dionisio would advise Vicky to turn down his invitation to dinner, guaranteed.

He had been ducking a volley of poison-tipped messages on his pager fired at him by Lupe, who was not happy. She needed to get out of the house but wanted company. There had been a seismic incident in the house in Puerta de Hierro. She wouldn't give him any details, but it was clear from what she wouldn't say that Federico had crossed into his grandfather's field of vision and got stuck there. Fixing on the boy in front of him caused Don Fabio to revivify the unpleasant events of his daughter's past. His equilibrium suffered. He tottered. Tottering induced anger. The anger aggravated his balance problem.

As the automatic gate opened to let Marc's SEAT sedan onto the grounds, he checked the window of Lupe's bedroom for the day's signal color. Lupe hung Turkish silk scarves in the window according to a communication system she had developed over the course of their relationship. It was up to him to read the colors.

The scarves came from Vakko, an upscale department store in Istanbul, where Marc had invited her on their first trip out of town. Don Fabio was recently enamored of the American diplomat, who was willing to converse with him without glancing furtively at his watch. That made it easier for him to respect the fiction that Lupe and her mother wrote for his benefit. His youngest daughter was traveling to Turkey to visit a classmate from the International School. Of course he remembered Makbule, an engaging multilingual girl whose father was a senior diplomat in the Turkish foreign service. Federico was sent to stay with a friend in Burgos. There would be no reason for Marc to call in her absence.

They stayed in the Çiragan Palace Hotel along the Bosphorus, a five-star hotel that stooped to celebrity endorsements, framing the autographs of American secretaries of state and CNN reporters and other high-watt guests. Money didn't matter to Lupe, not the way comfort mattered, but privacy did, and agreeable buffered spaces. She knew Marc wasn't wealthy, but she assumed the American government paid him well enough to afford a splurge; he bled out his life and time for the embassy often enough that they owed him.

Marc had planned on the stay at the Çiragan. The hotel was expensive, but he liked spending money on Lupe. It was like jumping off a cliff not knowing how deep the water below you was. What he didn't plan on was scarves. Their first day in the city she took him to

Vakko. The scarves were beautiful. She held up a paisley pattern. The bill in Turkish lira came to many millions. His credit card statement translated Lupe's enthusiasm into $959.

In their room at the Çiragan, the privacy and the scarves freed Lupe to make love with a hilarity she never reached at Marc's apartment in Madrid. She was like a teenager discovering her body for the first time, the molten pleasures of squeeze and stretch, the secret smell of sex oozing, a liquid lode she hadn't realized was there to plunge into. At night, the damask curtain open, watching gaudily lit Russian ships move down the Bosphorus toward the Sea of Marmara, they rested in a cocoon of exhausted sensation waiting for the urge to return. Because it was going to. Their hands were as hungry as their tongues. Everywhere he put his hand Marc touched a scarf.

Since Lupe started hanging her Vakko collection in her window, he had learned to associate a red scarf not with anger but with a curious mute elation. Anger came in black, and resentment in brown. Purple meant passion, either wished for or imagined or, on bad days, denied. Blue signified open-mindedness, or a desire to be entertained. A green scarf signaled that Federico was on his mother's mind. Pink suggested forgiveness, and white was the traditional truce color flown after battle. It got complicated when Lupe hung more than one scarf in her window. The range of possible meanings was too broad to be useful to him in the short time it took Marc to park his car and ring the bell.

There was a purple scarf tacked to the sill in Lupe's window. There was also a black one, and a green one, and a blue one. He wasn't fast enough to figure out what it meant before Gregorio answered his knock.

"Morning, Gregorio."

"*Buenos días, señor Marcos.*" There was a mild proprietary resentment in his voice, in his masked expression, in the small sweeping gesture with which he invited the American into his employer's home. It was a weird form of pride of place that depended not on possession but on occupying privileged space.

"Tell Guadalupe I'm here, will you, Gregorio? She called me this morning. She knows I'm coming."

"Guadalupe?" The valet thought he might recall someone with that name, if you gave him a few moments to sift through his crowded cranium for her.

"Don Fabio's daughter." Marc helped him out. "You may have met her. She lives here. So does her son, Federico." He wasn't sure why he liked taunting the guy except that Gregorio's attitude was as reactionary as the duke's, and there was no excuse for that in a man under thirty.

"Doña Inés asked that you see her the moment you arrived."

"Well, this is the moment, Gregorio. Fidel Castro—"

"What about him?"

"He's a Gallegan, isn't he? Like you? I mean his family, in the old days, before they went to Cuba."

The butler shook his head. "Castro is a Communist. Galicia is a traditional place."

"There are no more Communists, Gregorio. For better or worse, those days are gone. Now there are only circus clowns in costumes. Did you miss the movie?"

"Which movie is that?"

"The War Is Over, the World Is Changed."

Gregorio hadn't seen the movie. If they showed it on Spanish television, he'd change the channel. With ruffled grace he led Marc to Doña Inés's study, on the ground floor on the back of the house with a wide-windowed view of the territory leading to the Guadarrama northward.

"It's silly," Lupe's mother told Marc, standing up to shake his hand and allow herself to be air-kissed twice, once in the vicinity of each bony cheek. "Hanging those colored scarves from her window when she knows you are due to arrive. Harmless but silly. She thinks—"

"What does Lupe think, Inés? I'd really like to know."

Inés shook her handsome head. Sometimes the Spaniards made Marc think of thoroughbred dogs. They were Afghans, maybe, or greyhounds, or another of those sleek, high-strung, and self-regarding breeds that went for a lot of money. Alongside the *madrileños,* Marc was an American mutt. His father was a Serb whose own father, a watchmaker, suffered from Croat-induced depression long after he emigrated to the United States. His mother was a hybrid. Part Irish, part Sicilian, she was a superstitious Catholic who scrubbed the floors of the rectory because she believed each brushstroke on her knees erased an hour from the time she was sentenced to serve in Purgatory. In Esther Marie Karulevich's mind, sin and hard luck were two facets of the same heavy stone, which she carried around with her because she couldn't imagine she could just drop it and run free.

"I want to ask a favor," Inés said.

The favor was a form of placating. The duke was transferring his bitter feelings toward Federico to a safer outlet. He had made up his mind to write an honest letter to the American ambassador. But Don Fabio distrusted the embassy translators. They would subvert the letter's clear sense. Even worse, the letter, which was really a statement of principles, might fall into the hands of a Socialist employed by the Americans. Once it left Marc's hands there was no telling. It might be conveniently misplaced, set aside in an underling's drawer and forgotten until Duffey was recalled and an eager new fool sent in his place to be duped by the grandchildren of the Republicans Franco had beaten in battle in the thirties.

"If I left it up to you," Don Fabio groused when Gregorio led Marc into the library. He unloaded an accusatory finger in the direction of the American's unprotected chest, but the hand to which the finger was attached was heavy. It fell back into his lap.

"If you left what up to me, Don Fabio?"

"Birds of a feather, you and Guadalupe." He shook his head. "Two peas in a pod. No interest in politics, no interest in the great wide world around you. All you two seem to care about is where the next rumba band is playing."

Marc had never gone with Lupe to hear a rumba band play. He wasn't sure he would know one if he heard one. The duke was sitting behind his black walnut desk, a vast empty plain broken by a writing lamp whose soft light was trained on a stack of heavy bond writing paper and an uncapped fountain pen. Not yet written, the letter was still a perfect concept.

"I don't trust my English, you see, any more than I trust the Spanish of your embassy translators. I subscribe to the classical theory regarding the infidelity of translations. Their loose morals will not be cured by an iron hand. I propose to dictate to you in Spanish, Marcos. I'll go slowly enough to allow you to do a thoughtful job with the English approximation."

Sweeping both hands in sync, palms upward, to indicate resignation, the proud old man surrendered his place at the desk to the American. He looked like a rooster rejected by the cook. Tasteless, too tough to enjoy, the old bird was allowed to live out its years unthreatened by society's appetite. But Don Fabio had to know he was a relic, and knowing had to hurt. Marc did not begrudge him his outlet in political outrage.

Gregorio helped him navigate his way into a wingback chair that had belonged to a displaced Bourbon king. The valet knew better than to hover. He took up a position just outside hovering range, available if called upon. He remained in the library because he did not want to miss out on the lesson. The more completely he imagined the world according to his employer, the closer he came to God. Besides, he would not leave Don Fabio unattended with the American. The duke was too old, too formed in his opinions, to be susceptible to foreign influences. Still, it was prudent not to leave the two men alone. Looming above all political considerations was Don Fabio's health.

Translating into acceptable English the formal flourishes with which Don Fabio opened his letter to Ambassador Duffey was a challenge.

"The Left," lectured the old man, drawing in breath to inflate his thesis before launching it. He stopped, let out his breath in jetlike exclamations. He took another tack. "While the Spanish Left may appear, to the untrained eye, to be in a dormant state, while it may mask its true intentions in the guise of civil discourse, the cancer is in point of fact as malignant today as it was in the years that led us into war. You are the last person in Madrid, Mr. Ambassador, in need of a history lesson. Still, your much remarked perspicacity on the subject of contemporary Spanish affairs notwithstanding, I believe it incumbent on myself to refresh your recollection on one or two key aspects of the origins of the situation in which the nation finds itself today."

Here it came, the heart of the matter on a silver platter. Gregorio knew. He took one guarded step closer. He would commit the text of the letter to memory verbatim. Behind the big desk, Marc waited to learn exactly what he was to translate into plain American English.

In the back patio, Federico was kicking a soccer ball. Starting out listlessly, he gradually picked up the pace at which he attacked the ball until it went out of control and smacked the wall of the house. Stepping out onto the flagstones, Doña Inés flung a sharp, icy comment at the boy that reinforced the one sad fact he knew by heart. He had done something wrong. If Lupe ever went away with him to make a separate life together, Marc would have to learn to love an unlovable kid. Feeling bad for him at a distance wasn't enough.

Upstairs, Lupe removed the scarves from the bedroom window and laid them in a dresser drawer one by one. Picturing the drawer aroused the American: the smell of potpourri, the slide of silk across her fingers, a stack of letters wrapped in ribbon. Fencing with Vicky Sorrell at Sergio's had made him horny in a familiar way. It wasn't anger tangled into his desire, just an urge to take prisoners and interrogate them behind closed doors.

The duke cleared his throat. Although good breeding constrained him from letting down in front of an outsider, he couldn't help being a little testy. The infernal plumbing noises clanging inside his body, along with an ache in the elbow he didn't remember feeling last week, distracted him from crafting his message with the precision that was called for. He clenched his fists in his lap, unclenched them. He had it. The Spanish Left, he said again, more firmly this time. Gregorio applauded silently. They were on the verge of triumph.

"The Spanish Left," Marc wrote dutifully on a sheet of clean paper. He was concentrating on silk, and thinking about Vicky Sorrell, wondering whether she would change her mind and have dinner with him. So he missed it the first time when the duke spoke to him.

"Don Fabio?"

The old man glared fiercely at Gregorio, who realized he had finally overstepped his bounds and backed out bowing. No man on earth could have closed the door behind him as softly as Gregorio did.

"Money is not an issue," the duke said when he was gone. His voice sounded like a death rattle.

"I'm sorry?"

"If you marry the girl. Inés and I don't mind at all that you don't have an independent income. We'll see that both of you have enough. If you marry the girl."

He coughed to hide his embarrassment. In his prime he would never have spoken such words, not to anyone. He would never have pleaded. Only weakness made him do it now, weakness and that infernal son of Guadalupe's. But once he started coughing, he couldn't stop. There was bottled water on a silver tray on a table in the corner. Marc poured a glass and handed it to him, but his body had begun to shake with the force of the coughing fit. His face turned violet. Gregorio and Inés came running in together to rescue him. The valet couldn't resist a little flounce of recrimination in Marc's direction; whatever went wrong, it was the American's fault.

"Will you do it?" the duke hacked, looking up at Marc standing there uselessly with a glass of water.

"I'll do it," said Marc, but neither of them believed him.

9

The Lord is my shepherd."

For a terrorist, she had a strangely reassuring voice.

"I shall not want," he replied.

He had picked up the telephone in his room at the Palace with his right hand. Standing at the window, he noticed that his left hand was trembling, it was flapping like a fin. He smothered a laugh that would have made the woman on the other end of the line think he had completely lost it. If he was hysterical, he was no good to them. If he was no good to them, his nephew Benjamin's chances of staying alive dropped to nil. The ruthless logic of his own thoughts appalled him.

This was the call Jack had been told to expect. He had been waiting five days. He had done a respectable job for the Colombians. He had bullied Vicky Sorrell into hosting a party for him, setting her up to expect to hear from him again soon. Never mind that she thought he was either a flake or a complete and total narcissist. But he had flown from Bogotá and gone about doing what he was forced to do in a dazed state like a waking dream. None of it seemed real, least of all his encounter with a guerrilla leader whose name he didn't know in an isolated village in Colombia whose name he also didn't know. He thought about the captured boy being led away to his execution in the woods, the shots that sounded closer than they were, the argument over burying him, and it seemed like a play, something a person like Jack would imagine. Hearing the Colombian woman on the phone brought him back to where he didn't want to be.

"Very good, Mr. Baines," she encouraged him. "I hope you had a pleasant trip."

"Are you crazy?" he snapped at her. "You think I came here for my health?"

The calming voice took no offense. "I understand that this must be difficult for you. But I hope you haven't done something foolish."

"You mean like contacting the police?"

She hung up. He knew she was changing phones. In twenty minutes she called again.

"Go to the Abubilla Museum," she instructed him.

When she paused for a moment, he heard traffic in the background. She was calling from a pay phone on the street. Jack felt a cowardly urge to ingratiate himself with her. She should know he had nothing but contempt for imperial America. Instead he asked her a stupid question.

"How did you know which hotel I was in?"

If they were able to turn him up that easily, he might as well go out and walk naked around Madrid with a bull's-eye on his back.

She ignored his question. "The museum is on La Joda Street. Inside, there is a courtyard, with a garden. In the garden you will see a fountain. Next to the fountain is a bench. In forty-five minutes you must be sitting on that bench."

"What if I'm not?" It was another stupid question. He didn't seem to be able to stop them from coming.

The woman paused before answering, and the traffic sound behind her surged. She might be a block away on the Prado. There was probably some foot soldier chewing gum next to her on the sidewalk with a pistol in his pocket. Thinking of people who could hurt him being that close knocked Jack out of whack. To get through this ordeal he needed to stay on track, keep it simple, keep it clear. But the palms of his hands were clammy, and sweat trickled under both arms. He thought he might be coming down with something.

"In forty-five minutes," the woman repeated.

She spoke with the voice of a psychologist, a professional schooled to steer conversations toward positive outcomes. When he was a teenager, Jack had gone through a period of infatuation with honey slides—marijuana heated in a frying pan until the resin started smoking, then eaten with a tablespoonful of honey. She had a honey slide voice, sweet and smoky.

He stalled. Forty-five minutes. What if he didn't show? He looked for a notebook. He was a writer. What he wanted was a sentence, or part of a sentence. He picked up a Palace Hotel ballpoint pen but tossed it into the wastepaper basket under the desk. He had never been able to write with anything except a wood-barreled number 2 pencil on lined white paper in stiff-backed notebooks. There were pencils in the small leather backpack he'd brought to Madrid. He found a pencil, sat at the desk, and opened his notebook.

Forty-five minutes. He wrote a word, erased it. Wrote another, erased it twice. There was nothing there. That was what the woman had to be made to understand. There was only one J. J. Baines, and keeping him functional called for specific environmental conditions, including peace of mind. It wasn't his fucking war.

He closed the notebook. He thought he might be late. He didn't wait for the elevator. He ran down the stairs and out to the street, took a taxi to Salamanca, where the nineteenth-century villa that had belonged to the poet Abubilla de la Fuente was located. He had been there before, during a happier visit to Madrid. The city had taken over the family manse in the fifties, just as the poet was being rediscovered by critics, converting the building and grounds into a museum and archive.

Abubilla de la Fuente was known for the extravagance of his friendships. Waiting on the patio, surrounded by climbing vines, on the edge of a stone fountain, Jack read a chatty monograph that described the literary man's friends: a bony American who had repented late of the carnage he brought down on the prairie shooting buffalo for sport. A one-eyed Frenchman in starched khaki who had catalogued the diseases prevalent in the regions of Africa that fell under his country's sphere of influence. A Moroccan Jew who wore smoked-lens glasses and green felt slippers and chain-smoked a hookah in his shabby apartment, spending twenty years writing a book that sought to reconcile the Talmud with Darwin.

Forty-six minutes after the woman called, Jack put the book down. This time he knew she was going to make him wait. Next to him on the patio bricks, a cat with brittle gray fur licked its paws in a basin of sunshine.

Abubilla would have understood Jack's dilemma. He was an artist. Artists were singular by definition. There was only one Abubilla de la Fuente. There was only one Jack Baines. No one else could have written *Mario Moving*. It was precisely because there was only one of him that he had to be protected. And the Colombians had put him in an intolerable situation. They were forcing him to prove by his actions that the life of his nephew Benjamin mattered more than his own survival as a writer.

Could the world exist without Jack's novels? He understood the monstrous egoism of the question but couldn't helping asking it anyway. Why was he like that? It hadn't been a conscious decision. His readers admired the talent, the discipline, the craft of his writing. They loved the stories he wrote. They gave him prizes, and they made him rich. But they didn't have a clue how strong the force that drove him was, not a frigging clue. And they had no idea where the impulse came from. Jack had no interest in explaining it to anyone, but he knew exactly where it came from. It came from Samantha.

Jack and his twin sister, Eavy, seldom went to see their mother in her slow decline, south of Buffalo on the shore of Lake Erie. Alzheimer's wasn't the only disease represented at Cody's Bluff, but there seemed to be a disproportionate lot of it. The last time they drove out from the city they found Samantha outside attended by a lumpy girl who looked like a potato left too long in the pantry. The bulge in the pocket of the girl's skirt was a CD player. When she saw them coming she removed the earphones and waited to be scolded.

"You can leave Mrs. Baines with us for awhile." Eavy relieved her.

"Out there." Samantha gestured with a tired hand toward the lake, on the surface of which whitecaps rolled and broke in predictable patterns.

There were rings on all her fingers. Some of them belonged to her. Her helplessness made her look older than she was. Other women at seventy-eight were fit and formidable, but then their circumstances had not been too much for them. Powdery pale, with dark rings of sleeplessness around her blue eyes and cheeks whose muscles had lost their strength, Samantha Sturgess Baines sat on a bench under a grove of poplars on the lip of the bluff. She had lifted the lime-green dress she was wearing from the closet of a neighboring inmate, a widow from East Aurora. Mrs. Dashell had forgotten the sequence of events in a more privileged life than the beads and pictures and pocket change of her own that Samantha forgot and remembered and then forgot again.

The bluff fell down in a cascade of sand and low brush to the brown beach, where a squad of employees in matching green T-shirts raked the sand and piled debris from an earlier tide. The smell that came up over the bluff on the back of the breeze, breaking up in the flutter of poplar leaves above their heads, had lake water in it, and seaweed, and dead fish.

"What about out there?" Jack asked his mother.

He knew, from experience, that she was about to tell them a story. Even Alzheimer's hadn't gotten in the way of her telling stories. Jack recognized the force of the drive in his mother because it was the same in him. He didn't care how much of the story might be true, how much was sheer fabrication. Eavy cared. To Eavy, her mother's inventions were an annoyance. To Jack, they were sacred. The impulse to tell stories was what bound him to his mother and gave him his writerly life.

"You will recall the time my sister Elmira got her arm caught in the ringer washer. Awful awful awful." Samantha swung her head back and forth slowly. "Father flew into a rage at the laundry woman. We had household help, you see, so you couldn't blame Mother. Mother had very particular social obligations. To discharge.

That was how things worked in that era. Elmira was the one who fed that filthy street cat. The black one. I never fed it. I petted it, I admit that. But I never fed it once."

"The lake, though, Samantha," Jack insisted. They had never been permitted to call her Mother. "What about the lake?"

As she spoke, Samantha continued to stare at the horizon where water and sky blended into the same image of distance. The hovering presence of two strange adults disconcerted her. Good manners called for some sort of response, but she wasn't certain what it was she was failing to offer. She hid her chagrin. You didn't give yourself away. When she turned toward Jack, recognition was worse than its absence.

"Well, look what the cat dragged in. Hello there, John Jacob."

"Hello, Samantha."

"I told you, didn't I?"

"Tell me again."

"You were supposed to take out the trash."

"I took it out yesterday."

She nodded. If he had been standing closer she would have patted the back of his hand, her trademark sign of high approval. "I'd like to offer you something." She faltered. "A drink. Something to tide you over. Have you seen that sister of yours? She was the one that fed the black cat. I saw her do it. She coaxed the miserable poor little thing up on the back porch. I just watched."

"I'm here, too, Samantha," Eavy told her. "It's me, Evangeline."

But Samantha shook her head. They weren't going to pull a fast one on her. "My sister's name is Elmira. Like the city in the Southern Tier of New York State. Throughout the Civil War, North against South, Elmira was the site of a well-known prison. Terrible goings-on. The prisoners and the guards alike ate rats to survive. Lean rat meat fetched a high price. The name Elmira comes from the Greek, we were led to believe. When quite young. Father had a classical education. He enjoys the fruits of centuries of knowledge. Vast storehouses . . ." She trailed off.

Jack couldn't let it go. "Vast storehouses."

"That's what he calls his books. Where he dwells. The library. The shelves. Towers of learning. What say we take a walk? What do you think of the dress, by the way? I believe it becomes me."

"The dress looks great on you," Jack told her. "It makes you look like downtown."

"It's killing him," she confided.

"What's killing him?"

"The idea. The very idea that I might throw myself away on an irresponsible whippersnapper. No prospects, no ambition. Not even a proper handshake. He's looking for a soft landing on Easy Street, that's what Father fears."

"Bradford Baines?"

The name he pronounced startled her, or she was pretending. "Your tone of voice leads me to suppose that you have met the gentleman," she remarked, trying to draw Jack out.

"Out there," Jack pointed her back to the lake. He ignored his sister's angry flash that meant let it alone. He couldn't let it alone. In Samantha's mind, out there was where the story came from, and she had not yet told it. Eavy wanted to take her back to her room, but Jack wanted the story. Samantha decided for them.

"Take me down to the beach," she commanded, standing on her parental prerogative.

Jack and Eavy each took a listless arm and moved their mother slowly out from under the poplars toward the upper landing of the wooden steps leading down to the beach. The moment her foot touched the landing, though, Samantha stopped cooperating. Leaning into Jack, she studied a sailboat in the familiar middle distance as though it were one more piece of the vanished whole she had forgotten.

"Out there," Jack pumped her. He wasn't going back without hearing it.

"Not now, for God's sake," Eavy complained, but Samantha swatted at her daughter with a free hand and closed her eyes against the breeze, which made a silver helmet of the old woman's hair.

"It was my idea," she said rebelliously.

"What was your idea, Sam?"

"Taking the family to Alaska. Bradford bought the maps, but he was a timid man. When push came to shove, I was the bold one in that family. I said let's throw caution to the winds, let's pick up and go to the North Country." She shrugged, pleased with her own pluck. "So we went."

"How did you travel?"

Asking her concrete questions usually improved the narrative. The forgetfulness in which she lived since the Alzheimer's took her over changed only the pattern of the stories, not their usefulness.

"Overland in a Jeep, for the most part. Four-wheel drive. Terrible roads. Occasionally we encountered Indians."

"On the warpath?"

She shook her head. "On reservations. You had to be careful of them. Turn your back and they'd steal you blind. We made out pretty well, all things considered. We lost our good iron skillet to them. That was nobody's fault. They're sharp as two tacks, those ones. Not that we could replace the skillet, that far north. We were traveling on ice half the time. I recollect it had a blue cast to it, very pretty when the light caught it. Of course we didn't have much time to observe the beauties of Nature, what with the Indians and the bad roads and I don't know what all."

"Did the children go with you?"

She rounded on him. "That's a foolish question to ask, even for you, Jack. You were there, were you not? Always pestering me to ride in the front seat next to your father. Although I never minded riding in the backseat with Elmira." She shook her head with fond frustration. "My sister and her infernal black cat. However, I'd just as soon you not vex me. I asked you once already to take out the trash."

"I took it out."

"That's enough for now," Eavy tried to stop the replay. "You're tired."

"Which name do you prefer?" their mother wanted to know.

"What are our choices?" Jack said.

"The Aurora Borealis or the Northern Lights."

"I like the Northern Lights," Jack admitted.

"I always preferred the sound of the Aurora Borealis," Samantha admitted. "I blame the Eskimos."

"For what?"

"Please, Jack. Can't you see she's exhausted?"

"They planted the notion in my man's head about the best spot to observe the Lights."

Jack understood where she was going. He wanted to help her get there. "That was when he left you."

"Disappeared is more like it. The children were too young to make the trek. I had my hands full with that pair. The boy in particular was the harum-scarum breed."

"So Bradford took off to the place the Eskimos told him about."

But she had taken her story as far as she could deliver it. The effort to reconstruct what hadn't happened did her in.

His twins were seven when Bradford Baines discovered he wasn't built for life in the temperate zone and escaped to Alaska. For a long time Samantha made a joke of it with the same question every evening before prayers, after they had eaten and bathed and counted off the capitals of ten different states. Juneau, where your father is tonight? Turning thirty, with a wife who wore white gloves when nobody else did, Bradford Baines revealed a genetic defect. He was not equipped for ordinary life: broken porch steps. Punching a swing-shift clock at Queen City Beef. An always uneven number of dessert bowls with a rose wreath design. A stopped-up drain in a claw-foot tub with a rust stain around the drain. Persistent dandelions. Casseroles with crunchy cereal tops and leftovers in sealed plastic. Card parties with highballs and allusions to Johnson City, where all the Sturgess women had worn immaculate gloves.

By the time he was in his late teens and recognized a variation of the flight instinct operating in himself, Jack quit holding his father's abdication against the man. Besides, he had already learned everything he needed to know from his mother.

❁   ❁   ❁

After an hour and a half on the bench, Jack decided to leave. Let him flunk the test the Colombians were administering to him. Somewhere—inside the mansion or across the street at the bus stop—a plainclothes terrorist was watching for cops. How did he know what to look for? He had to distinguish between, say, the fussy bald man on the sidewalk in shade absorbed in peeling a bruised banana and the matronly woman with balustrade legs next to him fishing in her purse for a red herring.

But what if he guessed wrong? What if he decided that the woman with the purse full of red herrings worked for Spanish intelligence? So when the man with the banana called in his report, he told them Baines had disobeyed orders. If that happened, Benjamin didn't stand a chance. Neither did Jack. If they killed Ben, they had no leverage against the writer. Without leverage, Jack was useless to them. Useless, he was expendable. Expended, he was dead.

When he heard feet shuffling behind him, the hairs on the back of his neck stood up and his face flushed. But the shuffling feet belonged to a security guard carrying a bowl of bread and milk to the gray cat. Jack watched him place the bowl on the patio bricks, scratching behind the animal's ears as it lapped the mush.

Jack's eyes teared. This was the sort of thing people were supposed to do with their lives, feed and comfort, not surveil fellow human beings and take them out when they were no longer useful in your battle plan. He was losing it. He walked quickly out to the street and hailed a taxi.

The *taxista* was a yellowish man of thirty with flat purple lips who emitted an odor of Old Spice. When the driver did not return him to the Palace Hotel, Jack felt passive, as though he were being delivered to his own funeral, the eulogy already distributed to the mourners, who felt ambiguous about their loss. He quibbled for form's sake, but the driver shrugged and dropped him where he had been told to deliver his passenger, the Thyssen-Bornemisza Museum on the Prado.

"Edward Hopper," he told the American as Jack got out of the cab.

Inside the museum, there seemed to be only one Hopper painting. Jack studied *Hotel Room* for ten minutes before she showed herself, dressed to resemble a bank teller. Thirty-five or thereabouts, surgically neat, she wore a light blue suit and a white blouse with a round collar. On her feet, which were a little too large for the rest of her, were sensible shoes. She walked like a duck.

"The catalogue says the painting is about being lonely," she told him, "but all I see is a woman in a hotel room."

"What's with all the spy stuff?" he asked her. "I'm not the James Bond type."

The aggression in his voice surprised him. Aggression was better than panic, but neither was really helpful. Clarity would help, but he didn't have any.

"Neither are we, Mister Baines. This is about something bigger than Hollywood entertainment."

"Wrong," he said, furious despite trying to keep it in check. "You're dead wrong. I'll tell you what it's about. It's about a twenty-year-old kid being kidnapped."

"You're not as political as your writing, are you?" she decided. "You're an entertainer, after all."

"How do I know you won't kill my nephew even if I keep cooperating?"

"We're not savages, and we're not terrorists. We don't kill innocent people for the pleasure of it. Do what is asked of you, and your nephew will be released unharmed. You have my word."

"Your word."

They strolled with counterfeit leisure through the museum, which housed a huge collection. There were few people in the building except for a troupe of school kids in uniforms taking a quickie walking tour of Western civilization, observing what their grandfathers had wrought.

"Tell me about the woman," the Colombian woman said once, taking his arm as a swarm of kids broke streaming on either side of them. "The cultural attaché."

"She's intelligent," Jack told her. "Very quick. She finds my sudden interest in her a little strange. She doesn't trust me."

"She doesn't have to trust you, all she has to do is talk with you."

"About what?"

"We're interested in Ambassador Terrence Duffey. Anything she will tell you about him, everything. The slightest detail will be helpful. Does he work out at a gym, for example? How many times a week? Is it always the same hour? Does he go for walks? Who are his favorite Spanish friends? Does he ever slip his guard and go out on his own? Nothing you turn up will be insignificant."

"She won't buy it. She already thinks I'm strange. If I interrogate her about her boss, she'll know something is wrong. It's not a normal kind of thing for us to talk about."

"Then ask about the other Americans at the embassy, too. You're creative, you'll find a way to get what we want. We're not terrorists, Mr. Baines, but we are serious. You should understand that if you screw this up, your nephew will die."

"What if his parents decide to call the police? I can't stop them."

"They won't."

"What is that supposed to mean?"

She shook her head. "We are in the process of convincing them not to involve the authorities."

"You don't strike me as naive," he told her, "but you must be if you think you can drive the American government out of Colombia."

She looked at him as though wondering whether he had been born annoying or had worked to develop the skill.

"Stay focused," she advised him. "Sooner than you think, Señor Baines, this will all be over, and you and your nephew can go back to living your normal lives. That's a promise."

A promise. She left him in the Impressionist rooms, as though all that absorption with the sensual particulars of bourgeois light and life grated against her political sensibility, which had a single goal, getting the gringos out of Colombia. Eavy and Philip would be convinced not to call the police, she had told him. He thought about Benjamin. The kid was an odd duck, a loner. He didn't have enough friends, spent all his time drawing. He wandered. It seemed particularly unfair that the Colombians had kidnapped a nephew who was so much like his uncle, although they couldn't have known that. Under stress, Benjamin was likely to fold.

"Hello, Vicky, this is Jack Baines." Jack practiced the call as he walked toward the exit door of the Thyssen. "I'd like to come over and have you tell me everything you know about your ambassador. For the sake of efficiency, I'll take notes while you spill the beans. While you're at it, you may as well tell me about the ambassador's deputy, and the political officer, and the economic officer. Hell, tell me about all of them. I've got all the time in the world."

It no longer seemed like a play.

10

Erogenous zone."

Because of the highway noise and because Chick pronounced the words with a Spanish accent, it took Ben a moment to catch it, but as soon as he snagged it he knew where he wanted to go with it.

"Erogenous zone," he repeated carefully, trying to make it come out sounding the way a non-native speaker of English might pronounce the words. It was important to get on a wavelength with the guys who had kidnapped him. This was especially true now that they were on the road. Even if he managed, with his broken hand, to draw a picture that got their attention, they would be distracted by traffic and reading the map and deciding where to buy gas. Away from the little apartment in Buffalo, Ben felt more vulnerable. He felt more like a victim.

In Maryland, Quixote, who drove with more assurance than Chick, took the wheel to pilot them around Washington on the Beltway, which was rush-hour crowded in the middle of the afternoon. Across the American Legion Bridge into Virginia, Ben started smelling the South. Something about moving south excited him, as though he were going on vacation to a new place. They had switched vehicles, the kidnappers taking turns driving a butter-colored Lincoln. The big Town Car burned a lot of gas, but the ride was smooth.

Ben rolled his window down. Riding shotgun, Chick turned around once and smiled at him as though he had just noticed that they had a passenger. The smile, the distance, the southern air all increased Ben's sense of dislocation. It occurred to him for the first time that the reason he had been kidnapped might not have anything to do with Fearless Fly's marijuana.

Back in Buffalo, when Quixote took the call on his cell phone, Ben assumed it was over for him, if not when he hung up the phone, then a little later. Presumably Quixote was being given specific instructions about how and when and where to kill him. Ben hoped they would show some mercy and take him by surprise. He was afraid that, if he saw his own death coming, he would die disgracefully, blubbering and begging for his life. Even though there would be no one around to witness his shame, except of course his killers, he hated the thought of going out like a coward.

It would help to know whether Quixote liked what he was hearing on the other end of the line, but he disappeared down the hall with the phone on his ear, slamming behind him the door into one of the bedrooms. Ben wanted to believe that neither he nor Chick took any sadistic pleasure from being in the presence of the person they were assigned to kill. Most of the time they seemed indifferent to their American hostage, treating him like a slab of meat, but every once in a while they gave him the impression that they kind of liked him. Ben recognized that wanting to be liked by your kidnappers was normal but not a healthy impulse.

While Quixote finished his conversation in private, Chick hung out in the living room with Ben, picking his teeth. He held one hand like a fan in front of his mouth to screen the action of the other hand, which held the toothpick, so that his eyes looked out at Ben as from behind a veil.

"Okay!" he said when he noticed the panic rising in Ben.

He removed the toothpick from his mouth, tossed it into a dirty ashtray on an end table, dropped his screen hand, and grinned. "Okay, man. It's okay."

That night the two South Americans took turns standing guard over Ben as he lay on the sofa trying to sleep so that they could kill him unaware. He may have dozed, but Quixote and Chick went with him as he dreamed. *Muerto,* one of them was always saying, pronouncing him dead even before they killed him. But the tenor of their voices convinced him that he was right. They liked him. When the order came through, he wanted to believe they would take no satisfaction in the murder. Not that their state of mind was going to change what happened to him.

In the morning, the Lincoln had been parked at the curb under a large plane tree, and they let him know with curt, peremptory gestures that they expected him to go down the walk and get into the backseat of the car. On the sidewalk, in the pleasant early sunlight, Ben thought for just a moment about making a break. But there was no one in sight on the street; no witnesses, and no one to call for help. There was no doubt that if he ran, he would be shot. Getting shot in the back seemed, just then, a lot worse than being shot in any other part of the body. He got into the car.

"Erogenous zone," Chick read aloud from the Spanish-English dictionary he had tossed into the car when they left Buffalo.

"It's in Texas," Ben told him. "It's a place in Texas. Huge. There is a very big parking lot."

He thought that if he entertained them, they might have second thoughts. Was it harder to kill someone who made you laugh?

"*Un lugar de estacionamiento,*" Quixote said pedantically.

"That's right. A place of parking. As soon as you get there, your body begins to feel good. You feel so good you can't stand it sometimes. That's why they call it the erogenous zone."

"*Las casas,*" Chick wondered, rubbing the fingers of his right hand together.

"Of course," Ben agreed with him. "Houses in the erogenous zone are very expensive."

"Tierra del Fuego?" He pointed ahead of them, south down the interstate.

Now seemed like the right time to ask where they were going.

"Patagonia," Quixote told him, and that was the end of the conversation.

They had allowed Ben to bring paper and a handful of pencils. Left alone in the backseat, he drew a sketch of the Lincoln that wasn't bad, considering his hand; it had the kind of fidelity to the original that they would admire. But he thought they would probably see it as evidence, as though he were leaving behind a pictorial record of the kidnapping so the police could trace them. He tore up the paper but was unable to think of anything else to draw.

They had been pushing since they left Buffalo, stopping only for coffee that the two men drank like medicine. They never offered Ben any. Outside Turkey Run, North Carolina, Quixote left the highway and followed a series of small signs to a motel run by an Indian couple. The proprietors of the Vee-Jay Motel did not seem to find it strange that a pale young man with long black hair was traveling in the company of two Latin hardcases. Ben wondered desperately how he could signal them that he was in trouble, but the wife disappeared into a back office the moment they stepped into the little lobby, and her husband didn't look up as he pushed the registration form across the desk to Quixote and then fished in a drawer for a key.

Before they went to their room, Ben stood between Quixote and Chick for a few moments on a square of dusty grass, all of them letting the road buzz wear off. Behind them, a shallow creek burbled through a patch of scrawny woods that separated them from the interstate, along which vehicles rushed north and south. In front of them, seven peacocks crossed the grass like somnambulists. Four dirty orange cats with white feet watched them forage, while a black hound with tattered long ears sat on its haunches in the gravel of the parking lot. The sun grazed the western horizon, oozing color that was sucked up by clouds whose rims shone silver-gold as their centers darkened.

The relationship among the three men was rigidly hierarchical. Because he was king, Quixote showered first, using all the towels in the bathroom. Next in line, Chick went without complaining to the office for more towels. When he was finished, he left a single damp towel on a rack for Ben; the rest lay in a heap on the tile floor.

Ben rinsed his clothes in the tub and stretched them to dry on the towel rack and wrapped himself in wet towels. He wondered whether he could convince them to stop in Turkey Run and let him pick up a change of clothes. They might see that doing so was in their interest. Clean and normal looking, Ben would draw less attention to himself. But the thought of pleading with them in English and broken Spanish, and having them ignore him, was daunting. He didn't think he could do it.

In the mirror Ben looked older to himself. He looked like someone besides Philip and Eavy's younger son, or Darrell's little brother. That was good. He liked the idea of an escape clause in the family contract. But the older he got, the more he resembled his Uncle Jack. That was not so good. Hiding Fearless Fly's dope in the attic of his parents' house, Ben had come across an envelope of black-and-white photographs of Jack Baines when he was nineteen or so. Eavy must have taken the photos. The camera's eye had captured the artist as a young egotist. Ben knew it annoyed his father when someone pointed out the resemblance. In Philip Burke's opinion, famous writer or not, Uncle Jack Baines was not much of a role model.

A previous guest had left a blue plastic razor inside the medicine cabinet. Ben made a thin lather of soap and shaved carefully. But the blade inside the plastic head was old, and he sliced his chin. For a moment he stood watching the blood drip into the sink, where it gathered in a rusted out depression around the drain. It seemed like someone else's accident. He didn't mean to start laughing.

Once he started, however, he found it difficult to stop. He didn't stop because he didn't want to. The tears that made his eyes smart were not his idea, either, they were a contribution from his nervous system.

He would have bet money that Chick said *"Qué diablos!"* when he opened the bathroom and saw him bleeding and crying and laughing. But he and Quixote always spoke so fast it was impossible to know what they said, even if the words were easy. They had already begun drinking. Chick doused a wad of Kleenex with some Jack Daniels and pressed it hard against the cut on Ben's chin. The sting and the surprise made Ben stop laughing, although his eyes continued to tear and he tasted salt.

He sipped a little from the plastic glass of bourbon that Quixote shoved at him. It tasted like junior high school. Ben's bourbon phase had been short, beginning at a New Year's Eve party in eighth grade and continuing until he threw up a pint's worth of Old Grandad in Delaware Park in the middle of March. Now, the taste and the smell gagged him.

"*Está bien!*" Chick clapped him on the shoulder like a football coach, and despite himself Ben longed again for the man's approval. He thought he had it.

"*Borracho.*" He remembered the Spanish word for drunk when he was almost drunk himself.

Quixote had sent Chick out for food. Chick came back with fried chicken and a cardboard bucket of grits. But the food was not enough to absorb the alcohol, and Ben felt abandoned when the two men switched on the television. The cable system carried a Spanish channel. Two blonde women with large breasts clapped their hands and squealed every time a contestant on the game show got the right answer. Every few minutes the camera cut to a dwarf in a green suit carrying a wireless microphone around the audience to get their comments on the game that was happening onstage. Judging by the laughter, which wasn't canned, everything that happened on the show was hilarious.

They ate, they drank, they watched terrible television. During the commercials, Chick thumbed through his dictionary looking for words to test Ben with.

"Fatuous," he tried.

"Fatuous," Ben explained, "is the layer of fat on meat." He lifted the drumstick he was eating. "This chicken is fatuous. Fatuous foods are bad for the heart."

But he didn't want to play word games, he wanted to walk. He had to get out of the room for a while. He had to get away from them before they made up their mind to kill him. He stood up, tightened the towel around his waist, and lurched toward the door. They were on him before he found the handle. They laid him out on one of the beds like tired undertakers. Chick removed his sneakers, which he did not remember having put back on after he showered. His feet felt strangely narrow, as narrow as the blades of ice skates and just as hard to walk on.

Drunk and exhausted, lying on his back, for the first time Benjamin understood what the kidnappers were saying. *Let him sleep. Let the whiskey do its work. Work is work and nobody can make it go away. I miss my wife. I miss your wife, too. You bastard. It was a joke. So what's ever funny about your jokes? Forget it. I feel like shit. It's that damn greasy chicken. No, it's not, it's the bourbon. The King of Spain is a Bourbon. You think I didn't know that? The Queen of England is a pint of stout. I should know, I drank her health not three weeks ago. I don't have the stomach for this. Sure you do. Let the kid sleep. His feet stink. He didn't clean his feet. I'm telling you I don't have the stomach for this.*

The effort of translating wore him out. With no consciousness of having moved, Ben found himself at the edge of a dark ocean. The ocean had a whiskey undercurrent, and the waves lapped the shore in a reassuring rhythm. Being there like that was restful, but he felt apprehensive anyway.

He didn't feel the pain until the top third of his ring finger on the left hand was severed at the joint. He knew he was going to remember Quixote standing there with the knife in his hand. Chick, who didn't have the stomach for it, had pinned Ben's wrist and fingers on the night table next to the bed long enough for Quixote to chop off the tip. In the daze of pain and alarm, for a moment Ben thought the blood spurting from his finger was whiskey.

He wished he could be there when the package with his fingertip showed up at his parents' house. He wanted to cushion the shock for his mother. He wanted to tell her he could live without the tip of one finger, and to apologize for getting himself into another mess.

There was a lot to explain. More than anything, that was what he wanted to be able to do, explain it all so she wouldn't feel bad.

Chick went to the bathroom and came back with a towel to wrap around Ben's finger and squeeze off the bleeding. If it kept spurting, Ben was going to pass out. He closed his eyes. Fading from the fear, he was aware of Quixote still standing over the bed, staring at the knife in his hand. It's okay, he wanted to tell Eavy. Philip, too. And his brother, Darrell. It was no big deal to live without a finger.

11

Jack? This is Vicky Sorrell, from the embassy."

"This is pretty weird. I was going to call you, Vicky. Now. I mean I was just going to call you."

"I called to apologize."

"For what?"

"I was pretty hostile to you after the reception at my apartment. I'm sorry."

"Does this mean you dislike me less than you thought you did?"

"It means I want to make it up to you."

"How?"

"By taking you to see El Escorial."

"When?"

"Today. This morning. I took the day off. Unless you have to work."

"It's not healthy to write every day," he told her. "It has something to do with the lipids. There's a connection between cholesterol and karma. Only the prose drones believe you have to produce your five hundred words a day come hell or high water."

"So do you want to go with me or not?"

"I bet being with me counts as work for you," Baines guessed. "Am I right?"

"I'm leaving Madrid, remember? I don't want to be on duty anymore. I want to see El Escorial one more time before I go, that's all. Why do I have the feeling that you're the one who's being suspicious, not me?"

"Sure," he decided. "I'll go."

"I'm on my way."

"A rose."

"I'm sorry?"

"I'll have a rose between my teeth. So you'll recognize me."

Vicky didn't have a car. She could have borrowed one from Marc Karulevich but chose not to. It was bad enough colluding with him to carry out an interrogation of Jack Baines in the guise of a social outing. She didn't want to incur a debt with Marc even if it was to do him the favor he had asked of her. It was still difficult—no, it was impossible—to picture the novelist in league with the Badger and his Justice Concept. Jack was vain and self-absorbed and entirely obsessed with his writing. If he was involved with the Colombians, it was only because they had conned him. He was, at worst, only their useful fool. She thought maybe if she asked the right questions he would tell her what he knew, and that would be the end of it. She could go back to Karulevich and explain the whole misunderstanding and make her reservation to fly back to the U.S.

She should be thinking about what she was going to do for a living once she left the service. She wasn't. She was going to take a little time off. She pictured a beach somewhere, far enough away from anywhere that the stars were visible at night and there was no traffic noise. She could use two weeks of that, maybe three. After that, she had no idea what she was going to do, or where she would do it.

She overcame her reluctance and borrowed Wyatt's Opel for the trip to San Lorenzo. Working in the embassy, she and Wyatt could not avoid each other. They attended the same meetings. They had the same friends. When they came back from Sor Epi, Wyatt had put out the word that their relationship was passing through a rough patch. Nothing serious, but Vicky needed a little space to sort out her feelings, etc. People should let her do that in peace. So when she was around their friends, the subject of Wyatt Willis was conspicuously avoided. She was not close enough to any of them to bother telling the truth.

Wyatt was waiting for a change of heart. He was friendly with one of the Spaniards at the embassy's travel agency, so he would know that Vicky hadn't made a reservation yet, which he would interpret as meaning he still had a chance. Meantime he scoured his college lit anthology and transcribed love poems and sent them to her on the embassy email system, one a day. She knew if she asked to borrow his car he would take it as a sign. Maybe it was, it occurred to her as she put the key into the ignition of his beautiful automobile, maybe it was.

She picked up Baines on the street outside the Palace Hotel and then maneuvered north across the city to pick up the N-VI Highway toward La Coruña. Like a Baines character, she preferred not knowing what was going to happen next.

It was the end of June. The Spanish summer had thickened, coating the earth, dribbling through the dirt down to the roots of trees. The farther they left the capital behind, the closer Vicky and Jack appeared to approach an antique image of Spain, a Spanish state of mind that thrived in the imagination of romantic foreigners who craved a mysterious other, along with good red wine and appealingly presented seafood. Under a sun like revelation, sheep struggled through brambles on a brown slope. A thin man in a black beret smoking with understated pleasure rested on a round stone tower rising from the single standing wall of a castle on the crest of a fin-backed hill. In a village of umber roofs visible from the highway, motor scooters clustered like colorful gnats at an intersection, the drivers and their passengers waving their arms as though they had choreographed a chance instant and it was coming out perfect. Wyatt's peppy green car sliced through an invisible pudding of heat.

Neither of them said much. Vicky was not accustomed to conducting interrogations, and Jack was smart enough to know when he was being pumped for information. He was preoccupied, as though he couldn't make up his mind about something and couldn't do anything else until he did.

Then, as they approached San Lorenzo, the N-VI climbed and the garish gash of the Civil War monument was briefly visible against the green mountain. The colossal white cross erected by the Generalissimo looked more like a pair of crossed swords than an icon of Christian sacrifice.

"So is the guide book right?" Jack asked her.

"Right about what?"

"It says after the war, Franco forced Republican prisoners to build that monstrosity."

"For my Spanish friends the whole thing is an embarrassment," Vicky told him. "They'd just as soon not talk about it."

The sight of the monument wound him up a little. "Think about it, Victoria. You fight a just war to protect your republic from the rightists and the reactionaries and the royalists. You're some sort of idealist. You want democracy. You want the right to give your parish priest the finger in a public space. But you're captured, so you sit out the rest of the war eating rat tails. Your side loses, but the pricks who won won't let you go home and figure out how to rebuild some kind of life for yourself. A letter is smuggled in to you in prison. Your wife, you learn, is pregnant by another man, one of the rightists. Then, just to prove things can always get worse, Franco puts you on a chain gang building an ugly damn monument to every rotten thing you fought against."

"Even the scenery," she said.

"What about the scenery?"

"For you, even the scenery is political, isn't it? It's there in everything you write."

He shrugged; what she said made him uncomfortable, for some reason. "I've been accused of being an entertainer."

"Entertainment isn't a crime, it's a good thing. But you're doing something besides parlor magic in your work. Who told you that you weren't?"

"Never mind, it doesn't matter. The main thing is doing the work, getting it done, right? Writing is what I do. Everything else comes in second place. I can't help it."

"Everything?"

He nodded, and she had the impression it was a confession he was not often willing to make. "I always thought there was something worthwhile in it. Besides me, I mean. I thought I was on the right side, Vicky."

"What changed your mind?"

He looked at her sharply, and she realized it was too soon to step through the opening she had worked carefully to create. She waited until they reached the structured austerity of El Escorial, grim and gray, Felipe II's memorial to an idea of order huge enough to hold Heaven and Earth in their proper spatial relationship.

"Nobody ever said repression couldn't be elegant," she said as they got close to the place.

"Un-fucking-believable," Jack muttered. He tried to disguise his gawking to distinguish himself from the swarming tourists, who grazed lightly, nibbling at a cultural appetizer before sitting down to the heavy Spanish meal waiting for them in a restaurant that catered to busloads.

As they toured the grounds, the chambers, the chapel, Jack was openly resentful of the hold the place exerted on him, as though the Catholic king's cold stone statement of first principles and final explanations came so close to the sublimity to which he aspired that the only sensible response was to feel small. El Escorial always made you feel small, but it was always worst the first visit.

At the head of a flight of stairs down into the Panteón, Jack balked, pulling up like a horse that wasn't going to jump the ditch ahead of it regardless of the quality of persuasion applied. Scandinavians and Italians and Australians stacked up behind him. There was muttering in many languages. The obstacle in their way was American, of course. Who else? Bad enough that they owned the world, worse that they acted the part of landlord-boor with such relish. Give them a few more years and they'd figure out how to disassemble Spain, ship it across the Atlantic in numbered pieces, and put it back together in the Arizona desert so retired geezers could waddle to catch a bullfight.

"What's down there?" Jack demanded of anyone who could tell him.

An Italian man with his hands in the pockets of very blue jeans said something cryptic that made his chattering party laugh. Vicky took Jack's arm and pulled him away from the stairs so that he no longer blocked the traffic down. The outrage evaporated quickly, and people moved past them in a herd.

"The Panteón," she explained as if to a child who suffered from an attention deficit disorder, "is where they buried the royals who didn't rule and the queens who had no children and the children who didn't survive childhood."

"I can't breathe in here."

"We don't have to keep doing this, you know. Tourism is optional. I thought you'd enjoy it."

"I'm here." He shook his head as if he were seasick. "I'm a legitimate tourist. I'm telling you there's not enough air is all."

"There's more air downstairs."

Gripping the railing, he went down like an old man afraid of his ankles. Moving from room to room, tomb to tomb, he was overwrought, self-inflated, murderous. He was an artist. Tolerating him was tedious.

"So the idea is," he said, "you marvel at the architecture for a few minutes. You let the solemnity of royal prerogatives soak into your consciousness until you begin to understand how God thinks."

"How does God think, Jack?"

"He's arbitrary, and He plays favorites. Out of thousands of candidates in the Iberian Peninsula, he chooses a handful of families to run the realm. They can fight among themselves, but they have to band together to protect the system, which is a model of the celestial infrastructure. No wonder."

"No wonder what?"

"No wonder there are revolutionaries in the world."

"If you don't want to be here, Jack, we can go somewhere else."

Vicky disliked being put in the position of defending the death aesthetics of Spanish royalty. She was tired of being an official American, bridging between people who distrusted one another for similar reasons. To the Spaniards, she was obliged to explain U.S.

Middle East policy, and the depth of support for capital punishment across the United States. To the Americans, she talked about the Spaniards' obsession with being part of Europe, and why they were so reticent about their Civil War.

"Turn it off, Jack," she said.

But he went on hectoring. "This is what power does. It builds monuments to its own idea of itself. Which brings us back to where we started: the concept of the architect as whore. The guy who built this pile, he learned the hard way, they won't let you do your work clean. They drag you into their shit, and you get dirty, and then they turn around and say, See? We told you. You're donkey dung just like everybody else."

"Is this a roundabout way of talking about your writing, Jack, or your life, or what? If you want me to get it, you'll have to drop the metaphors. Approach me on a straightaway."

"Sorry." He slumped a little. "My nerves are bad, Vicky. It's a temporary thing. Any minute now I'm going to break out in reasonableness."

"Why are your nerves bad?"

The lag before he answered emphasized his evasion. "Let's talk about something else. Something that has nothing to do with me. Tell me about your work. Tell me what it's like to work in the embassy."

"Talking about the embassy is the most boring thing I can think of."

"What about the ambassador?" he said, inspecting a portrait of a bloody saint in religious ecstasy on the edge of an allegorical forest. "He's a political appointee, right? Is he also a human being?"

"Is that what you're really interested in, the management style of Terrence Duffey?"

"All right, forget about Duffey. Who do you like in the embassy? Who are your buddies?"

She looked at him hard, hoping intently that he wouldn't cross over a line that would prove to her that Marc Karulevich was right about him.

They were going into the last room of the Panteón, where there was a massive tomb in the shape of a wedding cake, the remains of royal babies buried throughout the stiff, gleaming mass.

"This place gives me the creeps," he admitted. "I'm a terrible tourist."

"Yes, you are. You're the worst tourist I ever saw."

"I give up. Why don't you just drive me back to Madrid?"

But on the drive down from San Lorenzo, all he wanted to talk about was Ambassador Duffey. Half the answers she gave were innocuous and random, nothing, she believed, that a terrorist organization would find useful for planning an attack. The other half she made up. She told herself it was still possible that Karulevich had Jack Baines wrong.

But when she parked the Opel in front of the Palace, the novelist took her forearm, wrapped his fingers around her wrist, grinned and grimaced. "This didn't turn out as well as we were both hoping it would, did it?"

She unfolded his fingers and took her wrist back. "No, it didn't."

"What do I have to do to get you to trust me, Vicky?"

"Tell me the truth."

"Okay, the truth. I told you I was working on a manuscript, right?"

"Seventy pages."

"I'm up to eighty. It's a kind of Americans abroad sort of a story. It's called *Expat*."

"Including an embassy type or two."

"Is it a sin for me to want to get them right?"

"Why didn't you say that the first time we met?"

"Because I fucked up. I usually do. If there's a smart choice and a dumb choice, I pick the dumb one."

"I'm still not sure I believe you, Jack."

"It's the truth. But not the whole truth."

"What's the whole truth?"

"I like you, Vicky Sorrell. I like your company."

Maybe he did, but the attempt to convince her of his virtuous intentions was so blatant it was like being slapped in the face. In response, she did something Karulevich wouldn't approve of. She threw Jack a lifeline. Marc would have said, *It's like a poker game. You don't tip your hand. You never tip your hand.*

But Vicky was not, after all, an intelligence case officer. She was a cultural attaché. Her specialty was using American culture to illuminate American society and the values that sustained it. She could talk democracy, higher education, Abstract Expressionism, the impact of an indie film sensibility on how people in Hollywood held their cameras. She knew enough to hold up a conversation on affirmative action, or hip hop, or how blues and country music had magically morphed into rock 'n' roll. What she didn't do, because she didn't want to do it, was play the kind of information poker that people like Marc Karulevich lived to play.

"What's up, Jack?" she said. "This isn't about a novel you're writing, and it's definitely not about being attracted to me."

"Nothing's up," he said.

He was looking at his fingernails. He saw a hangnail and peeled the strip of skin from the finger. A drop of blood appeared between nail and flesh.

"If you're involved in something, and you'll tell me what it is, I can help."

"You?"

"Okay, not me, we. We can help. The embassy."

She thought she had him. He shifted in his seat, watched the blood drop run along the edge of his nail. He whistled breathily, not a tune, exactly, more like an exclamation, what a man whistled when he hit the end of a cul-de-sac and couldn't turn around. But he looked at her sideways. His grin was malicious, almost a sneer.

"I had a lovely time, Victoria. May I call you again sometime?"

"Sure, Jack," she told him. "You can call me anytime you want to."

On the sidewalk he hesitated. He looked like a man who just might run. In his expensive shoes, his rumpled khakis, his dark silk shirt, he seemed out of place, as though he had dressed himself that morning thinking about camouflage but got it wrong. He looked at his hand, then up the street toward the Prado once before walking inside the hotel. Okay, Vicky heard herself admitting to Marc Karulevich, you were right. Jack Baines is into something big and bad.

12

Game point, am I right?"

With Juan Manuel Portillo it was always game point, and he was always right. He bounced the scuffed blue racquetball on the hardwood floor, letting Marc catch his breath. The Spanish intelligence officer looked charitably away from the American, hunched hands on knees and breathing like a gaffed fish in the floor of the boat just before it relinquished its sense of selfhood. For two years they had played against each other once a week. Marc had beaten Portillo maybe seven times.

"There's an expression in English," Marc told him. He didn't have enough air in his lungs to propel the words up and out of his throat. They blooped, dropped on the floor.

Unlike most of the professional Spaniards Marc knew, Juan Manuel insisted on speaking English with him. Practice was only part of it. Mastering the language gave him a tactical advantage. He spoke it well, storing up idioms, phrases, even puns, but the words had a certain odd sound, more burr than accent.

"I'm all ears," Juan said.

"I'll give you the second half first."

"Go ahead."

"And the horse you rode in on."

"Fuck you."

"Congratulations. You pass the cultural adaptation test. You're ready for your assignment to Omaha."

"Nebraska, am I right?"

If the Spaniards were thoroughbred dogs, Portillo was the champion of his class, a show animal with no visible defects. Two meters tall, with the build of a gymnast in his prime, he looked like a composite sketch of Zorro, the foxy lover who scaled the side of the evil king's house to whisper jokes into the ear of the princess, who'd been waiting for him. He was too good-looking to do undercover work.

"You ready?" he asked Marc.

"Fuck you and the horse you rode in on."

When the Spaniard served, Marc caught the ball off the wall with the edge of his racket so that it caromed weakly, giving Juan Manuel the time he needed to place it in a corner beyond Marc's reach.

"One more game, Marquitos."

"Isn't total domination enough?"

"It's never enough. One more game."

But Marc was played out. They went toward the showers. Playing racquetball in the middle of the afternoon let Portillo score another point in their marathon match. The point had to do with freedom, which had to do with dynamism. The American intelligence organism, he liked to point out, had atrophied into bureaucracy.

"Let's have a conversation," he proposed.

"There's only one subject I want to talk about, Juan Manuel."

"Me, too. And your subject is my subject. We're cooperating now, we're not competing. My boss talked with your boss. Madrid called Washington, Washington called Madrid. We're on the same side. We're introducing a new candor into the relationship. If you liked me before, you're going to love me now. It feels different, doesn't it?"

"What feels different?"

"You do. After the terror hits you at home, you understand what vulnerable means. It's no longer just an idea. Suddenly it's as real as, let's say, some ETA prick murdering a policeman who has three kids and his wife is pregnant with their fourth. How badly do you want to take the fuckers out, Marc?"

Portillo's hatred of the Basque separatist terrorist group, the ETA, was powerful and permanent. Juan Manuel was an anomaly in the Spanish service. He didn't come out of the military or one of the elite schools. He had no social connections. His father was a drunk in his home village in the Pyrenees, cadging cigarettes from tourists by performing sleight-of-hand tricks. As a starting place, Juan Manuel's story was close enough to Marc's in Dearborn that they should have been twins. But the American dream of social mobility and self-invention had no functional equivalent in Spain. Juan Manuel didn't mind who knew where he came from, but he probably didn't tell the story much; there was no audience.

The Spaniard's hard edge was harder than Marc's. If the service recruiters were smart, they would go looking for more like Portillo. The ultimate outsider given a pass into the secret center, he was the ideal watchman, fiercely vigilant of the order he was entrusted to protect. Marc wanted to believe there were fundamental differences that set the two of them apart, but he wasn't sure what they were.

"I want to take them out, Juan Manuel. I want to take them out as badly as you do."

Marc took a long time showering. He needed to wash Lupe off his body, inside and out. The night before, she had showed up at his apartment and bowled him into bed. She wouldn't talk, wouldn't even move. She lay on her back in the dark, locking his torso with her legs so that the oral sex she wanted but wouldn't ask for was pretty much the only option, from an acrobatic point of view. He gave and gave. She took until his tongue gave out. She would have taken more.

Afterward he had lied not to deceive her but to smoke her out. "I got my next assignment today, Lupe."

"Where are they sending you?"

He couldn't say Ouagadougou. She wouldn't buy it.

"Paraguay," he told her instead. Maybe they spoke Spanish there, but from Lupe's point of view the country was as remote as Africa. It was impossible for her to imagine herself in a South American jungle. She would picture them living in a tree, eating coconuts, traveling upriver in a dugout canoe to see the cannibal sights. Fede would have to wear a loincloth.

"When do you go, Marc?"

"Soon." In fact he had asked for two more years in Madrid, and they had told him yes. He was still settling in.

"How soon?"

"After the Fourth of July. Come with me. You and Fede."

"I can't."

"Why?"

"You asked them to send you to a hellhole, didn't you? On purpose. If you had asked for Rome, they would have given it to you."

"Come with me. Just the three of us. We can practice being a family."

But she was not willing to give him an answer. Yes would be a great answer, it might change his life. No would be an acceptable answer. Her chilly hesitation was no answer at all.

"Did you even ask for Rome?" she wanted to know, and he wondered which was worse, her indifference or her resentment.

"Spend the night," he said, but she got out of bed, dressed, and took a cab back to Puerta de Hierro, unwilling to forgive him for being assigned to Paraguay. He thought about telling her it was a lie, he was staying in Spain, but decided it would be more interesting not to change his story.

Meantime he was experiencing cluster erections thinking about Vicky Sorrell, who didn't seem to want anything he had to offer.

He left the gym with Portillo and they walked down the shady side of Serrano in the direction of Colón Plaza. The afternoon sunlight conceded the benefit of the doubt to the crowds of pedestrians moving on the sidewalks. Inside their shopping bags and packages and briefcases there was something for everyone. If looks counted, after centuries on the periphery, Spain had finally arrived in Europe.

"Did I ever tell you I was posted to Bogotá for three years?"

"Somehow I don't see you in South America, Juan Manuel."

Portillo's portfolio was the ETA, the Basque separatists who believed that killing politicians and policemen was a viable tactic in their struggle to create a Basque state. Residual pathology, Juan Manuel dismissed their motivation. But he thought about nothing else. Focused obsession kept people alive.

Marc noticed the women looking at Juan Manuel as they passed them. A tall, slender redhead in a summer suit and white clogs stopped and stared. It was like taking a walk with a movie star.

"I lack an English word for what I want to say."

"I'll give you one."

"An animal. It makes holes. Black and white stripes on the head. Gray fur. In Spanish, it's called *el tejón.*"

"Badger."

Juan Manuel nodded, added the new word to his stockpile. Marc remembered being that way with Spanish. Every word was an acquisition, every word had a gold glint. If he tried hard enough, he could recall the occasion of learning the word for greyhound, for hourglass, for the co-optation of dissent.

"Okay, under the new rules of the game," the Spaniard said, "we're not going to play cat and mouse, correct? I mean we are both going to speak directly."

"You're going to tell me what you know, Juan Manuel, and then I'll tell you what I know. Then we see what it adds up to."

"Let me start with what you probably don't know. The Badger's father was a clock repairman in Bogotá. When Paredes was a boy, a policeman shot the father with his service pistol in an argument over the bill for the repair of a grandfather clock."

"Let me guess. His father died, but the policeman wasn't prosecuted."

Juan Manuel shrugged. Like most Spaniards, he couldn't quite get past a certain scorn for Latin Americans. Like most Spaniards, he did his best to hide it. Disparaging *suracos* was politically incorrect in Madrid.

"So Paredes hates the Colombian government because a cop killed his old man?"

"Do you have a better theory?"

"The motivation doesn't matter. He's a terrorist. He wants to do harm to the U.S. I don't give a shit where he comes in, I care where he comes out. I want to be there when he makes a mistake."

"Then think about this, Marcos. When he was still part of the FARC, one of his jobs was liaison with the ETA."

He was right; Marc hadn't known that. And it was a fact that mattered. It mattered a lot. One of the things that had been bothering him was how the Justice Concept could pull off something ambitious in Spain, where there was no indication they had any infrastructure.

Juan Manuel looked at him sideways. He knew he had scored another point but was willing to let it go unrecorded. That way when the time came, Marc would cut him the same slack.

"Paredes was useful to the bastards," said the Spaniard, "because he was efficient at moving people around who were very difficult to move. In the process, some important personal relationships were established."

"And he took those relationships with him when he split to form the Justice Concept."

"Favors have been passed back and forth."

They had reached the Colón Plaza, where fifty tourists weighted with cameras had gathered to catch the flamenco riffs of a thin Andalusian guitar player in tight black pants. The guitar player had it down, an attitude of transcendent indifference that found expression in his fingers working up the neck of his instrument.

"Flamenco bores me," Portillo told Marc. "At least it does in a park for tourists. He's a whore. He's a beggar."

His anger was fiercer than the spectacle of a second-rate guitarist playing for change was worth working up. It had something to do with what Juan Manuel remembered about his father. Marc let the blue flame subside before he said anything.

"I understand favors, Juan Manuel. But the ETA hasn't touched the U.S. Helping Paredes goes beyond enlightened self-interest, it puts them in harm's way with us."

"Maybe this isn't about self-interest. Maybe it has to do with something different."

"Like what?"

"Like the way they see everything backward. They think they're the good guys. They think we're the bad guys. Maybe they believe the good guys have to stick together."

"It can't be that simple."

"Don't be too cynical. Cynicism can prevent you from seeing things as they are. Okay, now it's your turn to be, what's that word I want?"

"Forthcoming."

"Come forth, Marc."

"Our embassy in Paris has been surveilled. And Prague, and The Hague."

"You're not talking about some Islamic group, I take it. What else?"

"There have been some interesting intercepts out of Colombia—from bad guys who think they're good guys—talking about an operation in Europe. There's a phrase that keeps coming up."

"What's the phrase?"

"A handful of kings."

Juan Manuel nodded. "In other words, a handful of American ambassadors. It would be a spectacular accomplishment. Some of them are political friends of your president, no?"

"Let's have a cold drink."

They were walking on the long, green island that bifurcated the Prado, moving in the direction of the museum triangle and El Retiro Park. The city had the feel of a carnival, some kind of excitement happening around every other corner. Marc knew it was dangerous to feel the way he felt, as if he and Juan Manuel and a small number of people like them were the only thing standing between this festival of civic innocence and bloody ruin, anarchy, zealots with guns. It was dangerous because it magnified the role he played, which distorted his vision of what he could accomplish. He felt it anyway.

They stopped at a stall run by a man with the face of a wood-chuck and a surly manner.

"Why do you abuse your body with that evil liquid?" Juan Manuel criticized his Coca-Cola. He drank bottled water. In a bar he drank single-malt Scotch. "Sugar and carbonation and plastic that won't degrade in the environment—this is America's gift to the world. You can't really blame them."

"Who?"

"The population of nations subject to the United States of Imperial America. Their impulse to fight back is natural. It's even healthy, from a certain point of view."

"Do you have anything more you want to share with me, Juan Manuel?"

"Not today."

"Then we'll talk tomorrow?"

"The price of liberty is eternal vigilance, am I right?"

"You're right."

"We have a lot of people on this, Marc."

"So do we."

Watching him go, Marc counted. Two of every three women in his path down the Prado watched Juan Manuel coming at them. Most of them kept watching. A few of them turned around to stare at his back. He disappeared, and Marc thought about Lupe, about taking her to Paraguay to live in a tree. Second. First he thought about Vicky Sorrell.

He had this great idea to take her dancing.

13

The good thing about the telephone was how it wasn't ringing, just then. That meant his room at the Plaza could be what Jack needed it to be, a cocoon. It was a fine room, expensively appointed, with a street-side window and an oil painting in a severe style that looked like something he ought to recognize, although he didn't. The walls of the room were wainscoted, which was a little much, but the brocaded paper above the wainscoting was fawn colored and easy on the eye. There was a sitting room with an elegant, high-backed love seat. The bathroom fixtures were heavy and ornate. The stiff burgundy carpet absorbed sound. As cocoons went, the one he had rented was first rate.

He didn't want to leave the room. He didn't want to be touched or spoken to or, if possible, thought about by anyone on the planet. He wanted to be left alone for a little while inside his skin.

He called room service and ordered strawberries, a loaf of rye bread, a brick of cheese, and two bottles of ale. He specified English ale. It was the Plaza. They had English ale, and the strawberries were flawless, a pleasure to behold in their silver dish.

He opened a bottle of the ale and picked up a notebook. He took some notes. Not because he was in danger of forgetting what he knew, but because doing something so intensely familiar was as close as he could get to feeling normal, just then. His definition of normal had changed since he'd come to Spain. The new definition had everything to do with not being hounded by Colombian terrorists.

He had zero interest in writing a book like the one he had invented as an excuse to get Vicky Sorrell to talk about her embassy pals, but despite himself there was something there, a little hill of material was mounding for him. He had shown up at the embassy at lunchtime. Vicky had no choice but to invite him to have a sandwich with her in the cafeteria, through which, as they ate, wandered enough colleagues and characters and perplexed dry souls to fill a small book. Best, for fictive purposes, was the ambassador's deputy. Kemble came looking for Vicky's signature on something, and her comment on something else. In a perfectly tailored suit, fit at fifty, he was the sum of all the little things he knew. Kemble was hard, a career officer tested in bureaucratic battle. His eye glinted. He knew how to run an embassy, but he also knew how to run a political appointee ambassador like Duffey. When Vicky introduced Jack, he shook his hand as if the writer were there representing a new species, one they hadn't run tests on yet so it was safer to keep his distance. In the kind of story Jack wrote, there was always room for a certain kind of tiny-hearted villain. He knew he would use Kemble eventually.

In his room, sipping pale ale slowly and playing at taking notes, he lost himself for a few minutes envisioning a narrative situation into which he could shove a character like Kemble. But something distracted him, drew him out of the cocoon of quiet he had found. It was the telephone. It was his brother-in-law, Philip. It was more bad news.

"They cut off his finger, Jack."

"Slow down, Philip. What are you talking about?"

"Ben. Eavy went to the mailbox this morning and there was this package addressed to her. The kidnappers cut off part of his finger and mailed it to us in a refrigerated box."

"Jesus."

"There was a note inside the package. They said they did it to show us how serious they are about Eavy and me not going to the police. They said call Jack Baines in Madrid if we had any questions. They said what happens to my son depends on you. What the fuck is going on, Jack? Why did these assholes cut off my kid's finger?"

"I think you should call the FBI."

"And then what? Wait for Benjamin's whole body to show up in the mail so they can prove they were really serious?"

"It's a group of Colombian terrorists, antigovernment guerrillas. They're trying to do something horrendous that will force the U.S. government to get out of Colombia. They want me to help them do it."

"You? What the hell can you do? You're a writer, for Christ's sake. You can't do anything."

"I'm in a bad place here, Philip. I don't think I can give them what they want. I'm not sure, anymore, that I can fix this thing."

"Well, you better start trying harder."

"Call the police."

"I'm not calling the police, and neither are you."

It was a terrible conversation, and it wouldn't end. Philip wouldn't let him talk to Eavy, but that was okay. Jack didn't think he could take hearing his sister's voice. Talking with Eavy would push him over a cliff only he knew about.

"I have to go, Philip. There's someone at the door." It was true.

"You're a maggot, Jack."

"I'm doing the best I can," he said, but Philip slammed the receiver down.

When Jack answered the door, a bellhop handed him a padded manila envelope addressed to Señor John Jacob Baines.

"Who gave this to you?" Jack demanded.

The bellhop, a stooped man from the provinces with close-cropped gray hair, recognized a losing proposition when he walked into one. He backed down the hall scratching his head and mumbling colorful platitudes, putting distance between himself and an unpleasant American guest.

Jack closed the door and opened the envelope.

Inside were half a dozen color photographs printed on computer paper showing a massacre in a picturesque village. Someone with a digital camera had recorded the aftermath of the attack. There seemed to be as much blood sprayed on the adobe walls of the small houses as there was on the bodies of the murdered villagers, who had fallen in heaps. In the sky corner of one of the photographs, part of the fuselage of one lethal black helicopter was visible.

Clipped to the photograph containing the helicopter was an article from the Internet edition of one of the Bogotá newspapers describing an operation carried out by the armed forces in a town called La Babosa, where support for the FARC was blatant. Along with the article there was an editorial praising the operation. Giving aid and counsel to the outlaws, according to the editorial, was a provocation to all right-thinking Colombians.

Jack inspected the photographs carefully. His brain rejected everything except the photo of a girl in a bloody violet dress with wild dark hair, crumpled alongside a slaughtered pig. Attached to the photo of the murdered girl was a page torn from a paperback book. He had to read the underlined passage twice before he recognized the Spanish translation of *Mario Moving*.

When the first edition of the book came out, reviewers had fixed on that passage, a clean, angry scream that came close to rhetoric. An editor might have axed the paragraph, but for some reason the howl had stayed in, marking Jack as a passionate writer. If they ever put out an old man's revised edition of his books, he thought he might cut the passage himself. There were so few effective ways to tell people to fuck off.

Then, in the bottom of the manila envelope, Jack found a note on an unlined three-by-five index card. The note was in Spanish. You have the imagination of an artist, the note said. That is a rare gift. Use it, now, to imagine what it was like in La Babosa when the army stormed the town. Use it, also, to imagine what will happen to your nephew Benjamin Burke if you do not continue to cooperate with us.

Jack opened the door and looked down the hall again, but he knew there would be no one there.

14

I have two questions for you," Marc told her when he called Vicky at home. "One is hypothetical. The other one is practical."

"Ask me the hypothetical question first."

"If I invited you to go live with me in a tree in Paraguay, would you say yes?"

"What kind of tree?"

"See?" he said, marveling aloud to himself. "That's it. There's only one right answer to that question, and she gets it the first time."

"What's the practical question, Marc?"

"It has to do with dancing."

"What about dancing?"

"Will you go out to Tu Abuela with me?"

She told him she'd go with him to the dance club because she assumed the invitation had to do with something besides dancing. When she opened the door to her apartment for him she had just showered. Her hair was still damp. She was wearing a light, white summer dress. She looked as good as she was ever going to look in her life. She made him a Campari and soda and told him, "Jack Baines is pretending he's infatuated with me."

"Jack Baines is scum."

"No, he's not, he's confused. His judgment is off."

"We have to talk about J. J. Baines, Vicky. That's my job. Yours, too, for now. But how 'bout we dance for a while first, okay?"

They walked slowly from the Bilbao roundabout toward the Santa Ana Plaza. It was early. The day's heat hung like chalk dust, sticking to the skin, making it hard to breathe, wrapping the tops of buildings in a gauzy halo.

"I asked the personnel woman how much longer they need to process my separation papers," Vicky told Marc.

"So what did she tell you?"

"They won't spring me until after the Fourth."

Marc raised his hands, palms out. "Don't put that one on me," he insisted. "It's a coincidence. They have a serious warm-body re-quirement for the July Fourth party."

"I'm supposed to take that on faith?"

"You know the bureaucracy better than I do."

"This is Duffey's swan song. He wants to stand in the receiving line and be told he's the best American ambassador since Washing-ton Irving. His parties always have a theme. This time it's the Wild West and cyberspace. You know, the last American frontier?"

"Which means you have to go dressed as what, a cowgirl pro-grammer?"

"I'm going as a former foreign service officer."

Past Santa Ana, down a street closed to vehicle traffic, people with pink hair and people with blue hair were lined up to get into Tu Abuela. They were loud, with high expectations, but they were patient.

"I don't feel like dancing," Vicky decided when she saw the line.

"Sure you do," he said. "There's a reason I picked this club."

The house band was called Snarl: a drummer with spaghetti arms, a bass player with a tragic facial expression, and a keyboardist with hair that made him look like the Spanish Jesus, all of them a lit-tle too respectful of the American bluesman they were backing up. Cool Hand Lucas Carter liked Madrid better than he liked Chicago, which he liked well enough. His hands on the neck of his old electric Gibson were like claws. His shades, his guild identity, and his strong visual memory of Chicago streets at night protected him from excessive adulation in a crowded club. The music started out as blues but modulated into something like rock 'n' roll, totally danceable.

They danced. Marc was an indifferent dancer. He flapped, and there was only a theoretical connection between the moves he made and the music he heard. But for Vicky it was good to unplug the power cord from her brain and pay attention, for a change, to what her body thought. Her body had a better sense of what she felt. She danced hard, hard enough to forget the feeling of aversion that overcame her when she thought about Jack Baines and the Badger and the Justice Concept.

"I told you," Marc said when Snarl stopped for a break. "You're into it."

"I'm into it," she admitted. "But don't push your luck."

"Luck has nothing to do with it. You want a drink?"

"I'm in the mood for something different tonight. Bring me a nectar of the gods, if they have it."

When Marc went in search of a divine drink for her, the guy with the vintage gray ponytail who stepped into the small space he vacated had the look of a dissolute cherub.

"I'm Jebediah Thorn," he told her. He grinned, antagonistic as if she were the aggressor, she had hunted him up in his personal dark space and shined a light there. He was unhealthily thin. His T-shirted chest looked childlike, as though he would crush easily. His teeth were long. The yellowed whites of his eyes were crosshatched with red filaments, permanent distress signals. He wasn't high, but he was approaching the neighborhood. He knew how to pick the locks on the doors on all the houses there. "I wasn't always a merchant of death."

"You used to be an angel of light."

His hate grin increased in intensity. "What did they tell you about me?"

"That you had a problem with papal authority."

He snickered. "Get this, little sister: I came to Madrid as a favor. God and country. I still believe. They're paying my airfare. The rest is on me. Time out of *my* life, capital X. Believe it or not, fragging lieutenants while under the influence of acid was not a universal re-

sponse to the Vietnam conflict. The media fucked that up large."
He shook his head. His voice was oil resting on water. "I hate all
those phony friggin' movies."

"Are you going to tell me how Bill Tipton died?"

"I've got more brain left than you're giving me credit for, sister of
light. I used to think the tension was healthy."

"Which tension is that?"

"Between the public's need to know and the government's need
to keep a few important things quiet."

"But you don't think that anymore."

"National security." He rattled his glass at her, an accusation.
Something that mattered to him was her fault.

Marc wasn't coming back anytime soon. Getting the story she
wanted was going to take awhile.

"Spy versus Spy," he explained what he thought should have been
obvious to her.

Vicky shook her head.

"*Mad* magazine used to do this cartoon. One spy in white and
one in black? A Cold War spoof for kiddies. That was Vietnam." He
waved one long-fingered hand, sprinkling magic dust in the air.

"What about my father?"

Back onstage after his break, Lucas Carter was talking about
Hank Williams. Translating for him, the keyboard player struggled
to convey Carter's generosity, acknowledging his debt to a musician
from another genre. The Chicago guitar player took off his sunglasses, folded them away in a shirt pocket, wrapped both hands
around the mike stand. "What you can't say," he said into the black
fuzzy ball of his mike, "is where your music comes from."

"*Lo que uno no puede decir,*" the keyboardist pedaled.

"You can tell a few lies," Carter admitted. "Pretty ones, and some
not so pretty ones. But you know better. You know all the time.
About the triangle."

"*El triangulo,*" someone called from the dance floor.

Cool Hand Lucas nodded slowly. Behind him, his sidemen were
playing the blues edition of Hank Williams, half speed. "I'm talking

about the electric thing that goes from your heart to your brain to your fingers and then back to your heart again."

"*De vuelta al corazón.*"

"Do you understand what I'm talking about?"

Even if they didn't, they told him they did.

"The other thing about the music is how it never stops moving. You try and touch it, right, you think it's in your heart. Then it's in your fingers. You want to lock it in your brain and say, this is it. But you can't because it won't stop moving. So if you're wise, if you pay attention to the working of the mojo, you figure out this is how it happens. And it happens."

The keyboard player had given up translating. He was nodding over his retro Farfisa organ, conveying conviction and respect.

"There's no word for mojo in Spanish," Jebediah Thorn told Vicky, shaking his head as though that were the real problem.

"Sure there is," Vicky told him. "You just don't know it."

"Your father died trying to save a jerk. Nelson Ruff. Rough Nelly."

"Tell me."

"CORDS."

"CORDS?"

"Civilian Operations and Revolutionary Development Support. Sounds like the commies, no? But CORDS was apple friggin' pie. They were doing pacification work. Democracy building. That's where they sent your father."

"But he was actually an intelligence officer."

Thorn shrugged. "A week after he reported for duty, William Tipton, agronomist, was listed as killed in action on an inspection tour in Huang Doc."

"They wanted him listed as dead so they could give him another identity."

"Because his cover had to go in two directions, you know?"

She nodded; she understood. "Meanwhile they inserted him elsewhere, a new man."

"Your father was a star. He sucked up Vietnamese like a sponge. Listen, the people who asked me to talk to you said I should give you the true facts but not the names. Seems pretty fucking foolish, if you ask me. It's been a long time since this shit went down. But hey, it's their call. I'm far enough away from current events in Vietnam, I'm not going to second-guess them."

"Just tell me what happened to my father. I don't care if you make up the names."

"Keep your shirt on, Miss Vicky. I'm telling you now. They sent Bill Tipton to a place we're going to call Cleveland. Cleveland was an important city in what you might want to think of in your mind as the Vietnamese state of Ohio. He played the part of a renegade American preacher, so pissed off by the war he was working against his own side. He had this world-class ability to establish trust with people. In two months he had a chain of VC intelligence officers convinced the crap he was feeding them was real. The amazing thing was, he was working the other way at the same time. He ran this officer who gave him the best information we were getting from any source, period. Pavarotti."

"Because he sang like a nightingale," said Vicky.

He shrugged, his first self-conscious gesture. "Something like that. I'm not the creative type. I'm doing the best I can to tell you what you want to hear and follow their rules at the same time. Anyway, the main thing is, we were trying to get a road built between Cleveland and, say, Sandusky."

"So the North Vietnamese had a convenient place to sow their mines?"

He shook his head. He didn't think that was funny. She hadn't been there. "This was a goodwill gesture. There was a stretch of packed dirt highway through a swamp that flooded out every time it rained, which meant it had to be closed until the surface dried enough to handle traffic."

"This is where Nelson Ruff comes in?"

"Rough Nelly was into indulging his appetites. He did one tour early on, in 1965, maybe. He never saw any combat. The army trained him to maintain radio equipment, and he spent his free time chasing cheesy adventures in Saigon."

"But he stayed in Vietnam?"

"Nothing like it in Greenfield, Massachusetts: opium, gambling, and guns. Beautiful women expressed interest in his opinions. Exotic, you know? He let his hair go long and had it plaited in a pigtail, Manchu style. His accent was terrible, but he talked a lot of shit in Vietnamese. And he knew how to work with the bastards. That was useful when we needed to contract out certain jobs."

"Like roads."

"He could have walked away with enough to set himself up in Greenfield, if he kept it together. But when he wasn't high, he was kicking the shit out of village beauty queens. When he got the contract to pave the road through the swamp, it got out of hand. There were incidents."

"Incidents?"

"Away from city comforts he turned . . . cranky. He beat one of his workers real close to dead. With his belt. That kind of thing. A woman with welts on her back showed up at base camp with a story about how he tried to kill her when she told him she wasn't into animal sex."

"His workers complained to the other side, too."

"Good." He nodded. "You got it. VC dragged him out of his tent one night. They stuck him in a bamboo cage up in a goddamn tree."

"And my father used his connections with the North Vietnamese to try to get him released."

"Bad calculation. Tipton thought he was the Sunshine Superman. Thought he had more protection than he did. They shot him at the camp where they were holding Ruff. Then they shot Ruff. Hey, I'm sorry, Miss Vicky. They told me you wanted to hear the real story so that's what I told you." He adjusted his ponytail, pulled it over his shoulder, petted it lovingly. His hostile grin was the closest he could come to a genuine apology. He didn't say good-bye.

Vicky felt something going: hands stretching to touch nothing. It was not grief, because her father had existed for so long as an idea, and the death of an idea was not the death of a person. It was angrier than that, a slug of emotion that had collected inside so long it was as much a part of her as her elbows, the roots of her hair, her memory of sand in her sneakers on Virginia's eastern shore.

"They're fresh out of nectar of the gods," Marc told her when he came back. "This will have to do." He handed her something liquid. She drank it. It had no taste, but her lips burned. "You okay, Vicky?"

She nodded. "He's real, isn't he."

"Inside his own category, I guess you could say Thorn is real. His business card has a pictogram for merchant of death on it. He thinks that's cool. He made a bunch of money in the arms super-market in Central America during the Sandinista days. Dumb luck. He knew how to hold the big guys' jackets when they took them off to fight. Then he invested his cash conservatively. Now he spends his time procuring one-of-a-kind weapons for people willing to pay a fee for unusual services. You sure you're okay?"

"Let's get out of here."

She felt better on the street. The air was a little cooler, and the crowd out walking had thinned a little. They went past a noisy gay bar, in front of which a large man in a leather jacket was aggressively kissing a small man with slick hair holding a motorcycle helmet. Everyone was happy and smelled like alcohol.

"Do you want to go home?" Marc asked her.

"I want to hear what you have to say about Jack Baines."

"I had to ask them for a dispensation."

"You mean permission to tell me things."

"You're respected, Vicky. In a sea of mediocrity, you're known to be a serious officer. And they want you to keep on helping us. Me, too. I really want that. For several reasons."

"Then tell me."

"You ever hear of steganography?"

"It has something to do with hiding messages behind pictures."

"It's more than that. Here's the headline: we intercepted an email. The email had an attachment, a streaming video of a highly buff Latin woman working out at a gym. Behind the video, there was a message."

"Which says?"

"It contains the address of the gym where Ambassador Duffey works out. Then there's a very strange code, totally oddball, but it breaks down into the days of the week and the times of day that he goes to the gym."

She shook her head.

"You don't believe me, Vicky?"

"I believe you. What I can't believe is that Jack Baines is mixed up in this."

"I told you, he's scum. But like it or not, he's a bit player in this thing. Maybe he doesn't know it, but they're using him as a diversion. Ten bucks says he'll try and wangle an invitation to the Fourth of July reception from you."

"He already did."

"And you got one for him?"

"He's going as my guest."

"Good. But the whole July Fourth thing is probably a dodge. He's trivial in this operation, he's a gnat. But he's extremely valuable."

"Because he talked to the Badger."

"Exactly. Plus who knows who else he's in touch with right here in downtown Madrid? He's a gold mine of useful information. And the U.S. government is about to come down heavy on him."

"Don't."

"Why not?"

"I know him well enough to know that pressuring Jack Baines is exactly the wrong way to get him to cooperate. He's unstable, and he's not used to this kind of pressure. He's a guy who sits in a room and writes all day. He thinks about things. Thinking about things and writing them down has made him rich and famous. Now everybody wants him to be a terrorist. You do, and so do the Colombians. He can't take it. I think he's close to breaking down. If he breaks down the wrong way, you won't get anything from him."

"It's not my decision to go after him."

"Now you sound like a bureaucrat."

"Sorry, it's a fact. It's not my call. Maybe he'll come running to you for consolation."

"And if he does?"

"If he does, then you pump him like crazy. If he's on the edge, you push him over. Make him tell you what he knows."

"There's more to what's going on than you've told me, isn't there?"

"There's more. I can't give you all the details. We're operating under what you might call a limited dispensation."

She didn't really care, at the moment, whether he told her any more of his details. She was tired, suddenly, and overwhelmed with information that she did not particularly care to absorb. The image of her father that she had grown up with—talking rice production with a grateful farmer on the edge of a Vietnamese paddy—came back to her. But there was something wrong with the image. It was out of focus, or the colors were off, or the picture itself was torn. It wasn't the lie, it was the loss. It was the absence, which was absolute.

"Thank you, Marc."

"Are you talking about Jeb Thorn?"

She nodded.

"Does it bother you that your father was working for us?"

"It bothers me that he's not here. It bothers me that he was never here."

"He was one of the good guys, Vicky."

"Like you?"

"That's not what I mean."

"What *do* you mean, then?" It wasn't fair to take out her anger on Marc Karulevich, but he was the closest target. He was also smart enough to see that if he kept talking about Bill Tipton, he would wind up losing.

"Will you go with me to Paraguay?" he asked her gently.

"Is this still a hypothetical question?"

"Nope," he said. "This time it's real."

She gave him a real answer. "I don't want to live in a tree."

But she let him walk her home.

15

Jack didn't make up his mind to bolt until it became clear that the Americans were after him, too. They called him in his room. They wanted a few minutes of his time, that was all. Maybe he could help them clear up a misunderstanding; even better, maybe they could help him. He thought about making a run for it, but he wasn't sure he could get out of the hotel unobserved. The American world police were thorough; they practiced this kind of thing all the time. There was probably an agent covering every door of the Palace.

Undecided, he opened the door. The only person in the hall was a young black woman folding towels and placing them on a cart. Her long perfect hair, her remote smile, her dexterous folding motions, the intelligent accommodation she made doing her work but not surrendering to it, all of that flattened Jack. She looked at him and he felt rebuked by her quiet strength.

Okay, he told himself. I can do this. He took the elevator down to the lobby like a man who had nothing to hide.

The first one, the one who did all the talking, looked like the government. He spoke government-speak, fluency in which seemed to have damaged his ability to express himself in plain old American.

"Oliver Waite," he informed Jack, offering a hand the way the trainers had drilled him to do in federal finishing school, where he probably finished at the top of his class. "I'm the legatt here in Madrid."

"Legatt? That's a French cat, right?"

"Sorry." Waite quickly stood down, parade rest. He remembered that he was talking to an outsider, someone who didn't work inside his fascinating little world, where everyone used the same acronyms. "I'm the legal attaché at the American embassy. That means I'm an FBI agent. Do you want to see my badge?"

"Why would I want to see your badge?"

"This is my colleague, Marc Karulevich."

Less crisply, Karulevich offered Jack a hand to shake. "I work in Central Intelligence, Mr. Baines."

The representatives of his government did not give Jack a chance to cut and run. They walked him from the lobby, one on either side of him, into the coffee shop, where they commandeered a table in an empty corner away from eavesdroppers.

"You drink coffee, Mr. Baines?" Oliver Waite inquired as if he really cared. "I've been posted here six months, and the first thing I figured out is the coffee in Madrid stacks up with the coffee in Rome any day of the week. Don't let the Euro-coffee weenies tell you different. Same with the wine. Spanish red wine is one of Europe's best kept secrets. Do you drink the Rioja? All in all, Madrid is a great town to be posted in. My friend Marc here is a lifer. You couldn't pry him out of Spain with a crowbar."

Oliver Waite could not have been more than forty. Was that young to be a legal attaché in a European capital city? Jack didn't know, but Waite looked like accomplishment wrapped in a promise of more. His law enforcement career was at the take-off stage. African-American, fastidious, conscious of the positive impression he made on people and the way it was useful in his work, he wore a sober suit from an English tailor. His black oxfords were buff-polished like military patent leather. Even his glasses were conservative, the round rims mock tortoise shell. The expression on his thin, cautious face matched the suit. His pencil mustache was perfectly symmetrical, to the hair.

His sidekick was more rumpled. No jacket, and his blue chambray shirt needed pressing. The knot in his ugly-patterned yellow tie was a mistake of shape. His disheveled condition seemed natural, but maybe that was just a patina applied during CIA training because upper management saw the advantage of employing operatives who resembled normal people, the kind of men who wore ugly ties without affectation.

Limping like a bullfighter who had lost but lived to start a second career, a waiter with a tightly wound black ponytail took their coffee order.

"Mr. Baines." Oliver Waite tacked in Jack's direction again. He intended to be courteous regardless of how boorishly the writer behaved. There were rules governing how inquiries like this one were supposed to be conducted, and Waite knew them by heart.

"Let me save you some time," Jack told him. "I pass. I was just going out when you came in. I'm not interested in talking to you."

"We know about your side trip in Colombia." Waite stopped, scowled, then corrected himself quickly. "We know that Max Paredes had you abducted when you went to Bogotá."

"I don't know anybody by that name," Jack told him. It was a true statement. The ferociously ugly man who caused him to be picked up outside the tavern in Puente Perdido had never told him his name.

"They call him the Badger," Karulevich said, as if that might bring it all back to Jack. "He's ugly."

"Fuck you, spy boy."

"Please, Mr. Baines. That kind of hostility is completely counterproductive," the legal attaché inserted himself. It was his interrogation. Karulevich needed to be reminded that he was there in a supporting role, and Jack had to know who was calling the shots. "Let's go at this directly. You're here in Madrid because of something that happened between you and Max Paredes. Fine. You're in a serious bind. I don't blame you for not trusting us, but we can be helpful. If you'll work with us. If you'll cooperate a little. That's not a threat, it's a description of the state of play. Maybe you find this hard to accept, but we're not the enemy here."

Jack wondered whether the Colombians had someone watching

him now. Maybe it was the limping matador carrying coffee to them on a rectangular silver tray. They'd think, let's send someone who draws attention to himself, that's a sure way to make him invisible.

"You want me to sit here and talk with two guys who look like the running dogs of postmodern imperialism? You might as well be wearing a sign that says 'I'm a G-man.'"

He knew he was overreacting, but he thought he had earned the right. Head averted from the approaching waiter, he left the table and headed back to his room, where the walls welcomed him.

He needed a little time to think through his next move. Just that. Not a way out. A way out was not realistic. One move was enough. If he could decide where to set his foot down next, he would be able to breathe again. Breathing better would lead to thinking better. He dozed; his body clock was off cycle. When Oliver Waite knocked on Jack's door to finish the conversation they hadn't started, the FBI agent was alone.

Waite started out trying to placate him. "You're on edge, Jack. That's only natural. May I come in?"

"I told you, I have nothing to say."

"Then let me say a couple of things to you. All you have to do is listen."

Jack let him in. Waite sat in the desk chair while he paced.

"Let's go over what we know," the legal attaché began.

"What you know. You don't know shit."

"While you were in Colombia, you made contact with Paredes under circumstances that only you understand. Am I warm?"

"You're in Antarctica."

"Paredes was brought up in the FARC. You know what the FARC is, right?"

"Fucking Arrogant Revolutionary Communists."

"Something like that. Anyway, Paredes was a guerrilla golden boy. The founder of the FARC is a sweet guy by the name of Miguel Marulanda. Marulanda treated Max like a son. But then a few years ago there was some kind of falling out between the two men, and Paredes left the organization. He now runs an outfit of his own that goes by the screwy name of the Justice Concept. By all reports,

Paredes is a very intelligent individual, not your average revolutionary messiah. He won't have anything to do with the cocaine business. In Colombia, that makes him something of an oddball. Which is not to say he doesn't play dirty."

Listening to Waite, Jack realized that he wanted to confide in the man. He wanted to dump the whole mess in his lap and go away. He was exhausted, frayed, afraid. But he heard his brother-in-law calling him a maggot, ordering him not to contact the police. And he saw the stupid Colombian kid being led into the woods and shot for wandering into the wrong space.

"I didn't make contact with anybody," he said.

"Fair enough." Waite nodded, happy to get a response. Contact was established, which meant he was doing his job. "You didn't seek out Paredes, he came after you in a big way. You're a word guy. I respect the distinction. But you did spend some time in his company. There's a gap in the sequence here that I need you to fill in for me, but all of a sudden here you are in Madrid, scene of the crime-to-be. Some of the people following this case are convinced that you got involved with the Justice Concept for political reasons. They think you're trying to prove your politics are as kick-ass radical as your writing. Not me. I figure Paredes has some kind of hold on you. Tight enough that you can't imagine giving him the slip. Hey, if I were in your shoes, I'd probably do the same. It's not the politics, is it, Jack? What does the Badger have on you?"

"Do they teach you in FBI school how to disarm your victim like that, or were you born knowing how?"

"I guess it's true what they say."

"I don't know, tell me what they say, Oliver."

"That writers tend to be first-class pricks."

It was the first thing Oliver Waite had said that Jack did not resent. Waite was a little tougher than he allowed to show, a little smarter than standard operating procedure called for. The spiffy conservative facade served the useful purpose of hiding the interior of the building, the private rooms the legal attaché lived in when he was off duty.

"How many African-American legal attachés in American embassies in Europe are there, do you have any idea?" Jack asked him. "I thought I read something in the paper awhile back about a class action lawsuit of black agents against the FBI. You part of that?"

"Objection, Your Honor. Relevance."

"Sustained, I guess."

"This is where I start guessing. Paredes sends you to Madrid. What I don't know is how much he told you. My hunch is relatively little. My hunch is, you got on an airplane and came to Spain because you believed you had no alternative. How does that track with your reality, Mr. Baines? Is that how it happened?"

"This is your story, Oliver, not mine."

"What's the point of holding out now? We're doing everything we can to prevent something ugly from happening."

"Go to hell."

"That's pithy. I guess writers really do express themselves better than the rest of us unliterary schmucks. Tell me more, though. Even if you don't know what they're trying to pull off, what do they want out of you? If you tell me just that much, it will help a lot. And feel free to answer any other question I've been too dumb to ask you."

"Get out of here. This isn't the U.S. You don't have any inquisition rights here."

"You're scared. Nobody blames you for being scared, Jack. Jesus, anybody going through what you are would be terrified. That's it, isn't it? You're thinking if you work with us, Paredes's people will tumble to the fact that you sold them out and they'll nail you. But we can protect you. You're up to your neck in something much nastier than you can even imagine. You need our help, and we'd really like yours."

Reason was not the reason Jack threw him out. Fear factored its way in, and some blindness, the kind of blindness you covered a dead man's eyes with pennies to hide. And a certain certainty, that the belief structure of the Justice Concept included retribution. Jack knew what you did with loose ends, you snipped them.

"You're not hearing what I'm trying to tell you," Oliver Waite told him on his way out the door. "We can protect you, Jack. Work with us, talk to us, and we can protect you. I promise."

He tore up Waite's business card. He wasn't a hero, he was a writer. Nothing he did was going to save Ben. There was no point being killed himself. A train to Barcelona and then a flight to Mallorca. He knew people on Mallorca, trust-fund-baby sculptors with exacting requirements for light and space. Their work was important to them, it was cathartic. The woman was German. Her husband was from Boulder. They admired Jack's prose, which they saw as syllable sculpture, the words like so many stones piled into meaningful shape. They would turn over their beach house to him without asking questions. Inside the beach house, Jack would be able to think. He didn't bother checking out of the hotel. Carrying his backpack, he walked straight and fast to the Atocha Station.

Where he reacted stupidly, trying to shake off the two men with long steel arms who embraced him. What do you know? It's good old Jackie Baines, our old drinking buddy from the permanent revolution. *Jesús y María*, do you remember the time that miserable Contra unit had us pinned down in a coffee field in the blue valley along the border? Do you still feel the same tug of loss I feel when I remember how they wasted Che in Bolivia? It doesn't seem like yesterday, it's closer than that.

One of them stuck the muzzle of a pistol in the small of his back. Jack felt it push up against a vital organ but wasn't sure which one. He realized he should pay more attention to the basics of anatomy. That would make him a better writer, and possibly a better human being.

"*Véte a la mierda,*" he snapped when the gun barrel jabbed harder. He stopped struggling. "Go to hell."

In the backseat of the turd-brown car with no distinguishing features into which they folded him, a slight, dour man with the brisk demeanor of a lab technician poked a needle into his arm as though that were the last word in an exasperating argument they were having. The needle inserted, the technician looked satisfied. The corners of his mouth twitched. He was talking with the driver about

Enrique Iglesias. Jack caught the Spanish word for pussy. He tried to follow the conversation but was quickly transported elsewhere, a place he had already spent considerable time.

When he came to, he knew for some reason that he was still in Madrid. He was lying on a blue-and-white-striped foam mattress in the living room of a bare-walled apartment that had the feel of a way station. The only furniture in the room was a cheap wooden table and chairs. On one wall someone had tacked up a poster of a dove with luminous wings against a gray sky. The poster evoked something, even though it was not clear to him what the product being promoted was. Victory, probably. It had something to do with winning the struggle.

Tufo, he remembered. That was the Spanish word for musty air.

"Olor de tufo," he said as though he had unexpectedly cracked the Justice Concept's secret code.

One of the chairs had been pulled away from the table. The woman from the museum sat waiting for him. Jack watched her peel the foil from a roll of Life Savers and eat one. She was dressed like a shopper in black pants and a beige silk blouse.

"In the other room," she informed him, pointing toward the closed door separating them from the rest of the apartment, "there are men with guns. If you try to leave without permission, they will stop you. Do you understand what I'm telling you, Mr. Baines?" She spoke more loudly than she needed to, as if he were an invalid.

She wasn't a bank teller, Jack decided, and not a psychologist, either. She was a teacher with a need to communicate a major lesson to her dull pupil.

"The air smells bad in here," Jack complained, but she made no move to open a window.

Jack never wore a watch, didn't have to. But he wished he knew whether the snowy sunlight bathing the city meant morning or afternoon. A more resourceful person would know how to calculate an angle and pinpoint the time within fifteen minutes. Anatomy, orienteering, diplomacy; his shortcomings mattered more than they had before he came to Spain.

"Tell me about your friends."

"What friends?"

"The two Americans who visited you in the hotel. They looked like police officers, I'm told."

"Nobody visited me in the hotel."

She shook her head. "The straighter you talk, the quicker you'll be allowed to leave."

"The cultural attaché must have said something to them, I don't know. I didn't tell them anything."

"How can I be sure of that?"

"You can be sure of it because I know what this is about."

"Which is?"

"It's not about the liberation of Colombia, or geostrategic politics, or combating imperial America. It's about one kidnapped kid with a finger cut off. Getting him back."

"Then keep this in mind. If you attempt to leave the city again, or if you engage in another conversation with the American police—and I don't care who initiates it—your nephew will be killed."

"This is a nightmare."

"Don't exaggerate," she told him. "It's an inconvenience, not a nightmare. What would you do, Mr. Baines, if there were a civil war going on in the United States, and you woke one morning to find foreign helicopters touching down in the cornfields of Iowa? How do you imagine you might react?"

"That's a bullshit analogy."

She shook her head. He was wasting her time. "What about the American ambassador?"

"What about him?"

"You were able to secure an invitation to the Independence Day reception at his residence?"

"I have it."

"Good." She nodded, as if she had doubted his ability to succeed even with something so small. She stood up and stretched. She seemed distracted; she was thinking about something more challenging than the minor conundrum of J. J. Baines. On the other side of the apartment door there was a muffled sound of movement. Jack thought maybe they were changing the guard on him.

"*Esta gente,*" the woman said, not necessarily in Jack's direction. "These people."

"What about these people?"

"They live like kings."

"Who lives like kings?"

She shook her head, looked at him as though his Spanish were unintelligible. "You must be among the first to arrive at the reception. Guests are invited for what time?"

"Twelve noon."

"Then you will be there at twelve."

"Your master plan calls for punctuality?"

"We require of you just one thing, not difficult at all. You must get close to this friend of the American president, this ambassador Duffey." She pronounced it Doo-fay.

"How do you expect me to do that? I've never even met the man."

"You are a celebrity. North Americans are infatuated with celebrities. Use your star power. How you do it is up to you."

"Duffey probably doesn't even know how to read. They made him an ambassador because he gave money to the president's campaign."

"You are a resourceful person."

"What am I supposed to do once I get close to him?"

"You will deliver an envelope to him."

"An envelope. What's in it, a bomb? A disease?"

"The contents of the envelope are not your concern. I promise you that it will not explode. You will find the envelope at the reception desk of your hotel the morning of July four."

"What happens after I give him the envelope?"

"Then you are free. You go home to New York."

"What about my nephew?"

"He will be released as soon as you comply with your part of the bargain."

"I'd be a fool to trust you."

"You'd be a fool *not* to trust me. What do your instincts tell you?"

"My instinct system is broken."

"Then use your brain. Be a realist. You have no choice."

"You're leaving Spain before this all happens, aren't you? That's why it doesn't bother you to show me your face."

"You can't run away, Mr. Baines. You tried. Do what we're telling you to do and save your nephew. It's that simple."

When they dropped him downtown it was dark, and Jack was still groggy and confused. After it was too late, he remembered he should have noted the car's license plate number, although they would have thought about that, too, they would be changing vehicles every trip they made. Fuck it.

The drug the woman had given him in a glass of pulpy orange juice didn't quite knock him out, it only disoriented him so that the normal invisible lines connecting one place to the next went slack, like rubber bands that had lost their elasticity. There was a mild euphoria, too, that he could not resist. Every step he took along the sidewalk was like a little dive into a cooling lake of luxuriant sensation. A million tiny pleasure messengers skated every which way on the surface of his consciousness, which was glazed to a high shine.

He walked off the euphoria, which was replaced with exhaustion. In his room, sunk in a low place that shared basic characteristics with his body, he contemplated the choice they were forcing him to make. He supposed he would trade, if he could, any old rich man to save someone of Ben's age, a human being in the making rather than a demonstrated failure of the species. The family relationship only made the choice that much clearer.

I'm going to die, he told himself. He said it aloud. He repeated it, then said it slowly in Spanish. *Me voy a morir.* It didn't sound any better in a foreign language, it only sounded melodramatic, like a line in a Mexican soap opera. I'm going to hand Duffey his envelope. I'm going to leave the party. The Colombians are going to follow me. Whether they shoot me on the street or pick me up and dispose of the body discreetly doesn't much matter, does it? Then they're going to send a message to whoever it is they have holding Benjamin, and they'll kill him, too. He and his nephew were loose ends.

The funny thing, the enraging terrifying sublimely certain single fact about his situation, was that there was no way out of it.

16

Afterward, when it was too late for touch, Vicky wished she hadn't made Wyatt sleep on the couch in her living room the night he came to her apartment to offer her his spirit.

"I'm not sure if I have a soul, Vicky," he told her. "Not in the way the pope and my Catholic aunt are sure they have one. If I knew for sure I had a soul, though, I'd give it to you. That's how bad I love you, I'd give it to you on a silver platter. With applesauce. You love applesauce, right?"

Yes, she loved applesauce. He had her down. She sent him to the couch to sleep alone.

At five in the morning she woke feeling uneasy, as though she had left a chore undone before bed and now it absolutely had to be finished or the day would be spoiled. She dressed in jeans and a shirt, then undressed and put her nightgown back on. She went quietly down the hall to watch him sleep. He was stretched on her sofa, shirtless, in black jeans. The gold-and-green-striped afghan her mother had crocheted lay across his shoulders like a shawl. He was perfect, sexy as rainwater sin, and she wanted to touch him.

But she didn't. She didn't want Wyatt's soul or even his spirit. Since she left him at Sor Epi, she had admitted to herself that she still wanted his love, but she was afraid of the complications that came with it. It wasn't his fault, but she couldn't separate her sense of suffocating in the foreign service from being in an embassy with Wyatt. She watched his chest rise and fall and thought that might be enough, for a few minutes. Being and seeing was better than having. At least it was simpler.

Waking before dawn on Sunday in Madrid was like finding yourself in the world's biggest sarcophagus, the one where they laid out the king of creation. The royal wake was over, and all the parties that broke out when oppressed subjects heard the king was dead. The last owl in the city turned back to marble, dead adornment on a stone perch. The tapping of transvestite prostitutes' high heels on the sidewalks sounded like teenage rebellion. Vicky listened to the quiet clatter of a diesel engine idling at the Bilbao roundabout, probably a taxi, coming through the open balcony doors behind Wyatt. She heard first gear engage when the driver depressed the clutch, and the vehicle drove away very slowly as though the *taxista* were edging past an abyss only he could see.

Wyatt had called her at home the night before, but then he decided he couldn't say what he had to say over the telephone. He asked permission to come over, which irritated her, then he didn't show until midnight, sweaty, disoriented, and ragged.

"I went running."

"Out on the street? In jeans?"

"Listen," he told her. "I made up my mind, Vicky. Today. I've been thinking about this ever since you told me you were quitting the service. Then today I was in a meeting, and Kemble was being his normal rapacious self, and all the section chiefs were bowing and scraping in his direction, and I realized my mind was made up. I've had enough of this embassy shit. I'm quitting, too."

"I don't believe you."

"Believe me. I'm going with you. Same plane. Speaking of which, what flight are we leaving on? I need to make my reservation. And where are we going?"

It took an effort to picture Wyatt outside of the service. The hugeness of the sacrifice he wanted to make so that he could stay with her overwhelmed her. Having offered her what he had, what he was, he wanted to joke, to snuggle under covers with her, to heat some applesauce in a pan and serve it to her with cinnamon. He wanted her to help him figure out what he was going to do when he walked away from being what he was meant to be, a consular officer in the service of his country. She put him off, and eventually he took the invitation to spend the night on her sofa as half a victory and left her alone; at least she didn't send him home.

She had joined the foreign service out of curiosity. She wanted to see how the world worked. To see without a video filter. To apprehend the differences between Leesburg and a place like Madrid. And to observe power close up: the quiet compromises and the rush of winning big, the outrageous lies and the stubborn little truths. She wanted the juice in the glass and the dregs, too.

And she got what she wanted, but the isolation inside chancery buildings was hermetic. It was difficult to keep separate a sense of mission from a sense of privilege. It was just as hard to distinguish detachment from superiority. The bureaucracy became a jungle gym on which talented and ambitious people climbed toward power, strutting their best stuff. She performed well. She could perform still better in the future. But she felt herself changing, leaning in the wrong direction. Despite herself she was gradually becoming a creature of the official world of her work. She had a clear picture of the accommodations she would make to prosper inside it, and she was appalled by what she saw.

Rain began to fall in the thick, windless air, not dumped or driven, just allowed to drop as if by command of the dead king. She listened to drops slap the balcony softly, and the clean smell of city morning came through the doors. Wyatt stirred but didn't wake until thunder rumbled again, closer to the city but still muffled. He threw off the afghan but did not sit up.

"I was having this dream." There was a layer of gentleness around him as though he had come chastened through a trial of some sort.

"About what?"

He shook his head. "I was kissing your eyebrows. It was the sexiest thing I ever felt. What's going on, Vicky?"

"What do you mean, what's going on?"

"I was at a meeting yesterday. The emergency action committee."

"And?"

"The fucking spooks never tell you anything. The sky could be falling and they'd say they were still evaluating their sources. I hate their need-to-know crap. It's my life. I need to know. There's some kind of threat, isn't there? I mean now, in Madrid. Right here."

"Why are you asking me?"

"Because your name came up. It was a mistake. They tried to pretend nobody said Vicky Sorrell, but they did."

"I can't get into it, Wyatt."

"Are you working for them now?"

"I'm not working for them. It's a situation, is all. I'm kind of stuck in a situation."

"I mean here I was thinking you were practically on an airplane getting out of Spain, and by accident I find out you're into something spooky that you won't even tell me about."

"What did they say?"

"The same garbage they always say. They have credible information. The threat level is increased. Be very careful. Vary your routes. Keep your eyes open and report anything suspicious. Did you make coffee?"

"Not yet."

He sat up, pulled on his shirt, tucked it into his jeans. "I'll make it."

She let him work in the kitchen by himself for a few minutes. Waiting, she listened to the rain while throaty thunder rolled across the city. He came back with coffee and toast on a wicker tray. He had cut a lettuce leaf into the shape of a flower and tucked it into a crystal vase.

He placed the tray on the coffee table and poured her a cup of coffee.

"You know what bothers me, Vicky?"

"What?"

"I have this feeling that you're forcing yourself to move away from me because you think you should. Not because you want to.

You're changing, and I'm part of what you think you ought to leave behind."

"It's not like that," she said.

"Sure it is."

"Okay. It's like that, a little. But I do still love you, Wyatt. I'm still in love with you."

He nodded slowly, and she recognized that he was behaving with courage, stretching himself out in the middle of the highway knowing he might get run over. It would be much easier to hide behind the hurt. "Let's go to bed, Vicky."

"If you don't ask me to promise anything."

"Deal."

It was a deal. In her bedroom, she opened the window to keep hearing the rain, and Wyatt lifted her nightgown over her head. His hands traced the outline of her breasts. Then he brushed her nipples with his open palms.

"This situation you're involved in," he said.

"I don't want to talk about that, Wyatt."

She kissed him, but he pulled away.

"Okay," he said. "You don't want to talk about it. I won't push you. But tell me one thing."

"If I can."

"You're not in any kind of danger yourself, are you?"

"I'm not in any danger."

He pulled her toward him again, and they eased down together onto the bed, which seemed like the only place in the world she wanted to be, for a while. She didn't have any idea that he was asking the right question backward.

17

Y ou have some beautiful pieces," the diplomat's wife told Carlos Infante.

The palm of her hand caressed the base of a statue of Saint Christopher. In the crook of the saint's arm nestled a tiny traveling Christ. Carlos had always thought it unfair of God to disguise himself in order to test the intentions of humans who were so much weaker than He, so much less steadfast. But the statue was a find. He had picked it up on a scavenging trip to Lérida for so little money he had felt a momentary pang of compunction, a twinge of moral angina. But the pain went away, and he bought the piece knowing he would sell it for perhaps ten times what he gave for it.

"You like the Saint Christopher, then?"

He would not compliment her taste. She was not the kind of patron who needed reassurance. She would make up her own mind.

But she hesitated. "I'm not sure. There is something about the eyes of the Christ he is carrying."

"I know what you mean." He had to agree.

"The eyes upset me," she told him.

He nodded understandingly. "One does not have to be religious to appreciate the eyes."

If the eyes upset her, he was sure of the sale. She had made a connection with the statue.

She nodded just perceptibly and seemed to agree with him, and Carlos suddenly understood that she had not come to his shop to purchase a statue.

"I suppose you're right," she said softly, looking directly at him. "One does not have to be religious."

There was no place to run, or he would have tried, at least, to run.

He had assumed that the woman who liked the Christ's eyes was the wife of a diplomat or a prosperous businessman. There was something proprietary in the self-possession with which she inspected the antiques he had on display, as though her right to have rights were unquestionable. She was attractive in a duck-footed way that could grow on a man. She was Latin American, at any rate. Her Spanish sounded like home, like childhood and memory and deep green valleys.

She was in no hurry. She was cruel. She wanted him to pay for his sins by contemplating his death for a long little while. Or else she was waiting for someone else to show up to do her dirty work for her. But did it matter who killed him? He wasn't going to be around to give the Americans an after-action report. And whatever Mercedes learned, it would not be the truth.

"Are you waiting for someone?" he could not help asking the woman.

"Waiting for someone? Why should I be waiting for someone?"

He felt his face flush. He looked down at his ledger, which was completely current. His last sale, a nineteenth-century wooden cradle from Salamanca to a Norwegian woman adopting a Romanian child, was recorded there. Accurate record-keeping was one of Carlos's strengths.

"I don't know," he told the woman. He was floundering. "I just thought that you might be."

She shook her head and pretended to browse, and Carlos let her go on pretending. What else could he do?

In a quiet panic he ran though the lines he had planned to use to tell Mercedes about his decision. He had already hired a lawyer to make it happen. I'm not doing this for you, he would tell her truthfully, I'm doing it for myself. Everything he owned was in the process of being moved into Mercedes's name. He was without assets. Working it through with the lawyer, whom he didn't quite trust, he had stipulated irrevocable decisions. Not that he was going to change his mind; just the opposite, he wanted to demonstrate to Mercedes the depth of his feeling for her, and he could think of no other way to be sure that she knew, she really knew it.

Giving everything to Mercedes was connected in his mind with getting out of business with the Americans. They were two halves of the same decision. When both halves came together in a new whole, he had thought he would feel clean and free. All he owed Marc Karulevich was one last relay. He had called the American three times, left a voice-mail message on his cellular telephone each time. Karulevich and his partners in espionage would be chasing the same leads down as many roads as they could find. When Marc finally called Carlos back, it would be too late to learn that Paco Pacheco had told him the truth.

Homesickness for Medellín had warped Paco's consistently bad judgment. Scared, short of cash, in awe of the plan he was a reluctant part of, the house painter had confided in Carlos as if he were his father, or a priest in the confessional. If the Colombians pulled off what they were trying to pull off, it would establish a world record in the brass ball competition, Southern Hemisphere division.

The woman who was not a diplomat's wife opened the door of a hutch and ran her finger along the edge of the shelves as if inspecting for dust, a gesture that reminded Carlos of Mercedes. When she learned what he had done with his money, Mercedes would be grateful for his old-fashioned concern for her welfare. But her affections were incorruptible. She could not be bought. It was the same purity that had prevented him from telling her about 23-9.

In the Catholic Church, September 23 was the feast day of San Lino. More important, it was the birthday of Lino Larocha. It was also the date on which Bolivian police had stormed the university campus in La Paz and taken Larocha away to ask questions he couldn't answer.

The mutilated body of the professor of political science was buried before a conclusive identification could be made. In the little group of disciples he left behind, Julio Mateo took Lino's murder the hardest. That was predictable because Julio Mateo had been Larocha's anointed favorite: the quickest study, the dead-on shot, the only one among them who could tune a guitar and climb a peak in the Andes and parse Marx without a dictionary. Julio Mateo was the charismatic one who put into words, like stones you could pick up and throw, all of the reasons why armed resistance to injustice was holy, just, and necessary.

It was Julio Mateo who came up with the name 23-9, poorly coded homage to the leader they had lost. He also came up with their recruitment and expansion plan, and their plan to build strategic alliances with other organizations in Bolivia that were in resistance against the common enemy. Carlos became his best friend's de facto deputy. Practical where Julio Mateo was inspired, Carlos comprehended that the two of them together formed the perfect pistol, barrel and trigger, aimed at the fatty heart of evil.

It took a long time for Carlos to accept the fact that Julio Mateo sold out 23-9 in an act of betrayal that destroyed the organization before it had a chance to gel in action. Carlos cursed the flat tire that made him late for a summit in Sopocachi. Thanks to Julio Mateo, authorized representatives of the MIR had expressed their willingness to talk with 23-9. The MIR was serious resistance, serious Left; an understanding with them meant 23-9 would also be taken seriously. They were growing up.

Carlos hot-wired the most anonymous vehicle he saw on the street in Miraflores near the bus stop at which he descended, a VW bug the color of his girlfriend's Persian cat. Behind the wheel, he noticed that the odometer had turned over; the banged-up car was well on its way toward its second hundred thousand kilometers.

Badly out of alignment, the bug shimmied as he tried to keep it in the proper lane. Then the driver's side front tire popped, and he was late for the only meeting of his life that mattered.

Luckily there was a spare in the trunk, but changing the tire ate up minutes he didn't have to give. His hands, he noticed when he grasped the steering wheel of the VW again, were trembling, as though his body knew better, it had already come to an accommodation with cowardice. He followed his body's wavering lead, arriving on Calle Quepanada in Sopocachi in time to keep driving past the disorganized phalanx of uniformed policemen leading a line of men in handcuffs toward two dark-windowed vans.

He dropped his eyes. If the police had followed their own procedures, they would have pulled him over, making the connection between Carlos Infante in a stolen car and the handful of subversives they were rounding up. But the cops ignored the bug buzzing past them, and Carlos kept going. He went underground.

Where he reconstructed what went wrong. Working with disciplined caution, he dug a hole and burrowed in. From the safety of his hole, he probed gingerly, moving his hands along damp walls in the dark for three months, four months. In the fifth month the hole had become a tunnel. There were multiple passageways in the tunnel, and frustrating wrong turns. But as he moved through the dark, the way led inexorably to Julio Mateo. Someone who was trustworthy knew someone who worked in the prison to which the captured men were taken. That person reported that Julio Mateo did not remain long in police custody. After he was released, he was seen by another person of confidence conversing in a restaurant with a police detective.

The treachery did not stop there. Once he proved to his own satisfaction that Julio Mateo had sold them out, Carlos continued his research. He became a full-time student, taking on a program of betrayal studies with an earnestness that walled him away from the despair he knew was there as the ultimate option. He had to know how deep the treachery went. In a succession of safe houses, picking up and discarding false identities with a facility that suggested an absence of personality, he invented a tenuous existence for himself. Gliding, he lived a long lie, moving like a ghost among the scattered forces of the ineffectual Left. The only notes he allowed himself to take were in his head.

The thesis of his unwritten dissertation confirmed his original insight: what Julio Mateo did to 23-9 was part of a pattern of betrayal. The pattern was repeated so often it became a reflex, the way an atheist might go on genuflecting in church long after he had stopped propitiating God. In fact if Carlos had been religious, he would have written it all off to original sin, a structural hunger inside sinners born to do the wrong thing. But he wasn't remotely Catholic. He had never been moved by metaphysical parables. No sufficient explanation for what had happened was available to him. Absent an explanation sturdy enough to bear the weight, he left Bolivia.

Leaving the country meant abandoning what he had believed to be a universal struggle against the imperialists. Listening to Lino Larocha describe the putrefaction in Bolivian society, Carlos had clearly identified their enemies: First World capitalists and the local oligarchs who did their bidding in the Third World, priests with gold chalices preaching tin homilies, wealthy women who satisfied their sucking needs with honey and vipers, publishers who put out books that deflected attention from reality. There was no end to their numbers. They were the colluding classes, and he despised them. The struggle would go on. It would go on being betrayed. It would go on, he finally decided, without him.

In Madrid, he wandered into the Rastro by chance and stayed there, falling unexpectedly under the spell of old wood and visible history. Through his first few years in the antiques business, he was surprised to discover how much he enjoyed the work, and how well he did it. He could not have come up with better cover for his covert vocation, collecting intelligence on the liberation terrorists of Latin America. A neutral observer might call it revenge, but Carlos had no interest in exacting vengeance from anyone.

What moved him, what kept him juiced up to deal with losers like Paco Pacheco, was the imaginative exercise. This many years away from 23-9, Carlos could not grasp how such a thing had happened. Everything he did afterward was intended to come to terms with the fact that it had.

"I think I've made up my mind," the woman turned and told him.

She seemed happy, and calm, and focused. Her hands caressed the statue greedily. Her cruelty was abominable. She was playing with him just to see him squirm. She realized that he knew, now, exactly what was happening.

"How much do you want for the piece, Mr. Infante?"

"I think you'll be very happy with Saint Christopher," he told her. "The eyes—"

"Yes," she interrupted him impatiently, "but how much do you want for the statue?"

"I have to look up what I paid for it. For some reason I can't remember. I'm a little nervous, for some reason. The papers are in the back room."

Then he added, foolishly, as if to reassure her that escape was impossible, "There is no back way out. This is the only door. I'll only be a minute."

What he wanted, all he wanted, was a few moments more. He wanted to fix the picture of Mercedes in his mind. He couldn't do that in the presence of the woman the Colombians had sent to kill him. Turning, he felt a spasm in the small of his back, wondering whether she was going to shoot him there, before he had a chance to think.

But she let him walk into the back room, where without thinking he put his hand on the small wooden case that held the revolver. It was a six-shooter, a Colt Peacemaker. He had taken it in trade against his better judgment. The kind of people who shopped at Carlos's *taller* were generally not the kind of people who appreciated antique firearms. The revolver had sat on a shelf for five years.

He thought he remembered there were cartridges in the box.

There were. Three of them. Lord knew how old they were, how dirty the inside of the barrel of the Colt was, whether the spring was broken. Hands shaking, he loaded the cartridges into the cylinder. He pulled the hammer back slowly, then placed the revolver back inside the box. He closed the lid and placed the box on the work table.

And there she was.

"I'm sure that we can work something out," he told her.

He hated his voice. Facing death, he sounded like a shopkeeper, like a man who calculated the value of his life in a small stack of Spanish pesetas.

Only now did he see the pistol in her hand. For some reason she looked even sexier than she had when she walked into the shop. Green valleys, he thought nonsensically; green, green valleys. He would have liked to go with this woman—no, that wasn't it. He meant he wanted to go with Mercedes—to a green valley in South America.

He waited for her to say something. It seemed only fair that she say something, that there be an announcement, an explanation. Even a curse, an indictment of his treachery. But she said nothing at all.

"If you'll give me just a moment," he said.

She couldn't possibly still think he was looking for the paperwork on the Saint Christopher statue. She took a step in his direction to get a better angle. With a clarity that made him feel good about himself, Carlos lifted the lid on the box on the work table and picked up the Colt.

The question was whether it would fire. The other question was whether he could hit her if it did. The clarity went away and he felt clumsy.

"Put it down," she ordered him calmly.

"We can work it out." He didn't think he was pleading. He didn't want to plead. He wondered what he could offer her that might be of interest. A lifetime supply of religious statues? A discreet connection to American intelligence? His fidelity in all matters of politics and love?

Instead of putting the revolver down he lifted it. It fired in his hand. There was a terrible explosion. Before he went down, he felt an instant of irritation wanting to know whether the noise that was deafening him came from the old Colt or from the pistol with which she shot him.

18

If the decision had been his, Marc would have canceled the Fourth of July reception. Sure, you couldn't let the bad guys intimidate you. The purpose of having embassies was to represent American interests in the hostile world, and one way to serve those interests was by showing the flag on occasions like the Fourth. Sure, every time an event was canceled the terrorists opened a bottle of champagne and chalked themselves up another victory. Sure. But there was an unnatural tidiness in the way his side, working with the Spaniards, was able to scope out the Justice Concept's Madrid plan.

Standing with Lupe and her family in the receiving line to shake hands with Ambassador Duffey, Marc was on edge. He had no patience for his lover, who let him know in a furious undertone, "I'm not going to forgive you for this, Marc."

Ahead of her in the line, Doña Inés turned to shush her daughter the way she would shush Federico, who had stayed home with the maid because this was not the sort of event you took a child to.

"Your father is an old man, Lupe," Marc whispered into Lupe's ear. "You ought to respect his wishes."

"I can't live in that house anymore. I can't."

"Good," he said. "Then you'll come with me when I go."

"To Paraguay?" If a tone of voice could obliterate a whole country, poor Paraguay no longer existed.

Keeping up the lie that he was leaving Spain was the only way he could think of to get to the truth he needed to know. "Don't focus on the place, Lupe, focus on the wonderful guy you'll be living with there. Besides, there aren't any cannibals in the capital. When you leave Asunción, you take a gun, that's all. Cannibals are afraid of guns. I'll buy you a revolver with a pearl handle. We can go on picnics in the country."

"What are you trying to prove, Marc?"

"Love, Lupe. I'm trying to prove whether you have any of it inside you. Someday."

"Someday what?"

"I hope you'll finally figure out it's not a fairy tale word, it's real. If you let it be."

What she wasn't going to forgive Marc was telling the duke a second time that he and Lupe were going to be married. Don Fabio wouldn't let it alone. He brought up the question every time Marc visited his daughter. When Marc told him what he wanted to hear, he demanded that they set a date. Antique notions of respectability were involved. If the American diplomat did the right thing by his daughter, the mistakes of the past, including her exasperating son, Federico, would be canceled. He started to say that he could die happy then, but he couldn't quite get there. Saying the word *die* was more than Don Fabio could bring himself to do. It seemed to Marc that the old man associated his feeble condition with the same sort of treachery he had beaten back in his prime, during the war against the Republicans. But this time God, the ultimate field commander, had it in for him.

"It's not as simple as you think," Lupe told Marc. "What you call love."

In front of them, Doña Inés was propping up the duke, who resented being propped. Don Fabio was quite sure he was capable of getting through the ordeal on his own steam. To pass the time he was probably composing a little political rant. He would try it out on his valet when he was safely back home later that afternoon, recuperating in the study with a cool drink and a conviction that he was right about democracy. The whole thing was a sham, a ludicrous pretense. Face it, he would remind Gregorio. Some people were born to lead, the rest to be led. Refusal to admit it and govern accordingly was where the politicians went wrong. The astonishing feature of Gregorio was how he meant it when he said he agreed with the duke.

Inés narrowed her eyes and looked at her husband as though she didn't quite recognize the well-bred codger they had placed before her in a line she wished she were out of. Gregorio's practiced hand notwithstanding, getting the old man ready for the reception had used up Inés's monthly store of the sweeter domestic emotions. Her ability to persuade was gone, along with her patience. If she had been a more agreeable person, Marc would have felt bad for her.

"The American way," the duke turned to tell Marc. He was turned out nattier than normal. His cream-colored linen suit made him look oddly up to date, aware of the currents of fashion but not bent by their silly force. His head wobbled a little on his neck. Gregorio had recently trimmed the hair in Don Fabio's ears, and his eyes blazed. The combination of excitement and indignation was not good for him, according to one doctor. According to another, the feverish blaze of his internal fire was what kept him alive.

"Sir?"

"Invite everyone in Madrid. Include the rabble. Engage in flattery on a mass scale. This"—he raised a trembling hand to acknowledge the spread—"this is the diplomatic equivalent of bread and circuses, no? It's the American theory of empire in action. Convoke them all, every last unwashed beggar on the street. Bring them into your living room. Offer them a drink and hope one of them doesn't slit your throat in a fit of envy. But they will, of course, and now you know they will. If I were running this operation . . ."

"How would you go about it, Don Fabio?"

Lupe poked Marc in the small of his back. "Shut up."

Behind them in the stretching line, a military attaché from one of the Eastern European countries pretended to ignore their conversation. The man's hair was a silver helmet. He had a black patch over his left eye and a scar on his right cheek. When Marc stared back, he glanced down self-consciously at the medals on his chest.

The duke shook his head. "The first thing a government has to learn is the last thing they ever think about."

"What's that, Don Fabio?"

"Discrimination. How to tell cream from milk. There's nothing wrong with milk, mind you, but it has to be stored in a separate container. The cream, why, that's a different story altogether. Why do you suppose it rises? It's the natural tendency to distinguish itself from mere milk."

Marc shaded his eyes with one hand and looked across the sculpted, sprawling acres of gardens and green lawn for Vicky Sorrell. A thousand people had congregated at the Duffeys' residence. If Vicky was there in the bubbling crowd, he couldn't see her. There was no Jack Baines, either.

"Who are you looking for?" Lupe wanted to know.

"Just looking. It's a party, Lupe. Relax a little, get into the spirit of the thing."

The military attaché smiled blandly at him, wishing he were there with a woman as attractive as Lupe.

When it was Don Fabio's turn to be presented, Duffey grasped both of the old man's hands and pulled him toward him as though he knew his noble guest needed help staying on his feet. The ambassador waved at the blue sky, across the roof of which thin banners of cloud were nailed in a buffeted row.

"What can I say, duke? Glorious weather for the Fourth. Cordelia and I are delighted. On behalf of the president, allow me to say that we are officially delighted with how the weather has cooperated. Like an old-fashioned Fourth way back when, before the world went digital on us. I'm sure you remember those days, Mr. Karulevich, although perhaps just barely."

Duffey was expansive and sleek, permanently insulated by money and privileged access. His body was not yet aware that he had turned sixty, and he wasn't about to let it know. Not quite ruddy, he was pneumatic, beatific, proud to close out his tenure in Spain with a nontraditional July Fourth shindig. They'd be talking about it for years. American businesses in Madrid had pitched in cash and kind to help cover the costs of the massive reception. Although he didn't patronize them himself, Duffey had nothing against the fast food franchises that were providing complimentary hot dogs and hamburgers and pizza and roast beef sandwiches. And the idea for a virtual celebration had been his alone. Under a green and white tent, twentyish *madrileño* techies with intense facial expressions and round glasses offered the ambassador's guests an interactive introduction to American history: the Declaration of Independence, Martin Luther King's "I Have a Dream" speech, the Bill of Rights, the Electoral College, yippies practicing democracy in the streets of Chicago.

This was Terrence Duffey's moment. Next to him, his wife, Cordelia, shook a hundred hands with the air of a person who found herself, by a terrible mistake, at the wrong party in the wrong role. Never mind, she would tough it out regardless because that was what people like her did. Cordelia was thin, brittle as ribbon candy, accustomed to being entertained the same way that Doña Inés was. She was wealthy on her own account, which made for a kind of practical parity in the marriage, without which she would not have been able to survive her husband's hard-driven accomplishments.

"Don Fabio is the author of that thoughtful letter you received not long ago, Mr. Ambassador," Marc reminded Duffey. "The one with the very useful overview of the current political landscape."

"Of course," Duffey agreed. He held the duke by both his trembling, liver-spotted hands again. "I receive a great deal of correspondence, you know. Volumes of it. Lord, there's enough to write a book, which is something I would do if I had any talent along those lines, which unfortunately I do not. But the point of my comment is, out of the bushels of mail that come in, I save very little. Almost nothing. Your excellent letter, Don Fabio, will serve this embassy in good stead for quite a while. It's not every day one encounters such insights expressed with that sort of eloquence."

Don Fabio knew he was being put off. Duffey had overdone it. The duke bowed slightly and moved along.

"You see, Marc?" Duffey snagged him as he passed. His low hiss was conspiratorial, as though they had something sinister in common, when what they shared was only classified information on groups intending to do them harm. "We did the right thing today. I'm quite confident of that."

"I hope you're right, sir."

"I know I am." He nodded thoughtfully, and for the first time since he had known him, Marc admitted that the man must in fact bear a burden of decision that he did not take lightly. Duffey was more than his sheen, his money, his friendship with the president that went back to their days in college together. Somewhere in the man, hidden because he knew its value, there was reflection, self-knowledge, even a little doubt.

"I'm glad I'm here, Marc," he insisted. "When we leave Madrid, Cordelia and I are going to remember this party. My God, the weather is spectacular today. You'll remember it too, I hope. I'm grateful for the hours you and your colleagues have put into protecting us."

The embassy had doubled the number of officers assigned to Duffey's security detail, and the contingent of Madrid police outside the gates had also been bulked up. Plainclothes officers, Spaniards and Americans both, circulated through the crowd. No one on the guest list complained about having to step through the metal detector to get into the reception. The presence of a domestic terrorist organization with a horrific record of kills made the Spaniards more tolerant of security measures than people who didn't have the ETA to contend with tended to be.

After the party, the Duffeys were going to be driven to Barajas Airport in their armored Cadillac accompanied by a lead car, a follow car, and a squad of Spanish policemen on motorcycles. Cordelia had a summer place on the Outer Banks of North Carolina. Getting them out of the country for a few weeks would ratchet down the worry level.

Everything was tidy. For the first time ever, the Spaniards had established a no-fly zone above the city for the duration of the Americans' reception. There were sharpshooters stationed discreetly behind heavy curtains upstairs in the residence, and on the roof, and in other invisible locations where their presence and their guns would not upset the guests.

Three days before the reception, Juan Manuel Portillo had called to invite Marc to take a walk. He wanted to be the one to let his American friend know that the Spanish service had raided an ETA safe house in Madrid. They met in the Botanical Gardens and walked in sunshine up and down pleasant paths while Juan Manuel gave him an inventory. Inside the apartment they had found a number of interesting items: taped to the bottom of the medicine cabinet in the bathroom was a thin strip of paper on which a phone number in Colombia was written. The number in Bogotá was disconnected, but the American station and the Spanish office there were tracking it to see where it would lead. The Spanish police also found some automatic rifles, some phony identity papers, half a dozen stolen license plates, and a disk copy of the Badger's Blue Book.

There was also a newspaper photo of Ambassador Duffey. The photo appeared on the society page of *ABC*. He was shaking hands with King Juan Carlos at some sort of official reception. The unusual thing about the photo was the crown that someone had drawn on the American ambassador's head with a ballpoint pen.

"So what do we do now, Marc?" Lupe asked him when they were finally through the line.

"We've done our duty," Inés decided, but she was unable to convince her husband to leave.

Don Fabio had spotted a couple of acquaintances in the crowd. No one of his generation, exactly. There were so few men left who had actually fought in the Civil War, and on the right side. But a small number of mature, right-thinking individuals had accepted the invitation to the American party, men who permitted themselves no illusions regarding the farce of democracy. Their responsibility was to keep alive a certain point of view until such time as reason prevailed and the politicians showed up begging them to reconstruct society along the lines it had been meant by God to follow. Don Fabio informed his wife that he had more than enough strength left to chat with his friends.

Lupe took Marc's arm. Her nails gripped and bit him. Her smile was the culmination of a lifetime's effort of subterfuge. "Marc will take me home," she told her mother.

"*La fecha,*" the duke reminded Marc with a cold smile as they parted. The date. "Don't forget, you owe me a date. We want to make a party of it."

"Do you want a drink?" Marc asked Lupe when they were free of them. A waiter dressed as a high-plains drifter, with a red bandana around his neck and a large straw sombrero on his head, struggled past them with a silver tray loaded with plastic glasses.

Lupe shook her head.

"Then how about we go under the tent over there and look at the computers?"

She shook her head again. Computers did not interest her. Marc had been unable to interest her even in email. She was the last completely analog woman he knew.

"Then what *do* you want, Guadalupe?"

She looked at him puzzled, her face crinkling attractively in the harsh sunlight, wondering why he was leaving himself open that way. "Does my father know you're leaving Spain?"

"I haven't told him yet."

Somebody somewhere had probably written an insightful book about the relationship between sex and money. Lupe wasn't trying, but she was the most striking woman at the Duffeys' party. She understood simple, how it worked in complicated ways. She was wearing a light blue dress, belted with thin gold rope. No rings. The only jewelry she showed was a necklace of flat gold links. All the men in the crowd stared at her, and the military attaché who had stood behind them in the line seemed to be shadowing her from a prudent distance.

"What you want," she said to Marc when another waiter disguised as a cowboy offered them red, white, and blue canapés arranged on a tray to resemble a fireworks pinwheel exploding in a patriotic burst.

"What I want?"

"Maybe it isn't there, Marc. Did you ever think about that? I give what I have."

In fact, she had been more generous lately making love, and more passionate, as if she knew the relationship was ending and she had to seize what she could from it. Sometimes her generosity seemed to be a form of aggression. She was demonstrating how good the sex was so that his regret would be that much keener when he went to Paraguay, or wherever the Agency sent him when they pushed him out of Spain. Without her. Sometimes he knew he was wrong. She was only being Lupe.

A few days earlier, she called him at nine in the evening. "I can't eat dinner with them tonight," she complained. "Inés says she's tired of looking after an old man. Fabio says no one has taken him seriously since Franco died. Both of them are picking on Fede again. I can't take it."

"You should send the poor kid away to school somewhere, Lupe. He'll be better off away from them, don't you think?"

"I didn't call you for advice on how to raise my son."

"Then why did you call me?"

"To tell you to meet me at Los Galgos."

"Now?"

"Now."

When he got to the hotel, she had already booked a room in his name. She used her own credit card.

"Neutral ground," he guessed when she opened the door. "That's what you want, isn't it?"

"*Tierra de nadie*," she admitted. No-man's-land. She took his hand and licked the nails of each finger separately.

"*Diáfono*," he told her.

"What?"

"You're supposed to be wearing a diaphanous robe."

In fact she was in her underwear, lemon yellow, parallel strips of bright and pleasant color against her alabaster skin. She opened a flask from her purse and mixed him a Scotch and soda. She served the drink with an imitation of docility that she had picked up from her mother, who had it completely down. Watching her lick the spoon she stirred the Scotch with, he was completely aroused. But he wanted more than sex, he wanted her to say she would go with him to the ends of the earth, and love him there. In a tree. Subsisting on coconuts.

"Give me one good reason," he said.

"A reason for what?"

"Why you won't come with me. It's not like you're all that happy in Madrid. All your friends are married, and they shop. What kind of a life is that?"

She shook her head. "What do you like best about me, Marc?"

"Your acute social conscience."

"What's that?"

"Exactly. And I like your nail polish."

She waggled her fingers at him. He was the slum she visited by night to score some speed. It started because they had both liked the thrill that gave her. But the buzz wasn't enough to keep it going. To keep it going you needed more love. You needed to be able to say it, to pronounce the word. The sex was great—it was sublime, sometimes—but the silence inside which it happened was so cold Marc felt himself freezing.

As soon as he tasted it, Lupe took back the drink she had mixed him. The air in the room was blue and thin with edges sharp enough to puncture flesh. She embraced him, a sign of change and proof of the end. She believed her role and her right was to be held. They stood that way for a few moments, her hands locked together against the small of his back, which felt tender to the touch. When she was ready, she waltzed him backward to the bed. She pushed. He fell on his back, and she fell beside him.

What she did with her hands was not like caressing, although it was not untender. It was more like discovery, with all the intelligence, the acuity of perception, gathered in the palms and fingers and kneading knuckles of Lupe's hands. They moved over his body as though he were a planet she hadn't read about in school. When she reached his penis he felt a sensation of purifying panic. If she were not there holding him, he would not exist. Remove her touch, just then, and there would be nothing left of him.

She reached across his chest to turn off the light on the bedside table. The darkness intensified the comfortable traffic noise filtering into the room she had rented. Climbing onto him, she made a scouring sort of love to him.

She knew he disliked it when she smoked after making love. She lit a match, waved it out, snapped the unlit black tobacco Ducado cigarette in two and tossed it onto the floor.

"If I go to Paraguay," she said softly, and he realized she would never go with him, not anywhere.

But it was important to keep pretending, because this was maybe the one elegy moment they were going to get, when both of them knew it was over between them and neither of them was willing to say it, and the sadness of that was so fresh it was almost sweet. "We'll go on picnics in the jungle," he offered.

"Can Federico come with us?"

"I wouldn't go on a picnic without him, Lupe. I'll get him his own pistol. With silver grips. All the boys Fede's age in Paraguay know how to handle firearms. He can take a walk and shoot a few cannibals, and while he's gone we'll make loco love."

"And then," she began.

He waited for the rest, but in a few moments he heard her breathing slow down and regularize, and she slept.

At the reception, Lupe turned down the patriotically colored canapés the cowboy waiter was offering her. "I'm ready," she told Marc. "Take me home now."

"I can't, Lupe. I'm working. I told you this is not a social occasion for me, it's work."

"No one will notice if you slip out for a few minutes."

"Sorry. You'll have to take a taxi if you want to leave."

But she pouted as they strolled through the crowd. Lupe didn't like going anywhere alone. She was uninterested in the people the Americans had invited to the reception: politicians and business-men, academics and artists, military and police officers of a certain rank. High-cholesterol bankers and two cat's-eye actresses who thought their English was strong enough for Hollywood. Diplomats who worried about the turnout at their own national day receptions, and a handful of priests who believed in ministering wherever spiritual need existed.

Marc had lived in Madrid long enough to recognize some of them: the Lebanese ambassador whose collection of pre-Columbian pottery rivaled a small museum's. The police captain who lost his right arm and the sight in his left eye to an ETA attack while he was posted to Zaragoza. The art dealer with copper hair and a tobacco-addled voice who made a living of introducing new diplomats to un-dervalued Spanish artists. The bottle-blond TV anchorwoman who produced snappy video vignettes of drug abuse along the highway between Madrid and the southern beaches. The ascetic molecular biologist who wrote a manifesto condemning the state of research at Spanish universities. And the duke of Albino, a social progressive who bankrolled projects to integrate economic immigrants from North Africa into Spanish society.

It had to be Alex Barnes who looked them up. Barnes wanted an excuse to stand next to Lupe. He pretended to be glad, and a little surprised, to see Marc Karulevich at the reception.

"I didn't think this was your sort of party, Karulevich."

"Command performance."

"So introduce me to your sister."

Barnes worked in the political section. His personal style was contemporary European Union. His burgundy suspenders held up pinstripe pants in which the crease was perfect. His face was flat and hard. Barnes believed he wrote the best analytical prose in the embassy. Maybe he did, maybe he did. If the State Department tried to send him to some hellhole in Africa, he wouldn't go. Timbuktu? Even the name was ridiculous. He was in Europe for the duration of the duration.

"This is my sister Fatima," Marc introduced Lupe. "We were separated at birth, so we're allowed to kiss."

Barnes probably didn't see the cold contempt with which Lupe sized him up. They shrugged him off as quickly as they could, and Marc's cell phone rang.

"That was a woman's voice, wasn't it," said Lupe when he hung up.

"A woman, yes. I believe she was a woman. She had a woman's voice."

"Speaking English."

"An American woman."

"Let me guess."

"I hate to do this to you, Lupe."

"Do you?"

"I have to go. It's important. Will you go home with your parents?"

Better this way. There wasn't time for an explosion. She smiled, and he saw exactly what he was walking away from: her singular beauty, and the love that she refused to give herself to, the love she wouldn't say.

"Good-bye, Marc Karulevich," she said to him in English, pronouncing the difficult syllables of his last name carefully. She offered a hand to shake. He allowed her to be the one to make the break.

"I think it's happening," Vicky Sorrell had called him to say.

"You think what is happening?"

"The Colombians. We had it wrong. Meet me at El Retiro. At the Estanque, that lake thing, by the statue of Alfonso the Twelfth. That's where I'm going. Now."

Halfway through the throng at the reception, down the sloping walk on his way to the gate, Marc stopped to take one more look at Guadalupe Farrón. No chance. There were too many people. And Lupe was too quick to disappear. He saw again with blinding clarity what he no longer had. She was everything he wasn't. He jogged toward the Castellana to flag down a cab.

19

In an instant it was too late for hypotheticals, but Wyatt couldn't stop asking them anyway. What if he hadn't done Alex Barnes the favor he asked? Then Wyatt would not have been out on the street where strangers could ask directions to the Opera House. What if he had gone directly from the Hotel Cristál to the Fourth of July reception at Duffey's residence instead of going home to change? If something about the car, or the woman with the map in the passenger's seat, had made him think twice? What if Barnes were not such an asshole so totally full of himself, which if you thought about it was another way of saying he was full of shit? Or if Wyatt hadn't taken the foreign service entrance examination and found out he liked consular work as much as he did? Or if he hadn't bid on the Madrid job and been assigned to Spain?

If he had seen the Bullet coming.

If he were not terrified. But he was.

The chancery building was closed for the Fourth. Alex Barnes was the duty officer, worse luck for both of them. When the Bullet called, the marine on duty at Post One transferred the call to Barnes at home. The political officer was on his way out the door. He didn't want to bother with a gringo lunatic even if he was on duty and supposed to respond to the emergency situations people like the Bullet were always getting themselves into. He called Wyatt.

"It's not that hard, Alex," Wyatt told him. "Everything you need is in the duty briefcase. You can try working something out over the phone. Maybe you won't even have to go to the hotel to see the guy. Use that impeccable Spanish of yours."

"I'm on my way to the reception."

"So am I."

"Come on, Willis. You put up with this kind of crap from lowlife freaks every day. That's what they pay you for. Not me. Besides, I'm no good at it. You can fix this thing in ten minutes. It would take me three hours to straighten it out and it still wouldn't be right."

Wyatt let Alex whine at him longer than he should have. There were zero valid reasons for him to back down and do Alex Barnes a favor of any size. On righteous principle he believed it was healthy and instructive and a step toward justice in the embassy workplace for reporting officers like Barnes to deal with the kind of human mess that consuls had to clean up every day. They called them substantive officers, people like Barnes, who had one time looked around a meeting table in the embassy and said aloud, wonderingly, "Am I the only substantive officer in this room?" If Barnes was substantive, that made the rest of them . . . insubstantial. There was no reason to cut the guy any slack just so he could get to the reception in time to schmooze with his favorite Spaniards.

"Never mind," Wyatt told him. "Forget it. I'll do it."

He agreed partly because Alex was right. Barnes was likely to botch it regardless, which meant a consular officer would have to come in and solve a bigger problem than was really necessary. But the main reason Wyatt went along with him was because he was Wyatt Willis. Almost despite himself he could understand Barnes's anxiety, and his refusal to get his hands dirty with consular crap. He could even understand, a little, Barnes's deep need to schmooze. Wyatt understood because he had too much of what Barnes lacked completely. Empathy, maybe, or the kind of imagination that let you see and feel and think as though you were inside another person's head. It was what made him a good consular officer. He knew when people were lying to him.

"I owe you one, Wyatt," Alex told him, and Wyatt understood perfectly that he didn't mean it. He'd forget the favor by the time he got to the reception.

He took a cab to the Cristál, a cut-rate dump near Atocha Station that attracted problematic citizens from everywhere, not just the U.S.

"He's quiet now," the desk clerk informed Wyatt. He was a pale, puffy man of maybe fifty-five with dainty hands, a pressed white shirt, and unrepressed disgust for his clientele.

"Is he in his room?"

"Upstairs. He paid for one night but he won't check out. This is the fourth day."

"But you didn't call the police."

The clerk shifted his puffy body on the high stool it rested on and brought a flyswatter down hard on the counter. The body of the dead fly stuck to the swatter, which he shook over a wastepaper basket until the tiny mangled carcass dropped. He seemed pleased with his aim.

"You called the embassy instead of the police," Wyatt prodded him.

He shifted again on his stool, shrugged, then studied the business end of the swatter. *"La policía."*

"What about the police?"

"I had an uncle in the Guardia Civil. This was in Galicia, way back when. My mother's older brother. He played the bagpipes. Drank too much. He had one glass eye but wouldn't admit it. Said it was a lazy muscle in the brain that made it look that way. Some woman's jealous husband put it out." He shook his head reprovingly.

"What about your uncle?"

"I saw him shoot crows in the woods once. Two or three of the damn things. What kind of man would go out and shoot crows for fun?"

"I'd like to talk with this American for a few minutes before you and I agree how we're going to handle the situation."

"Room three-o-five." He pointed toward the stairs and reached for a key. "The elevator's out of order."

"Thanks."

"Get him out of there, or get him to pay up, I don't care which. Otherwise—"

"You'll have to call the police."

"You know, playing the bagpipes is not that unusual a thing to do in Galicia. Lots of people have that talent. There was nothing special about my uncle."

A knob clicked to the on position in Wyatt's head. This was why he had joined the foreign service: to watch a dainty, discriminating man swat flies in a fleabag hotel while refusing, unpredictably, to call the police on a deadbeat Yankee drifter because his mother's brother killed crows in Galicia. The desk clerk, the moment, the particular prickle he felt, all of it would have been wasted on Alex Barnes. This was what he could not imagine living without.

In fact, Vicky didn't believe that he could. But she was wrong. There had to be some kind of work out there that would make up for what he was losing by leaving the service. He wanted Vicky more than he wanted his work. It had taken the threat of losing her to see it and decide, but he saw, and he decided. When she left Madrid he'd be on the same plane. He had a friend at the airline who would give them courtesy upgrades to first class. He wasn't going to tell Vicky about that. It would be a symbol of the way they were going to put a different life together, first class all the way.

There was no answer to his knock, so he opened the door. In room 305, the Bullet was speeding in a prone position, flat on his back in one of the crummy narrow beds the Cristál provided their guests. He lifted his head from the pillow, shaded his eyes with one hand as though the American vice consul were glare itself. "Who the fuck gave you the key to my room?"

"My name is Wyatt Willis. I'm a consular officer in the American embassy here in Madrid."

Mentioning the embassy was like jolting him with electric juice. He sat up and shook. His upper body vibrated; a chest tremolo. His arms flopped. The heels of both feet tapped on the floor in an uncoordinated rhythm. The Bullet was a stone cowboy, an outrider on the world's high plains. Maybe twenty-five. His hair was dirty sand, his eyes were green glaze, and his ears were disconcertingly small, as if he had heard too much already. He needed a shave, a bath, a full-body reconditioning package.

"I didn't do it," he told Wyatt sullenly.

"Didn't do what?"

"Steal them nukes. I'm not a terrorist."

"We've got proof."

If there had been any food, any kind of fuel in his body except the drugs, the Bullet would have smiled.

"What's your name."

"I'm the Bullet."

"As in deadly. Right?"

He was on his feet and across the room at him before Wyatt thought to defend himself. His body gave off a sour smell, the smell of a sick man unattended. But there was more strength in the arms wrapping around him than any road-wasted speedophiliac had a right to. His lips on Wyatt's were dry. His tongue bored, but Wyatt locked his jaw and the venomous snake did not get inside.

"Bang," said the Bullet when Wyatt pushed him away.

"You prick, you've got AIDS, don't you?"

He grinned, shrugged, and shrank into himself. "I have a fever, that much I know for sure."

Wyatt brushed his lips with the back of his hand. If the Bullet's lips were dry, and if he didn't stick his tongue into Wyatt's mouth, was there any way the disease could get to him? He didn't think so. He brushed his lips hard with the back of his other hand. He spat on the floor. The Bullet giggled moronically.

From the questions he wouldn't answer and the lies he was too lazy to conceal, Wyatt got enough of his story to make a decision. Naked at the wrong moment, the Bullet had been infected. Infection gave him a reason to nurse his sense of the injustice being done to him by enemy agents. He couldn't see them, but they were everywhere, and they knew where he lived. So he skipped. He got a passport, stole a little money, went out not to see the world but to give back as bad as he got. The gender of his victims didn't matter. It wasn't a sex drive, it was a death drive. Momentum was important. So was attitude, sustaining it. The music in his head was all high lonesome. It was always cold wherever he happened to be.

"What you have is what you give," he explained to Wyatt. "Pass it on, you know? Like the plague only on purpose."

Wyatt worked out an arrangement that pacified the desk clerk, and the Bullet was tranquilized by the prospect of an airplane ride back to the United States even if it meant surrendering his passport and a heart-to-heart with immigration authorities in New York. He kept repeating the word *repatriate* as though it meant something else to him: a cure, or a quiet place, or a stab at justice. He promised not to kiss anybody, even the ones he knew from looking into their eyes wanted to be kissed. He was lying about that, too, but there was no purpose served in challenging him.

Wyatt went home to shower and change. He'd catch the tail end of the reception, which was more than he wanted of it anyway. Vicky would be there. He'd convince her to go out for dinner with him when it was over. They could talk about the future, how different it was going to be in the U.S., and what they were going to do there. New Mexico sounded like a nice place to live. So did Vermont. In New Mexico they'd have a horse. In Vermont they'd live in a house with a white picket fence.

He gargled with mouthwash, then with warm salt water, then with mouthwash again. He didn't think the Bullet's dry kiss could kill him, but the embassy doctor would also be at Duffey's reception. Wyatt could wrap it in an anecdote, but Dr. Fernández was smart enough to realize he would be asking for a serious answer to his question.

Wyatt's apartment was only a fifteen-minute walk from the embassy. He never took a taxi. Besides, if he walked he saved himself a few more minutes of cocktail tedium. If anybody dunned him for being late, he had the perfect excuse. He had been nicked by a speeding bullet. If Dr. Fernández had left the party, Wyatt would call him at home just to be sure. One thing he would not do was tell Alex Barnes anything, not a goddamn thing.

Intense white sunlight dried the sweat on Wyatt's skin as soon as it formed. When he got to the reception, Ambassador Duffey would say something trite about how the weather was cooperating with the cause of American independence. A year earlier, a woman in the economics section had built a list of the clichés that Duffey used. The list circulated on internal email for a while, everybody adding Duffeyisms until a nervous supervisor ordered it deleted from the system. But not even Duffey could be wrong all the time. There really was something festive about the weather.

It was a Peugeot. Rusty brown, new or near new. A nice-looking car but not as hot as Wyatt's Opel. The driver had a mustache and the sharp, stressed features of a bird of prey. The guy behind him in the backseat, his legs folded to fit in a small space, was clearly disgusted with his traveling companions' incompetence. He chewed his lower lip, looking out the street-side window pretending he wasn't there, lost in the middle of the street, when any fool should have known where they were going.

Next to the driver, a short-haired woman with a map looked sheepish and peeved at the same time. She was younger than the men. They had designated her navigator and she screwed up. She was lean, dark, too intense for Wyatt. She wore a throwaway camera around her neck. She spread the map on the dash and asked Wyatt, *"Conoce Usted Madrid?"*

Sure he knew Madrid. "Where are you trying to go?"

"We want to see the Opera House. We're not from Madrid."

"I can see that. Actually, you're pointed in the wrong direction."

Hearing that was too much for the guy in the backseat, who didn't want to see the Opera House badly enough to waste his whole day getting there. He got out of the car.

"Luís? Where are you going?" The woman navigator didn't want to lose him. If Luís left, the whole outing would be spoiled.

"*Vaya,* Luís," the driver muttered, hands wrapped around the wheel. Embarrassed, he smiled sideways at Wyatt, who was standing helpfully and patiently next to the car. He was born to be a consul, born to serve, trained not to register a reaction to what people couldn't help revealing to him. The driver lifted his hands from the wheel, palms up and out, and repeated what Wyatt already knew. *"No somos madrileños."* They were not from Madrid.

"Let me see the damn map," Luís demanded. It didn't make sequential sense, any kind of sense at all, really, for him to throw open the rear door behind the navigator, but Wyatt was accustomed to the illogic of people's actions when things weren't going their way. Consular work schooled a person in the limits of reason. He did not particularly want to be there if the lost tourists were going to have it out, but he couldn't walk away once the woman asked him for help.

She handed him the map through the window. "I'm sorry. You're not Spanish, either, are you?"

"North American."

"But you know the city, and your Spanish is wonderful. People always say that North Americans can't learn foreign languages. But that's not true, in your case it's definitely not true."

She got out of the car herself, anxious to follow Wyatt's directions. Which meant there were two of them, one on either side of him, to shove him quickly down and into the backseat of the Peugeot.

He was bent over, chest on knees as if for an air-raid drill. They were driving fast but not too fast. Luís lay heavily on top of him, holding his arm in such a fashion that the pain was intolerable if he tried to move.

"Ni una palabra," the woman with the map warned him. Wyatt's Spanish was good. He got it. Not a word.

Eventually the fear would make him start crying. That was the most likely reaction. But not yet. His lips burned. That was the Bullet's fever, or else just the way Wyatt's empathetic lips imagined the speeder's sickness must feel. He thought for some reason about a glass-eyed policeman in Galicia shooting crows for sport. He thought about Vicky, about a mole in the small of her back that symbolized his personal definition of female beauty. Thinking about Vicky brought on serious vertigo. His brain blurred, but he understood with brutal precision that they were not on their way to the Opera House.

20

Coming through the gate, she jogged a little, then stopped to catch her breath. There were so many people in Retiro Park that Vicky worried she wasn't going to find Jack Baines, or that he was going to change his mind and bolt before she got to him. She walked fast through the multicultural crush out for sun and company and a chance to feed the black squirrels with pointed ears that had colonized the park. The day was immaculate, hot and dry and fresh. She headed toward the Estanque Grande, the artificial lake where Jack had told her he would wait for her.

A Peruvian band with panpipes and some odd, fur-backed stringed instruments had collected a crowd. Farther along, top hat upturned on the walkway for donations, a mime in white face and striped suspenders performed for anyone who would stop. Children on bicycles and inline skates cruised by in secret syndicates. Many of the people Vicky passed were Latin Americans or Africans or Asians. Among the foreigners, the strolling *madrileños* looked sleek and satisfied, like landlords comfortable with the concept of ownership.

She resented Jack Baines: his ego, his petulance, his conviction of entitlement. He had trapped her. The only reason she was still in Spain was because he had walked into a mess he didn't know how to walk out of.

As she approached the statue of Alfonso XII overlooking the Estanque Grande, a bony boy in bright, baggy green shorts and matching hair came at her on Rollerblades. He smiled and slowed in front of her, and for a moment she thought he was a teenage terrorist under orders to eliminate her. But he dropped a piece of hard candy in her hand and speeded up again, and she realized he was only flirting on skates. She tossed the candy in a trash can.

Jack was too keyed up to stand still. She found him pacing the stone overlook along the edge of the artificial lake, across which tourists in paddleboats made noisy looping circuits. In the lucent sun the green water looked thick, like Sunday soup.

He had cut his hair short, which must have been an attempt to disguise himself. But it didn't work, it only made him look younger and even less responsible than he looked before. His purple sneakers were ridiculous.

"Jesus, it took you long enough to get here."

"What's going on, Jack?"

"What's going on is I finally figured it out. The Colombians don't want your ambassador, Vicky. They were never trying to get him."

"If they don't want Duffey, then what *do* they want?"

He stopped pacing. He was wringing his hands unconsciously, which made him look like a boy in trouble. "You, me, anybody from your embassy they can get their hands on."

"How do you know?"

"After your FBI friend came to see me, I got scared. I panicked. I tried to run."

"You were going to leave Spain." She knew it sounded like an accusation. She couldn't help it.

He nodded, still defiant even though what he had undergone since coming to Madrid had worn him down. He wasn't going to apologize for respecting his self-defense instinct.

"Okay, so I was leaving. Running away. But the Colombians picked me up at Atocha and took me to some crummy hideout apartment they have. It's here in town but I couldn't tell you where. They drugged me. When I woke up, a woman who talks like a psychologist gave me my orders. She told me I was supposed to go to the reception today and deliver an envelope to Duffey."

"What envelope?"

"She said they'd leave it for me in the hotel, at the reception desk. I was supposed to pick up the envelope before I went to the reception, but I didn't. Because all of a sudden I figured it out."

There was a strange shine in his eyes, and she realized he was seriously afraid. Some of his fear communicated itself to her, and for the first time she felt herself at risk. That was preposterous. There was no reason to go where he had already gone.

"Figured what out? You're not being precise, Jack. Now's the time to be specific."

"When they picked me up and took me to the apartment," he told her, frustrated to have to spell out what was already clear to him when all he wanted was to be elsewhere, across a border, "the woman in charge said something strange. I thought it was random, just something she thought of and it came out. She said, they live like kings."

"Who lives like kings?"

"You do, your friends do. All the Americans in the embassy do. I don't know, for chrissake. At the time it didn't make any sense. Now it does."

"Not to me, not yet."

"They were always asking me questions about people in the embassy."

"Which people?"

"I think they had a list." He waited for a moment, but he couldn't wait forever. His blunder was king size. "If they had a list, Victoria, you were probably on it."

"And you never told us?"

"Don't crucify me. I told you, I didn't get it. I thought all that stuff about the other people in the embassy was cover for the Duffey plan. The envelope was just a distraction. If I broke down and started talking to you, you were supposed to think it was a bomb, or they put some kind of disease inside it. I'm sorry. That's the best I can do. I'm leaving. I left my stuff in the hotel. I went down to the kitchen and out a back door. I'm taking a bus to Barcelona and getting the fuck out of Spain. This time I'm going to make it."

"I called someone from the embassy. He's on his way here. Wait for him. This kind of thing is his business. He can help."

"Don't forget I did this."

"What?"

"I took a chance, Victoria. I stayed around long enough to give you a heads-up. That should count for something."

"Why did you do this to us, Jack?"

He shook his head, uncontrite. "I can't get into it. Someday I'll call you up and tell you what this was about. Not now. Right now the cost is too high. I'm out of here."

When he looked around, Vicky looked with him. Listening to the Peruvian band lament the mountains they had left behind, she observed a bearded man in a turban berating his traditional wife as she sat next to him on a picnic blanket with her head averted, dispensing sandwiches in waxed paper and coffee from a green thermos. They didn't look like people on the Colombians' payroll. The moonstruck couple with cotton candy? The mechanic in a dirty blue uniform smoking a briar pipe on a bench and contemplating the duck-studded lake? She felt a minor panic rising.

"Wait," she pleaded with Jack.

But he was already fixed on Barcelona. He had done his duty. A wiry man with stubby, hairy arms carrying a black canvas bag was coming toward them. They both noticed him at the same time. Black pants, pale blue shirt with short sleeves, he had the kind of appearance you would never be able to describe when he was gone. If a person could look like a hit man, this one did. He was trying to get their attention. From the expression on his face he seemed to suggest he didn't want to trouble them, maybe just ask a question. Or else he was confused, he was looking for someone else, another couple of lovers.

"I'm not done writing," Jack said calmly, as though what finally mattered was how many books he produced before he died.

But they were lucky. A pair of policemen on patrol were there, suddenly, on the path behind the lake. And they were walking in the right direction. Lover-like, Vicky took Jack by the arm and steered him toward the police. She refused to look at the nondescript man with the black bag, but on the periphery of her field of vision she saw him slow down. He hung back a little and looked away.

"*Señores,*" Vicky announced to the cops when she flagged them down. They were young, bristling, professional. "We need your help."

They listened patiently, politely, carefully to what she told them. They were trained for this sort of thing.

Jack let Vicky tell the story. Her Spanish was better than his. She continued to hold his arm as though he might still cut and run.

"Fuck this noise," he said softly once, in English, out of the side of his mouth. She recognized it as a prayer, devout and deep.

When she was finished, the policemen looked at each other, then at Jack. The writer was a hard man to defend. He provoked antipathy in people without even opening his mouth. It had something to do with his outrageous sneakers, more to do with his personality. But the cops were professionals. They knew their duty. They did it. The smaller one made up his mind first. He was a fine-featured man, more delicately constructed than his partner, who was a hulk.

"Come with us," he said peremptorily. "You don't have to worry. There is a police van on the street. We're changing shifts. You can ride with us to the station. There is a telephone in the van. We will call your embassy and they will send someone to get you."

"Thank you," said Jack. He managed to make it come out sounding sardonic. Vicky wondered whether he knew how unlikable he was.

"There was a man," Vicky told them. "Here, in the park."

"Where?"

"He was coming toward us when we saw you. He had a bag."

They looked, but the anonymous man with the black bag was gone. He would have detoured when he saw the *Policía Nacional* on patrol.

"Relax," said the hulk. "Nobody's going to touch you." His smile made Vicky believe in the possibility of effective communication across cultures.

As if to make good on his promise, the two police officers walked on either side of Jack and Vicky. People picnicking glanced at them. They thought they were being arrested. But the two Americans didn't look like criminals, they weren't the kind of people cops picked up and hauled away.

"If it's not too much trouble," the slight one apologized, "I'd like to go over all of this once more. We can talk while we're walking." From his accent, she guessed he was from Andalusia.

"This will save you some time at the station," his partner explained.

Vicky thought it would be a good idea if Jack went through it the second time around. He would probably remember things she had not thought to include, or see things from a separate angle. The more angles the better. The hulk smiled again as if apologizing for the inconvenience of having them rehearse their story again. There was no sign of Marc Karulevich. She decided she would call him from the phone in the police van.

21

Richard Nixon had the longest tail.

Lying on his side in bed, facing the wall, Ben waggled the big toe of his left foot. There was not much motion involved, but it was enough to stop the cold-blooded Nixon in his tracks. On the alert, the gecko hugged the wall, head cocked, throat stretched. Ben waited for the red sliver of color to appear along the lizard's neck, but it didn't show. Years ago, on vacation in the Dominican Republic, Ben's mother, Eavy, had explained what the red meant, but Ben hadn't paid attention. Now, when he cared, he couldn't remember. Mating? Hunting? Ennui? He didn't have a clue. All he knew was what he saw: every once in a while, a gecko passing through the room breathed out a slice of brilliant red, then retracted it and moved along to its next meal.

Nixon had the longest tail. Carter was darker. There was something about Father Bush's feet that made him stand out. Clinton was thicker in the body, and Reagan's peculiar shade of green was obviously his own, not to be confused with any other president's. Once he began to look at the lizards with disciplined focus, Ben had no difficulty distinguishing among them. He wished there were somebody around to test him. He would like to prove that captivity had not driven him crazy, it had only strengthened his powers of observation. In that way, confinement was better than dope. His eyes were knives.

Naming the lizards after twentieth-century American presidents wasn't crazy. Anyone in Ben's situation would do the same thing; not that he would wish his situation on anybody else. Crazy would be naming the cockroaches. Naming them would give them an individuality they didn't deserve. Palmetto bugs, he remembered someone used to call them, but they were roaches plain and simple. During a late-night radio talk show back in Buffalo, when he couldn't sleep after mixing speed and hashish, Ben had learned that cockroaches, not the meek, were going to inherit the earth. He was in seventh grade at the time, and for weeks afterward his dreams were infested. Roaches went blithely in and out of the orifices of his body, attacked and retreated and then attacked him again.

You could group the roaches according to size: *pequeño, mediano,* and *grande.* Then look out, here comes a *grande,* you'd be tempted to think. But Ben wasn't going there. It was healthier to think of the filthy bugs generically, a gazillion iterations of the same awful idea.

He was being held in a room with no windows, but every once in a while he picked up sounds from the outside. It was a working-class neighborhood. He never heard any English, just Spanish that was usually a beat too fast to catch. The room had no air conditioning. Because the door was locked, the air got staler by the hour.

The harsh treatment was how Ben knew that Quixote and Chick had been given the order to kill him. Driving south, the closer they came to Miami the unfriendlier they became. After they cut off his fingertip in North Carolina, they stopped letting him out of the car when they pulled in for gas. They took turns going to the bathroom, getting themselves something to eat, making sure one of them was with him in the car, which they parked where it was not likely to draw attention. In a combination of English and Spanish and the universal language of intimidation, they made sure he realized that if he tried to make a break or to signal a passerby in the parking lot, he would lose a lot more than half a finger.

Ben wanted to believe that they were sorry they'd had to cut off his finger, even if they went ahead and killed him now. They followed orders because they were guys who followed orders.

But their hostility increased as soon as they arrived, in the dead hours of a cool blue night, at the little house in Miami. The streetlights were out, but there was enough ambient brilliance for Ben to make out adobe walls and painted wooden shutters. The tiny lawn was enclosed by a ridiculous wire fence. Inside the miniature yard there were jasmine bushes. The white flowers smelled sweet and remote, like the memory of a smell. When Chick opened the door, a gray cat with a stumpy tail barreled its way out.

Cooped-up cat was not the only bad smell in the house.

"Mother of God," said Quixote, and Chick opened windows in the living room.

In the stagnant air were congealed grease and sweaty clothes and half a dozen other ingredients not so easily identified. With the window open, Ben thought about screaming, or diving through it, but it was late, and it didn't seem to be the kind of neighborhood where people turned out to investigate noises in the night.

Without asking permission, he sat on the vinyl sofa in the living room. That was a mistake. Quixote cuffed him in the head with the back of his hand and gestured down the hall to his room. His room was the one with no windows. If you were thinking about killing somebody, you had to put some distance between yourself and your victim.

In the gray-walled room there was an old-fashioned coil bedspring, the kind of thing people tried to unload at garage sales for seventy-five cents so they wouldn't have to haul it to the dump. Silver flakes of old paint fell on the floor every time he lay down. There was a mattress on the bedspring. The foam inside the mattress had crumbled into lumps, and the lumps had edges. Folded on the mattress was a ratty pink sheet. Apart from the bed, the only other item in the room was a four-drawer dresser, in the top drawer of which was a stack of old Spanish-language magazines. The women in the pictures were made up to look heartless and sexy. They all wore too much makeup, and there was an unreal sameness to their tremendous cleavage.

In the second drawer of the dresser Ben found a stack of plain bond paper, but there were no pencils, not even a ballpoint pen, to draw with. He wondered whether they would offer him a last meal, and if they did, what he would choose. Maybe they would let him trade food for a pencil. He didn't think he'd care much about eating, knowing he was going to be killed, but it would be good to draw something, even though drawing increased the pain in his hand.

He knew it was important to keep track of the days. If you didn't, you lost your grip on reality and your sense of connection to the world. When Chick brought him a plateful of rice with a lump of lard resting on it, he asked him for a pencil, but Chick pretended not to understand. He made a vaguely threatening gesture and closed the door.

When they picked him up in Buffalo, he had a penknife in his pocket. He could have scratched marks on the wall to keep track of the days, but somewhere on the trip south the knife had slipped from his pocket and disappeared. He lay on the bed dejected until it occurred to him to turn the dresser on its side. Yes. Three of the four feet had those little round plastic pads to prevent the floor from being scratched. The pads were like big-headed tacks, driven into the dresser feet with sharp pins. It took a long time to pry one out. His nails began to bleed. He made no progress until he went at it with his teeth, gnawing a space around the plastic pinhead until he could work it out. On top of the dresser, where the wood was soft, he scratched a line to mark day one.

The cruelty of Chick and Quixote was also evident in the way they ignored him. His beard grew, but they didn't let him shave. He stank because they only allowed him a shower every other day, acting baffled when he asked, in his best small Spanish, to be permitted to clean himself. Unwashed, unchanged, his clothes became torture. All they gave him to eat was prisoner food, rice and lard, beans in grease, hard stale bread or a short stack of dry tortillas.

On the evening of the fourth day, Chick brought him a slice of pepperoni pizza and a can of orange soda. The pizza was on a rose-colored plastic plate. Next to the slice lay three pencils, all of them sharpened to a fine point. The ravenous way he scarfed down the pizza shamed Ben deeply. He wiped his hands on his pants and began to draw.

He had counted the bond paper in the dresser drawer. He had forty sheets, which meant nineteen practice sketches for each man, way more than he needed even though his nerves were bad and he was out of practice. He was going to draw their portraits. It would not stop them from killing him, he understood that now, but it was the only way he could think of to say something to them that they would have to understand.

He started with Chick. He wasted two sheets of paper right away, but that was only nerves.

At the same time, he knew that he should keep trying to engage his captors. If they talked with him, if they acknowledged him in any way at all, they might find it harder to pull the trigger when they aimed a gun at him. But talking with them was not practical. When they dropped off food or escorted him to the shower, they might as well be walking a deaf dog for all the notice they paid him. For a while he tried shouting at the closed door. They spent most of their time in the living room watching Spanish TV, but that also back-fired. Whenever his voice hit a certain level, one of them coasted down the hall, unlocked and opened the door, and hit him on the side of the head or in the gut. *Cállate,* they ordered him.

He was learning. He knew it meant shut up.

He knew he shouldn't, but he gave up, pretty much, trying to win them over. Getting inside their dreams was an accident. He wasn't sleeping much, no matter how many pushups and jumping jacks he did during daylight hours. He knew you were supposed to keep yourself in shape. The room had electricity, one overhead bulb, but his confinement grated harder on Ben at night. He paced, he lay down, he dozed, he got up and paced again. After a few nights like that, he realized that he had stepped without warning into Quixote's dream.

It was a harsh environment. The lights blinded, and the bright colors glared. The fish in the rivers all had teeth. The exact opposite of his outward demeanor of calm control, inside Quixote's dream everything was angry chaos. The animals looked human, and the humans looked like something else again. The air was full of weapons, flying blades and bullets. As soon as Ben realized where he was, he cut out fast, before he got hit. He ducked, shrank himself to nothing, held his breath. He was out.

Chick's dreams were nothing like Quixote's. They were so gooey, it was hard to walk. The landscape was peopled with women, lots of them, like trees in a forest. The women had long dark hair and large breasts. If Ben stretched out a hand, it was licked, slobbered, and fawned over. He felt his gorge rise. It didn't make sense, but turning a round, wet corner he ran into Chick, who was hiding in his own dream. He was apologetic. He seemed to be on the verge of explaining something important, except that Ben woke up. He got out of bed and wasted another sheet of paper on a hasty sketch of Chick's head in profile.

Once, late at night, he overheard them talking in the hall outside his room. The Everglades, he clearly heard Quixote tell Chick. He pronounced the word as though it were Spanish: *los* ey-vair-glah-days. So that was the plan. When the time came, they would dump his body in the Everglades. He wondered whether they wanted him to know, and that was why they let him eavesdrop on their conversation.

It went on. He scratched day markers on the dresser top but didn't count them. He craved candy bars and women without makeup. He did his exercises. He refused to masturbate, although the right women crowded his imagination. He did more exercises. He stank. At least once a day he asked for clean clothes, and for something to draw with. He salivated over greasy beans. One evening they gave him a cold can of Pepsi. He understood that it was for contrast, to make the lack of amenities that much harder to bear.

He continued to draw their pictures.

What's your name? he asked Quixote. What's mine? he asked himself. He wasn't going crazy, he was just conforming his mind to the shape of the room. He began to understand how arbitrary the division of days into hours and minutes was. He wasn't going crazy, he was learning to live on less.

Cuatro de julio. He knew it was the Fourth of July because kids in the neighborhood were excited, running around screaming *el cuatro de julio, día de independencia.* He was overcome with a wave of appreciation for the patriotism of new immigrants. Their enthusiasm was a beautiful thing.

The firecrackers started early and went on intermittently all day. The kidnappers didn't come for him until late evening.

"Cuatro de julio," he said when they opened the door to his room.

He was ready for them. He handed each man the final portrait he had done of him. They were good. Under the circumstances, they were better than good. He felt a strong sense of accomplishment, especially because the pencils Chick had given him were not really meant for drawing portraits.

Quixote hardly looked at his before he crumpled it and tossed it on the floor. Chick stared a little longer at his, and Ben knew he liked it. He watched him fold it carefully and put it in his pocket.

"Vamonos," said Quixote brusquely, grabbing Ben's arm. *"Vamos,* we're leaving."

"Dónde?" Where?"

He didn't expect an answer, and he didn't get one. In an instant they were out of the house.

He was a wreck: disoriented, dirty, frayed. Mostly. It was the difference between mostly and completely that he was depending on.

They were driving yet another car this time, a boatlike Buick with Florida plates and a rusted chassis. There was no one in the street. They must have been waiting for the street to empty out. Ben wondered where all the kids who'd been lighting firecrackers all day had disappeared to. They were letting him down. If he thought about it, he would weep. But crying wouldn't help. He focused on what was there around him: heavy wet air, a purple sky, Cuban music on a radio in somebody's window. Overhead, dry fronds dangled on a row of spindly palm trees.

Quixote slid into the driver's seat. Chick gestured for Ben to get into the back and then eased in beside him. There was an odor of garlic coming off his body.

The two men took turns being perfectly clear.

"Keep your mouth shut," Quixote ordered Ben. "Got that?"

"*Tengo arma,*" Chick advised him, letting him see the blunt, ugly pistol.

"We're going to drive for a little while," Quixote said, pulling away from the curb, like a father explaining something simple to an exasperating child.

"Just a drive," Chick said. "We need some fresh air. You need some fresh air. You've been inside too long, no?"

"But if you do something stupid," Quixote said, "he will shoot you."

"*Sí,* I'll have to shoot you." Chick nodded.

"Do you understand what I'm saying?" Quixote wanted to know.

But there was no answer. Ben closed his eyes, which seemed to be the correct response, and Chick reached across him to lock his door.

At the stop sign on the first corner, Ben opened his eyes. He was mostly destroyed, but not completely. His body was perfectly still. He wondered whether they were heading toward the heart of the city or away from it, in the direction of the Everglades.

It didn't matter. There was only one right moment. Quixote came to a complete stop. The last thing he wanted was to get pulled over by a cop just then. It was the right corner. There were people on the street, luminous and glittering. One moment, one motion.

Which began with lifting the lock on his door. Then rolling out the door as he pushed it open with his shoulder. He hit the pavement, stumbled up the curb, and ran. It was the difference between mostly and completely.

He ran, powering up. There was wind in his lungs. He could have done five hundred jumping jacks. They were right, the experts who counseled prisoners to stay in shape.

He knew they were coming after him, Chick on fat feet and Quixote in the Buick. There was an unspeakable relief in not being the only object of attention. Running, he was aware of a pair of sexy red high heels. Then an old woman's string bag of groceries and her bagging mahogany stockings. A man in a fedora, his thin brown cigarette flaring. American and Cuban flags side by side in a shop window. A yellow dog. A fire hydrant. A barber pole spinning for business even though the shop was closed. A chain saw and a toolbox overflowing with hand tools in the display window of a hardware store.

"*Alto*," Chick called behind him, closer than Ben thought he should be, given the difference in their ages and physical condition. While Ben had been doing calisthenics, Chick was eating pizza and drinking beer on the sofa, watching Univisión on TV. But Chick had to be desperate. If they let Ben get away, he would probably be killed himself.

There was an alley. It was tempting because it was dark, but Ben went past it because he couldn't see to the end of it. A block farther and he came to a walkway between two office buildings. He thought he heard Chick coming up behind him, but he took a chance, ran down the dark walkway because at least that way Quixote couldn't follow in the car. At the end of the walkway was an iron fence with a gate. He jumped it but came down wrong on his left ankle, which made a popping sound. His eyes teared, and he felt a burst of hot, white anger at the men chasing him.

Along the street on which he came out, all the buildings were businesses, and all the businesses were closed. Except for Tío Pepe's butcher shop, specializing in Argentine beef, direct from the Pampas, and sausages and chicken and suckling pigs.

Tío Pepe was behind the counter wiping up for the evening. It was time to go watch the fireworks. He looked more like a surgeon than a butcher, lean and wolflike. He did not look like anyone's uncle. When Ben came into his shop, he was pouring hot water from a thermos into a brownish gourd. In the gourd was a silver straw. He sucked on the straw as though that were how he got oxygen into his lungs.

"Help me," Ben said.

He didn't recognize his own voice.

Saying it, he realized with a pang that he looked like a wild man. For the first time, he had an idea of how he must look to other people.

"Please," he said to Tío Pepe. "They're going to kill me. Help me."

The butcher pointed with one white thumb to a narrow space between two long freezers in the back of the store. Ben squeezed behind them. The cold metal against his back and his stomach made him feel more vulnerable than he had felt on the street with Chick gaining on him. But the butcher shop was the only place he could have gone.

In a moment Ben heard the door open, causing a bell on the jamb to tinkle.

"We're closed," Tío Pepe informed the kidnapper. "Come back in the morning. *Mañana de mañana.*"

"Did you see a kid come by? A gringo kid, crazy looking, like he's on drugs?"

They were speaking Spanish. Ben understood every word, or at least the idea behind every word.

"I didn't see anybody," Tío Pepe told Chick. "Sorry."

"He stole my wallet. Came running up out of nowhere. He knocked me down and took my wallet. I just went to the bank. The punk cleaned me out."

Wedged between the meat lockers, Ben was able to see the butcher but not Chick. Tío Pepe picked up his thermos, poured more water into the gourd, sucked on the straw. Ben saw the deliberate way he was thinking things over. After draining it, he set the gourd on the counter next to the thermos.

"Did you call the police?" he asked Chick.

"Screw the police. *Que se joda la policía.* I want to catch the goddamn kid myself. I want my wallet back. I'll teach him a lesson. The police don't give a fuck about my cash."

"I'll call nine-one-one," Tip Pepe offered. He reached for the telephone.

"Don't," Chick ordered him. There was that something in his voice. He was thinking about everything he stood to lose if Ben walked away alive. Ben thought he must be on the verge of pulling his pistol.

"He's in here, isn't he?"

"Who's in here?"

"The kid. The crazy one who stole my wallet."

"The only thing in here besides you and me, *mi amigo,* is dead animal parts. You want a kilo of ground beef before you go? I've got some nice beef, very lean. Grain-fed cattle. You ever try Argentine beef? It's the best in the world."

The bell over the door jingled again, and Quixote came in behind Chick.

"We're closed," Tío Pepe said in his confident proprietor's voice. The customer was almost always right.

"I think he's here," Chick told him. "In the back somewhere."

"Then go get him."

"We're closed," the butcher reminded both of them as though he were realizing that this was one of those rare times when the customer was wrong. "Now get out of here."

Ben wished he could see more of what was happening. What he did see was the swift grace with which the Argentine butcher reached for the shotgun that had been resting out of sight against the counter.

"Out," he said, pointing the gun at the men who thought the gringo kid they wanted was hiding somewhere in the back.

"You don't know what you're doing," Quixote told him.

"Out," Tío Pepe repeated.

He was calm, patient, convincing. He was the most reasonable and deliberate man in Dade County. His finger was curled around the trigger of the shotgun. No sane person could have disagreed with him.

"I'm calling the police."

There was something of a standoff then, but the shotgun, and the possibility of the police, persuaded Chick and Quixote to back out the door. The bell above the door signaled something like liberation.

It was over.

It took a long time before Ben came out from between the freezers. Tío Pepe didn't appear to be in a hurry. Ben cried a little. He waited for his tears to dry, then waited a little longer.

"You want me to call the police?" Tío Pepe offered, but Ben had to make another call first. What he wanted was a back way out, which was something the butcher also had.

"Those men are gone, but you had better get yourself some help just the same," the butcher told Ben as he unlocked the back door.

Ben stepped out into the smoothest black night he remembered in his life.

"You don't look good."

"How do you say velvet?" Ben asked him. "I mean in Spanish."

"Terciopelo. Are you all right? Maybe I should call an ambulance."

Ben shook his head. He didn't want an ambulance. The Miami Fourth of July night was like *terciopelo.* He heard firecrackers. Somewhere not too far off, cherry bombs were going off in celebration.

Seven blocks away, in a drugstore that had a special on mentholated throat lozenges, Ben found a pay phone on the wall next to a rack of prosthetic devices. There were enough replacement body parts hanging in packaged rows to build a whole new person from scratch.

He had changed his mind. He was going to call the police. He had figured out, or he would figure out by the time he called, what he was going to tell them. How it happened. He wanted Quixote and Chick put away somewhere.

But first he had to make a collect call. He dialed the number. A recorded voice asked him to say his name. That threw him. Saying Benjamin Burke like that was like an admission of guilt. He hung up the phone.

No one in the drugstore noticed him.

He dialed the number again. This time, when the automated operator asked him for his name he got it out. There was a pause until his mother accepted the charge for the call. From inside the drugstore, he could hear the controlled explosions of fireworks. *El cuatro de julio.*

"Oh, my God, is that you, Ben?" his mother was saying. "Are you all right?"

"I'm okay, Mom."

"You're all right? You're free? You're safe? Where are you? What happened to you? What did they do to you? Are you nearby? Does your finger hurt?"

He owed her an answer to all her questions. Then he would call the Miami police. But he was having a hard time finding a starting place.

"Ben?" she said, panicking when she didn't hear his voice.

"I'm here, Mom," he reassured her. "It's okay. Listen, you know that marijuana in the house?"

"I don't care about the marijuana."

"It's not mine. It doesn't belong to me. It's not what you think."

For a moment, the sound of the fireworks distracted him. The Fourth of July. He wanted his mother to understand why it was his favorite holiday. He felt a burst of patriotism. His half-finger ached like fire again; he had forgotten about it for a while. He brushed the stub with the fingers of his other hand, but overall he felt pretty good.

In another moment, he would find the words to tell his mother everything.

22

Maybe it was the way they wore their uniforms. Or their lockstep, which wasn't quite. Everything was right about the two officers from the *Policía Nacional* walking on either side of Vicky Sorrell and Jack Baines toward an exit from the park onto Calle Alfonso XII, but something was wrong. Marc kept just enough distance and crowd between himself and the four people he was following that Vicky would not see him if she turned around to look. If Marc was wrong, if the cops ahead of him were the real thing, there was less of a problem than he expected to deal with.

But they weren't. On Alfonso XII Street, he watched the two uniformed men feed the two Americans into the backseat of a battleship-gray van waiting curbside that did not belong to any police department anywhere in Europe. Baines went in first, stupid and sheeplike. Vicky hesitated a moment. Her instincts were finer than the writer's. But even if she had any doubts, she knew it was impossible for even the most accomplished Colombian terrorists to get hold of a pair of Spanish national police uniforms. What she didn't know, because Marc couldn't tell her, was that the ETA could. There was something disturbingly final about the way the van eased into traffic, as if a truly appalling premise had just been successfully tested.

The taxi driver who picked up Marc was a middle-aged woman in jeans and straw sandals and a light summer blouse. As soon as she realized he was an American, she wanted to talk politics. "You can't be the world's policeman, you know. For every terrorist your military people kill, ten more will jump up to take his place. You have to address the conditions that create the hatred. The Middle East . . ." She shook her head.

"Listen. This is important. I'm a police officer."

"Not in Spain you're not. The only police we have in this country are Spaniards."

"Then pretend I'm a Spaniard. What I want you to do is stay behind that gray van there. See it?"

"I see it."

"Not too close, but we can't lose them. What do I have to say to convince you this is serious stuff?"

If she was going to wear makeup in the cab all day, her eye shadow needed touching up. Her pale face was haggard. She was working too many hours. She had high monthly bills to pay, some private aspirations, and hunger for a little luxury in her life. She was following the van without difficulty. "Congratulations," she told him.

"For what?"

"The radio just said today is your national day. But the United States of North America needs to reexamine its foreign policy."

"In my country the taxi drivers talk about crime in the streets and tax cuts for working people."

"In your country the people are fat from bad food and too much television."

"What's your name?"

"Macarena."

"Macarena, the only thing I care about in life right now is staying exactly the right distance behind that van. Can you do that?"

"I'm low on gas. I was just going to stop and fill up."

If he stopped long enough to hail another cab he would lose the van. "How far can you make it?" he asked Macarena.

She shrugged a perfect Spanish shrug, full-bodied and understated at the same time. They didn't shrug that way in the United States, not even in New York City.

"Until it runs out."

"Drive, please."

She was a good driver. She managed to stay where he wanted her to stay. In the early-afternoon traffic flow there was no reason for the driver of the van to start thinking he was being followed.

"How's this?" she wanted to know.

"This is perfect."

He called the station chief on his cell phone. The line was busy; he got Ray's voice mail. He called the deputy. No answer there, either. That was impossible. He dialed both numbers again to make sure he had the correct digits even though he knew he did.

"Shit," he said aloud.

"*Mierda*. That's what shit means. I used to know the German word for it. I spent a summer in Valencia once. All you hear anymore in that part of the country is German. They're very red, aren't they? *Físicamente hablando*. Pinkish anyway. How do you say 'Go to hell' in English?"

"What's your best guess, Macarena? How much longer is the gas going to hold out?"

But she wasn't going to be trapped into a guess that might not be accurate to the half minute. "*Scheisse*. That was it. Shit in German. What's your name?"

"Marc."

"Like Marcos, more or less. You know what I think, Marcos?"

"What's that?"

"Shit is an ugly word in any language."

He called the marine guard at Post One in the embassy. It was Corporal Oakton on duty, a weightlifting vegetarian who carried in his wallet a picture of the classic Pontiac GTO he had left behind in South Dakota when he signed up for Parris Island. A nondrinker, Oakton usually sounded, for some reason, like a binge alcoholic at the tail end of a three-day drunk.

"Sir," he said when Marc identified himself.

"What's going on there, Corporal Oakton?"

"It's not anything I can get into on an open line, sir."

"This is an emergency."

"That's what I'm telling you, sir."

"Patch me through upstairs to my office."

"Sir?"

"What is it?"

The marine corporal hesitated a moment, trying to come up with a formulation he could use on an unsecured phone line. "People are disappearing," he said finally.

"I know that. I'm in a taxi following two of them. You got a pencil?"

Oakton had a pencil.

"Listen up."

He gave Oakton a description and the license plate number of the van, and told him where they were in the city. He told him what he had to do to get through to someone who could get the Spanish police moving in the right direction.

"Roger that, sir. You got a weapon, sir?"

But Marc didn't have a weapon. In his business there was no reason to carry one. South. Out of town. That was where they were going. As they approached the cluttered edge of Madrid the traffic was still heavy.

Macarena and Marc watched the van make a hard left, then travel under an overpass and up an access ramp onto the Valencia highway.

"We're not going to make it much farther," Macarena warned him. She shook her head as if she cared, after all; she really would have liked to stay with the chase.

"Mind if I smoke, Marcos?"

He didn't mind if she smoked.

"So you might as well go ahead and tell me what all this is about," she suggested after she lit up. It might be a short one, but a trip was a trip and that was what people did on trips, they talked to each other to pass the time. Even an American undercover policeman could be sociable.

They were traveling across high, open territory, huge plates and long planes of arid earth. The sense of space and distance was discouraging to Marc. The van was moving faster. There was almost no chance he could stay with it, and nothing he could do once he caught up. He looked behind, hoping to see a police car coming at them, but there were other ways to travel south. He took it out on Macarena.

"It's about," he told her, "doing exactly what you're doing, which is exactly what I need you to do."

That wasn't the answer she wanted. She pointed to the needle on the gas gauge as though they had been arguing and now she had the clincher, she had objective reality on her side. The needle hovered just above the red empty line. She let the van gain on them a little, a demonstration of her power, their joint weakness, the simple facts of the matter.

"I can do lots of things," she told him. She worked hard to sound more sullen than she really felt. "Computer programming, for example. I can do that. And I'm a better mechanic than *mi viejo.*"

"Your old man?"

She shook her head. "My husband. He's not that old. It's just a way of speaking. I can tell when a politician is lying, every time. That's easy. What I can't do is make this car run on air."

They passed a sign for a BP gas station, alleged to lie two kilometers ahead on the right and to offer speedy service. If they stopped for gas they were going to lose the van. If they didn't stop, they were going to run out of fuel before the van got to wherever it was going.

It was better not to think.

"Pull in," Marc told Macarena as they came up on the exit for the gas station.

She was happy he decided to stop. It was all right to ask for her help, but not if he wasn't going to offer even a minimal explanation about what the hell he was doing chasing an unmarked van across Spain, not even an entertaining lie. Marc understood her complaint even though he couldn't help her out. At the end of the day she wasn't going to have a whole story, just the opening chapter. As she coasted to a stop at the pumps he threw money on the seat and jumped out.

"Call the police."

"I got the license number."

"I knew you would."

He jogged toward the only car at the pump. Better not to think. There was a winning smile on his face. "Just a moment," he raised his hand.

Given a choice he would not have stolen a Mercedes. Not that he had an ideal make and model in mind, as though taking a humdrum Ford sedan without permission might somehow be a lesser offense than ripping off a European luxury automobile. Nor would he have stolen a car from an inoffensive elderly man with a giant head of white hair, a patrician face like Don Fabio's, and a sense of outrage the size of the Autonomous Region of Castilla–La Mancha. But business was slow at the British Petroleum outlet where Macarena had dropped Marc. It was the Mercedes or nothing.

"This is a police emergency," he told the old man whose dream vehicle he was about to hijack. Marc could tell he loved his car; he had spared no amount of time or attention to keep the burgundy-colored Mercedes coupe in cherry condition.

The old man made an admirable defensive stand at the driver's side door, but Marc shoved him aside hard.

"Talk to the taxi driver," he said. "She'll explain it. Go ahead and call the police."

Marc didn't recognize all the names the owner of the Mercedes called him as he jumped inside and started the engine. He had been in Spain a long time, he'd picked up a lot of local culture. He didn't mind being cursed at so much; what bugged him was not knowing what he was being called. The Mercedes, he noticed, had a full tank. He was already in fifth gear by the time he merged into the traffic flow south.

23

Next to Vicky on the back bench of the Colombians' van, Jack Baines was melting. A puddle of disintegrating novelist had begun to collect on the floor at his feet. The puddle shimmered in the dark.

"Jack," she spoke to him sharply, "don't lose it. Keep it together, Jack. If you keep it together we can get out of this."

Like a dog, he seemed only to register his name. The rest of what she said washed over him uselessly. His face was blanched. His body shivered. His head drooped. For a moment, she thought he was going to heave.

"Jack," she said again, but he would not look up.

There were no side windows in the van, which probably should have made Vicky think twice before climbing into it, but why would a person assume a police van had to have windows all around? That was silly. Kicking herself was wasted effort. She kicked herself.

As soon as they were inside, the smaller of the two police impersonators had begun trussing them. While his partner pointed at them what looked like an authentic National Police pistol, the one with the rope tied their ankles, their wrists, and then strapped their upper bodies to the back of the seat. He had evidently practiced the maneuver. Vicky felt like a drill dummy.

"*Tú,*" snarled Jack to the one with the gun. "You." He couldn't help himself. His sense of the enormity of the injustice being done to him overpowered his self-defense mechanism, normally his strongest instinct.

"Shut up," the one tying the writer ordered him matter-of-factly.

Jack opened his mouth, but his jaw went slack. He stayed quiet while the two Colombians took turns stripping off the police uniforms. They stuffed the uniforms in a laundry sack and dressed civilian. They could be anyone: small-time government functionaries who knew about stamps and seals and the rituals of official permissions, or your second cousin from Extremadura, the one you didn't really know too well, or licensed insurance adjustors, or professors of earth science from a provincial university somewhere in the Andes.

When they had dressed and settled themselves, pistols in hand facing their prisoners, Jack started up on them again. "Who the hell do you think you are?" The question sprayed like bird shot.

"Shut him up," the driver suggested. He was younger than the two fake cops, maybe eighteen but definitely no more than twenty. He wore a beret at a jaunty angle over long, dark, curly hair. There was a spare cigarette tucked behind his ear. He looked like a wise-ass cicerone, the unlicensed kind who collected in front of famous churches looking for cultural victims until the cops showed up to move them along. This was his first major action. The boost he felt was awe-inspiring, more addictive than other drugs. He couldn't stop grinning.

Under duress, Jack's Spanish deteriorated. Untethered words got loose inside his sentences, which broke down halfway to their destination or got sidetracked on their way to a full stop. "It's not my fault," he struggled to say clearly.

The tour guide in the beret looked at him curiously in the rearview mirror the way, Vicky assumed, you looked at a dead man just before the sentence was pronounced by a judge who had no doubt he was doing the right thing.

"We don't want to hear that shit," the smaller man with a pistol told Jack. He made it sound like a cultural difference, an unbridgeable gap between privileged North Americans and Colombian revolutionaries.

"What you don't get," Jack told him anyway, "what you'll never understand, *la pequeña burguesía*. That's where most of the real artists come from. The social class. I'm talking about. They're the ones who look out of the shop window and get angry. Their art. In some cases, words. My father was an Eskimo. There are different ways to move out of the class you were born into. Take Charles Dickens."

"Jack, this isn't doing us any good," Vicky told him in English. "If you piss them off, they'll only go harder on us."

He looked at her as if surprised to find her there, sharing the same awful experience. He spoke to her in his fractured Spanish. "They don't realize. They think they're striking a blow for national liberation. It's not, though, it's cheap fucking theater is all. You want to do something that really counts? Write a book. Let them try to do that. Mario is in my head. Consistently. What's in their heads? God-damn empty slogans, dirty straw, video dreams. It's not my fault."

They let him go on longer than Vicky would have allowed him to continue if she were in charge of the abduction. Eventually, though, the driver pounded the dash with the flat of one hand and whistled a few bars of what sounded like a Mexican *bolero*. That was the signal for the hulk sitting facing Jack to lean forward and press the barrel of his service pistol hard against Jack's cheek.

"No more," the Colombian said, and Jack understood that it was time, it was really time this time, to shut up. He did. He closed his eyes, and the gun barrel was removed from his cheek, down which a few tears washed.

"Where are we going?" Vicky asked the Colombians.

"To a safe place."

Vicky couldn't help thinking of them as renegade cops, police officers gone bad, although she knew they weren't. "What do you want from us?"

But the question was incomprehensible. One at a time she looked at them for signs of hate, a sign of passion of any kind that would explain their being there, running a risk they must have known was huge. If the anger was there, they had it under control.

The rush they were experiencing was logistical. It had to do with the van, two snared Americans, a destination, a sequence of actions to be executed. The ideology that motivated them was hidden.

After a few minutes Vicky was sure they were leaving Madrid. She fought a sense of passivity that wanted to take her where she shouldn't be going. Strapped to the seat, her body was almost pleasantly lethargic. Her feet were okay, but the blue plasticized rope around her wrists and hands was pulled too tight, cutting off the blood flow. She tingled. It was good to have Jack there. He needed a keeper. Trying to stave off total breakdown in him made it easier not to let the fear overwhelm her. But she could not quite shake off the urge to nap.

She lifted her hands so the Colombians could see them. "Too tight," she showed them. "Will you loosen the rope a little?"

They ignored her. The driver was whistling again. This time she recognized the tune. It was "Guantanamera." Translated into English, the lyrics came out farcical, banal. "I am a sincere man from where the palm trees grow . . ." What kind of message was that supposed to convey? No wonder the separate Americas failed to communicate. There wasn't a radio station in the U.S. that would play a song like that if the lyrics were in English. Anger bit her in a soft spot. That was helpful, it was an antidote to the urge to nap under stress.

The van was picking up speed. That meant they were out of the city. She was not going to sleep although she felt profoundly indifferent about where she and Jack were being conducted. That was a lie, but she couldn't penetrate its hard shell to get at something true. Her hands buzzed and burned.

"What do you want?" she asked the two men facing her again, as if it were a new question only then occurring to her. Now that they were moving safely away from Madrid, they seemed to relax a little. They held their pistols in their laps as though their primary purpose was sport, not terrorism. At the same time, the driver's mood changed. He was subdued, almost pensive. Bound next to Vicky, Jack continued to leak vital personality fluid onto the floor of the van.

"*Colombia libre,*" said the smaller of their guards. He grudged the answer, didn't care to give it away. He was going to remember what it cost him and charge her later.

"The United States out of our country," said his partner, the hulk, making it sound like the most reasonable political demand a person could make in an unjust world.

"Just that," the driver agreed enthusiastically with them, head bobbing on his neck like a plastic toy. "It's that simple."

"Very simple," the phony policemen nodded.

Vicky wanted to believe them, that it was simple. For a moment she fantasized being strong enough, or worth enough as a bargaining chip, to give them what they wanted, the U.S. out of Colombia. Colombia for the Colombians. A fair fight among factions of their own kind.

But that was impossible. The world didn't work that way. Power seeped. It bled across borders. Contrary to what the terrorists sitting across from her believed, there was no conspiracy. Just the opposite. The United States of North America was a giant. When pushed at just the right pressure point, the giant stumbled. He regained his balance, but in the dangerous few moments when he put his foot down without looking, anyone might get stepped on. All that was required was being in the way. Vicky saw it coming—the momentary stumble—and she flinched.

24

As the gray van traveled south and east toward Cuenca, Marc had to take a few chances. There were still plenty of vehicles on the highway, but the farther they moved from Madrid, the lighter the traffic became. The Mercedes coupe he was driving was conspicuous by design. Every couple of kilometers he dropped back and allowed a few cars to pass him. Then he worked his way up close enough to get a glimpse of the van, which stayed within the speed limit. Whoever was driving was not going to be pulled over for speeding.

Castilla–La Mancha was rural Spain, its dull, stretching plains capable of inducing depression in an emotionally exposed tourist crossing them. Cuenca Province was handy to the capital but far enough away from the metropolis for them to come across a tractor on the highway, a farmer in high brown boots along the berm, hands in his pockets, a hawk in the sky with no memory of a cityscape spread below its wings. Flat cultivated fields ended in light-absorbing stands of woods, and the towns along the road looked like places where the news in the Madrid newspapers had the limited significance of distant events, not as remote as Anatolia but not as significant as a local cup of coffee. Cuenca was hunting territory. Spanish friends with property outside Tarancón had given up inviting Marc out to shoot quail on property they owned there. He was not opposed to shooting game birds, but he had no interest in a long weekend in the company of shooters who believed the rituals of hunting were more fundamental to their existence than the Judeo-Christian religious tradition.

Just past Cascadas Nebulosas, a traditional town where residents gathered on weekends to gossip on the grounds of a ruined castle, the van's left turn signal began blinking and Marc hesitated. He slowed down, then came to a stop on the side of the highway. The road onto which the van turned was a lane and a half of glistening gravel. It led uphill between enormous tilted fields of wheat and beans across which a million yellow-and-black butterflies foraged in a fluttering drove. There was no credible reason for a red Mercedes with Barcelona plates to travel uninvited up a road like that. He counted slow seconds long enough for the van to disappear from view up beyond the fields, where the road bisected a copse of yellowish-green woods. Then he drove slowly up the hill.

He climbed in second gear. The car complained. The Mercedes he had stolen wanted an autobahn to perform on. The road narrowed as it ascended into the woods, which were nothing at all like the woods in the Upper Peninsula of Michigan where Marc's father took him to fish for muskellunge. In the UP, the woods were huge and still wild. The woods around Cascadas Nebulosas were more like thick parks dedicated to hunting and aesthetic contemplation. For the first time in a long time, a pang of homesickness weakened him. It was a distraction. He shoved it aside.

He parked the Mercedes below the crest of the hill, set the parking brake, and walked to the top of the grade under cover of oaks and poplars and a line of lindens. Below, where the woods ran into fields of brushy grass, he watched the van turn up a long drive toward a long, low whitewashed house with a roof of brick-orange tiles that looked like a hunting lodge. Behind the house, a handful of outbuildings clustered, a couple of sheds and a small barn. From the security of a fence in front of the house, a black dog with a stiff back bayed at the vehicle as it approached.

The dog barked until the van stopped moving and the side door opened. After a few moments, Vicky and Jack Baines were removed like cargo. Marc watched them frog-marched toward the house with their hands tied. The two counterfeit cops had changed into civilian clothes. They unlocked the front door of the lodge and shoved their prisoners through. The driver of the van, thin and hyperactive in a black beret, picked up a stick and threw it for the black dog to fetch.

Marc had no weapon, not that having one would change much. He had no plan, other than calling for the Spanish police, who had not shown up despite his stealing an expensive automobile and asking Macarena and Corporal Oakton to call for help. One thing bothered him more than the rest of what was wrong. The lodge might be just a pit stop, and they would be gone in twenty minutes.

After the dog brought the stick back to him, the kid in the beret patted its head and jogged toward the barn. The dog ran with him. The wide front door of the building was closed. He unlocked a padlock and shoved open the door just enough to squeeze through. If they were only making a pit stop, there would be another vehicle inside, gassed up, with legal plates, innocent looking as a dog chasing a stick in country sunshine.

If they left in a second car, they would probably take the back way out. The gravel road went on past the hunting lodge through more fields of brush in the direction of a ragged stand of trees, where it would connect to another highway, or to a dirt road that led to one. He waited for a few moments for the driver to emerge and prove something, but he stayed inside the barn. Then he returned to the Mercedes, coasted downhill through the woods, turned the car around and drove very fast to Cascadas Nebulosas.

Where the sergeant on duty at the Guardia Civil outpost seemed to be waiting to arrest him. A large man with big feet and a low center of gravity, he had reinforcements. His two corporals looked like graduate students in green uniforms, studying at night for an advanced degree in criminology. But their sergeant was rooted in Cuenca Province. His grandchildren lived too far away to visit on weekends; distance cheated him out of the one consolation of aging.

The post was small, two rooms stacked one behind the other shotgun style. Half of the back room was a low-tech cell. The telephone looked old, but the computer on a desk in one corner of the front room was a Pentium 4. Someone had installed a Disney screen saver on the machine. Images of the Magic Kingdom formed and dissolved and reformed on the black screen.

"Mi sargento," Marc tried, but Sergeant Lorca was not about to be appeased by a proper display of respect, however surprising, coming from a foreigner. Knowing the forms was a nice touch but not enough to change the basic facts of the situation, which did not favor the American.

"Is that your Mercedes automobile parked out front, the one you drove up in?" The voice was a mismatch with the man. He sounded like a radio news announcer except that the filter smoothing the voice was in the man, not in a microphone. His corporals stood at opposite ends of the small room, alert as teenage cats.

"It's not my car," Marc admitted. "That's what I came to talk to you about."

"Here in Spain a confession is not like a confession in the United States of America," the sergeant warned him. "In this country, a person who confesses to his crime goes to prison."

"I'm not confessing to a crime, I'm explaining a situation."

"I have a description," Sergeant Lorca informed him. "It just came in over the computer. I have a description of a Mercedes coupe stolen at a BP station on the Valencia highway. The description matches the car you are driving."

Both corporals nodded. Eagerness and caution contended in them, producing a stalemate.

"If you let me," Marc told them all, "I'll explain."

The sergeant held up a muscular hand. The fingers were callused. His hobby had to be woodworking, or gardening, something that took his mind off police work and human malignancy. "I also have a description of a man, an American, who stole that Mercedes."

"I took the car," Marc admitted, trying to make it sound not like a confession but like the opening to a story they were going to want to hear.

They didn't.

"As of this moment," Sergeant Lorca informed him, glancing at his watch so he could record the time when he made out his report, "you are under arrest."

The corporals drew their sidearms. They had been practicing this one.

Marc tried to explain what had happened, and the help he needed from them, and the consequences of delay. If he had been the one listening rather than the one explaining, he would not have believed what he said, either.

"Listen," he tried. "If I stole a car just to steal a car, why would I drive it to a police station and ask for help?"

While the question had no easy answer, it did not undo the crime.

If Marc called the embassy again, whoever was on duty in security or at the station might get through quickly to a contact in the Spanish police. Or not. Corporal Oakton, security conscious on an open line, had told him, "People are disappearing."

"Put your hands behind your back," Lorca ordered him. He was not as distracted as he sounded. He fished in a drawer of the desk for handcuffs.

"We will help you find a Spanish lawyer," he offered as a corporal fastened the cuffs. It was a concession to Marc Karulevich's foreignness. Perhaps a lawyer would be able to convince a judge his unbelievable story should be believed.

"Gutierrez?" he wondered aloud to his men. "Gutierrez spent a year in New York. That was a long time ago, but he says he speaks the language. Not that I would take at face value every last thing Gutierrez told me. Look up his number, Aquino."

It was the cool feel of the metal around Marc's wrists that brought Juan Manuel Portillo's cell phone number up from the memory hole where it had been stashed.

"One call," he asked politely.

The sergeant shook his head. He had seen the American cop series on television. They were entertaining but irrelevant. "It doesn't work that way here. The law in Spain is more sure of itself."

But Corporal Aquino, who knew how to manage up the chain of command, tactfully persuaded his boss that a phone call might be in everyone's better interest. The sergeant was a mature man. He was not offended by the suggestion. He uncuffed Marc and steered him to the telephone.

"Juan Manuel?"

"Where in the hell are you, Marc? Do you have any idea what is going on?"

It took less time than Marc could have hoped for Juan Manuel to convince Sergeant Lorca he was on the verge of making a mistake. Rubbing his wrists to rid himself of the feel of the cuffs, Marc was aware of fireworks exploding above a castle on the screen saver on the computer on the desk, while an image of Mickey Mouse as the Sorcerer's Apprentice coalesced in a lower corner of the dark screen.

Corporal Argaña was more conservative than Corporal Aquino. He agreed with Sergeant Lorca that they should wait for reinforcements from Cuenca before they ventured out to the property where the Colombians had taken their American prisoners.

"It's called El Refugio," Lorca told Marc. He shoved a heap of office clutter aside and unrolled a map on his desk. "The property sits in the middle of what the old folks around here called *la cuadra*, back when they first built the roads."

He pointed with an index finger. "Years ago we used to hunt out there. The place belonged to a gentleman from Madrid, a wealthy man but the kind you didn't resent so much. He never cared about losing a few birds to us, especially when he wasn't around to worry about it. He died a few years ago, a shame. The new owner didn't want any local people traipsing around on his land. He was opposed to hunting, that was what he told me whenever he came to register a complaint. Opposed on principle. What principle is that, I always wanted to ask him, the principle of too many game birds?"

"*Mi sargento*," Corporal Aquino prodded him, but Lorca was not easily budged.

"The property changed hands again last year. We never got a look at the new owner. I was told he was a foreigner."

"What I'm afraid of," Marc interrupted him, "is that maybe these Colombians are only stopping at El Refugio to change cars. If they are, then we don't have time to wait for help from Cuenca."

Corporal Aquino told Sergeant Lorca, "He's right, *mi sargento.*"

Outside, an engine backfired, and a motorcycle with a two-stroke engine whined past sounding self-important. Inside, Tinker Bell sprinkled pixie dust over the uplifted heads of Peter Pan's lost boys on the computer screen, and the minute hand on a battery-powered clock advanced with a tiny tick.

"Then we'll go," decided Sergeant Lorca. "We'll go now."

But his *we* did not include Marc.

"There's still this question of the Mercedes you stole," he pointed out. "As a courtesy, I prefer not to lock you up. The key, please." He opened his hand, palm up, and Marc surrendered the ignition key to the Mercedes.

"What about if I just go along with you?" Marc asked him. "I'll stay in the backseat. I'll keep my mouth shut. We're talking about American citizens, don't forget."

"American citizens," he agreed, "in a jam on Spanish soil."

Burdening his operation with an unarmed superfluous American made no tactical sense. "Wait here," he told Marc. "It is my duty to inform you that if you leave the premises while we are away, I will have you arrested, with all due respect to Mr. Juan Manuel Portillo's high opinion of you. That's the way it is. Trust me."

"I trust you," Marc told him.

Sergeant Lorca tucked a cellular telephone into his breast pocket. He and the corporals each took a rifle from a rack in the back room, along with a box of cartridges. They were gone quickly as if this, too, were something they had drilled to perfection and had only been waiting for an opportunity to make it work. It was finally happening. Marc wished that Sergeant Lorca had not ordered his driver to use the siren as they left Cascadas in a rush toward El Refugio. He was out the door before the noise faded on the street.

Never having stolen anything before, Marc was surprised how easy it was to commandeer a second vehicle. The owner of the truck he took left the engine running while he stopped for cigarettes. Marc was relieved not to have to face the man. He knew from experience that his explanation would be unconvincing. After the coupe, the truck drove like a truck. But it drove, and the gas gauge registered half a tank. And, wedged between the passenger door and the seat, he noticed a shotgun in an unzipped case.

It was an old Volvo diesel, the color of Dijon mustard, built sturdy for hauling freight, not for speed. There was no point going in behind Lorca and the corporals. Instead, before he reached the gravel road that led to the hunting lodge, Marc turned left onto a dirt road that paralleled it. The truck labored up through more fields, crested the hill going through trees, then down again along what must have been one perimeter of *la cuadra*.

When the dirt road ended, he turned right onto the macadam highway it intersected. Pushing the truck hard, he approached the back road out of El Refugio, which lay out of sight behind a rise. He parked the truck along the berm and pulled the shotgun from its leather case. It was a beautiful weapon, the kind of gun before which Marc's Tarancón friends would genuflect, a 12-gauge over-and-under Regata, its walnut stock polished to a deep, rich shine. The shotgun was older than the Volvo, cared for the way no one cared for a mere vehicle. The owner of the truck might be indifferent to the loss of his Volvo; he would be homicidal over the Regata. If nothing else, with Lorca and the corporals blocking the principal way out of El Refugio, when the Colombians came his way Marc could try to shoot out the tires on whatever they were driving.

If there had been any shells. But there were none. Marc rummaged twice through the leather case, then through the glove locker, which was stuffed with junk. The owner of the truck was anything but a neatnik. There had to be a loose shell, one shell, somewhere in the pile of things forgotten there. There wasn't. He looked under the seats, behind the seats. He felt carefully with both hands where he couldn't see. He got out of the truck and looked around the flatbed. He looked inside the toolbox that was fastened there. There were no shells.

Sergeant Lorca must have changed his mind and decided to go in quietly. Corporal Aquino would have pointed out the advantage of stealth. Marc sat in the cab with the windows open, the useless shotgun next to him on the seat. He listened to a breeze scrape across the brush in the field next to him collecting summer sound and depositing it on the dry, full air. Bees droned over purple clover patches. Butterflies clustered, fell and rose together across the field and up the rise. Out of sight, a donkey brayed once. It was the kind of day on which nothing happened but weather.

When the shooting started, Marc felt a new kind of helplessness, worse than being naked. Unarmed, he couldn't take the truck toward the lodge. He had one option. He waited. There were only a few shots, and they were spaced at intervals. It sounded less like a firefight than a hunting party not wasting ammunition.

He knew it was the gray van before the car came down over the rise fast toward the macadam road. He considered getting out of the truck and brandishing his unloaded shotgun at them as they blew by him. But that would be an empty gesture. He stayed inside and exercised his option. As the van approached the intersection he barreled toward it in the Volvo. They were not expecting a kamikaze run. As the van pulled onto the hard-top road, he aimed the old truck and smashed it into the front end of the escaping vehicle. Having slowed to make the turn, the van was knocked sideways. It jolted, skidded, and the engine died. The van's front wheels went down into a shallow culvert.

It was time for the empty gesture. Marc grabbed the Regata 12-gauge and stepped out of the truck onto the highway. But before he raised the shotgun in the direction of the scuppered van it was already clear that there was only one person inside it, behind the wheel, and that she was Vicky Sorrell.

She did not seem surprised to see him, or surprised that he had driven her off the road with an old truck. She was in shock, not taking anything new in.

"It didn't have to happen," she told Marc. She shook her head slowly.

In a few moments the stress would catch up to her, and she might wilt. But for now the main thing on her mind was what she was telling him. She looked down at her hands and told him again that it didn't have to happen.

She wasn't talking about the collision of their two vehicles. Her face was blanched. Butterflies gusted around her, and the sound of one more shot came from beyond the rise at El Refugio. It sounded, for some reason, like the last one. And Marc knew that she was wrong. It had to happen.

25

Even his name was old-fashioned, and he brought flowers. Modern Spanish mothers didn't name their sons Fulgencio. The name was a throwback to a time when the plague was Europe's only globalizing tendency. His father's father had also been named Fulgencio, and that grandfather's grandfather, and so on back to the local Fulgencio who witnessed the miracles worked on Sor Epi in 1492, when a woman of undefined origin appeared in the village in the cove and declined to say whether she was a Jew. Some of the villagers believed she was a Moor, but her description of the Virgin who appeared on the beach where she slept thrust aside the question of her identity. Over a period of months, there were miracles and cures, there were tears of ecstasy and testimonials from the heartsick, there was renewal. The current Fulgencio understood himself to be one link in a long chain of witness to God's presence in the place he grew up.

Vicky had run away from Madrid. Coming back to Sor Epi was an impulse of pure escapism, as though the distance she drove could obliterate what had happened. But she couldn't work in the embassy, and just hanging out in her apartment in Madrid, waiting for news, was intolerable. She came back to the place where she had told Wyatt she was leaving him because the village was a long way from the city, and because people there remembered Wyatt from the drunken tantrum he threw in the plaza the night she tried to leave him.

She was comforted, in a small but valuable way, by the villagers' sober solidarity. Whenever she went out for a walk or to get something to eat, people stopped her on the street to ask about him.

"Yes," she told them firmly, "my friend is one of the American diplomats the terrorists have kidnapped. Yes, he is the same man I came with the last time I was in Sor Epi. You're right, he does look like a *torero*, doesn't he? An American *torero*. His name? *Se llama* Wyatt Willis. Wyatt is a vice consul at our embassy in Madrid."

Talking about him, describing the work he did and what he looked like, was one of the ways she kept him alive. She understood that she had an important part to play in keeping Wyatt alive. The police and the intelligence types, Americans and Spaniards both, had the primary responsibility for finding him and bringing him back to safety, of course, but what Vicky did mattered substantially. Keeping faith took a physical effort as much as an effort of will. She was as strong as she needed to be.

After every chance encounter with a villager on the street, though, she felt sick to her stomach, and sometimes her legs trembled for a moment before she was able to walk on, as though somehow this time she had narrowly missed losing Wyatt, letting him go.

She wasn't going to let him go.

Vicky was lucky. There were no tourists in the village when she showed up. She rented a room with three windows in Las Palomas, a *pensión* run by Covadonga, a widow with allergies who kept the windows closed and played solitaire in three-hour stretches. What the doctor had told Covadonga was simply not true. There was no connection between cigarettes and allergies. In fact, she had noticed that cigarette smoke coated her lungs with a protective film that made her ailments more bearable. The more she smoked, the better she held up. The doctors were interested more in treating a person than in curing him. It was only force of habit that she continued to offer Vicky a smoke every time she came into the room.

Fulgencio was harmless, Covadonga insisted. He was a romantic with exaggerated ideas about love and duty, a man of twenty-two with no ambition except to demonstrate fidelity to an ideal that was not yet fully defined in his imagination. Slight and lithe and prematurely weathered, he lived with his parents west of the village, where they cultivated a few hectares. Until he caught a glimpse of Vicky, he came to town rarely. After he saw her walking up a stone street from the beach on the afternoon of the second day of her stay in the village, he was there every morning. With flowers.

"He's not courting you," Covadonga explained. "He's paying tribute to your trouble. Once he saw you, the plight of Wyatt Willis was no longer abstract to Fulgencio. It became very real to him, and now he must express what he feels."

"The flowers make me uncomfortable."

"They shouldn't."

"I can't help thinking he wants something from me that I can't give him."

"This isn't Madrid, Victoria. It's not even Sevilla. This is Sor Epi, and he is Fulgencio. That's the way it is."

The flowers he brought her were wild, some days, although sometimes they were clearly purchased from a florist, and Vicky worried because he was spending money he shouldn't. He dropped the flowers off early, before she came down from her room for breakfast, leaving a bouquet in a basket or wrapped in ribbon on the doorstep, where Covadonga retrieved them. The widow took them from their wrapper, clipped the stems, placed them in a vase, and placed the vase on the table at which her American guest drank her coffee and ate her rolls with butter and marmalade in the morning.

"They're beautiful," Vicky said reflexively the first time she saw the flowers.

"They're for you," Covadonga told her.

Vicky shook her head. Someone had made a mistake.

On the second day, the bouquet was twice the size of the first. Flowers spilled from the vase.

"I don't want these," Vicky told her landlady. "How do I send them back without offending him?"

Covadonga shook her head. She lit her fifth cigarette of the morning, coughed, and absorbed a little of the protective smoke down deep into her lungs, where its coating action soothed. "So what's the problem? You don't like flowers?"

Vicky liked flowers. In fact, after one bouquet included damp sprigs of a flower with tiny pale purple blossoms she had never seen before, she began to experience a kind of visual addiction to them. As soon as she woke, she anticipated her bouquet. While she showered, her eyes craved seeing flowers. She began taking them to her room after breakfast. She picked a petal, crushed it between her fingers, and inhaled the fragrance from the bruise.

On her third day in the village, Vicky's mother had called. "I want to come wait with you."

"No, please. Not now. I'll call you when I'm ready."

"Are you sure?"

"I'm sure, Mother. Do you remember that story you told me about my father?"

There was a hesitation, as though even now it might be a security breach to talk about her dead husband's line of work. "What about your father, Vicky?"

"A friend checked into it for me. You were right. He was a spy."

"If it hurts, honey, then I'm sorry I told you."

But William Tipton's desertion no longer bothered Vicky. She didn't have room for it. She had her own story. She didn't need her missing father's anymore.

At the end of the fifth day, Covadonga told her, "Fulgencio called. He would like to come by and read you some poetry. Don't worry, they're not his own poems. Fulgencio couldn't write a poem to save his life. He has picked out some of the classics."

"I don't want to encourage him."

"You don't understand yet, do you?"

"Then explain it to me."

"Fulgencio's mind doesn't work the way you think it does. Neither does his heart. If you say no, you will wound him as no man deserves to be wounded."

"But what does saying yes mean?"

The landlady looked up from the playing cards arranged in front of her on the desktop where she kept her calculator, her sign-in book to register guests, her telephone, and a pad of paper to write notes to herself. "It suggests that you are a woman in trouble, and the civilized response is to express his fellow-feeling with you."

Vicky wasn't sleeping well. The most she managed was an uneasy state more like a daydream than sleep, in which awareness of her surroundings prevented her from any real rest. It was as though her consciousness had been divided in two, and the strong half was assigned guard duty. Lying in bed the night before Fulgencio visited, she pictured the face of an American Studies professor from Grenada she had met at a conference.

"Of course you prefer Andalusian Spanish," he was informing her. "That's because the Spanish we speak in Andalusia sounds so similar to the Spanish your ear was accustomed to hearing in Latin America."

She should have known. In Retiro Park, she and Jack should have run screaming from the Colombians in National Police uniforms. Instead, she let the wrong inference register. They spoke a certain way, so they must be from Andalusia. She kept walking and got into the van even though it struck her as odd that there were no markings on it, nothing to indicate that it was an official police vehicle.

She got out of bed and broke Covadonga's house rule about not letting environmental contamination in. She threw open the window and leaned out to breathe. The *pensión* was three blocks up from the beach. The intimate percussive sound of the waves satisfied the ear.

Nothing about the Justice Concept suggested that they would be willing to compromise. They got Vic Flagler, the consul general. And Vicky's boss, Art Harris. And Mike Mara, a junior guy from the political section who had arrived from Chad three weeks before he was picked up by the Justice Concept, exhilarated by living in a place in which things worked: telephones, water faucets, public buses; in Madrid, everything worked. And the press attaché, and the administrative counselor, and a woman from the economic section who had once played bucket bass in a jug band and added numbers in her head with the precision of a calculator. And the guy from the foreign commercial service who spent his vacations walking across the provinces of Spain taking black-and-white photographs of chapels. And, perhaps by mistake, an English teacher from the American School of Madrid.

And Wyatt Willis. Over and over Vicky imagined the Colombians hurting him, and Wyatt working out a plan to get away. He was so good with people, so convincing. He knew how to read all the signals people sent to one another. If there was a way to escape, Wyatt would find it.

She didn't think, really, that there *was* a way.

Because she thought so much about Wyatt, most of the time she was able not to think about Jack Baines. She didn't want to think about Jack.

When he came to read, Fulgencio was courtly and formal. After six poems, none of which Vicky knew, he cleared his throat.

"The people of Sor Epi," he began. But he stopped to cough self-consciously. "The people of Sor Epi wish to express their great sadness."

"Thank you," she said.

She was surprised how badly she wanted to hear what he had to say.

"We have read in the newspaper, and we have heard on the radio, that the government of Spain is cooperating with the government of the United States to rescue the American diplomats and bring the terrorists to justice. It is our sincere hope that these goals will be accomplished very soon, and that you will be restored to the company of your friend Mr. Wyatt Willis, vice consul in the embassy in Madrid. As you wait for that much desired conclusion to this sad affair, please know that the people of this village wait with you. We in Sor Epi shall wait with you no matter how long it takes."

She wanted to cry in gratitude. But she thought Fulgencio, representing the whole village, might expect her to demonstrate her strength with reserve. When he left, he kissed her hand, and Covadonga cried in Vicky's place for her.

Two days later, Marc Karulevich called from Madrid. She took the call at Covadonga's reception desk on an old black rotary phone with an echo in the earpiece. The landlady knew she should let Vicky carry on her conversation in private, but she couldn't quite bring herself to leave the room. She lit a cigarette and paced back and forth, twisting a blue handkerchief into knots with her free hand.

"Are you okay, Vicky?"

"I'm okay. Is there news?"

"Yes. I have some news for you," he told her slowly. "But I can't get into it on an open line like this. Come back to Madrid and we'll talk. Don't go to the embassy, though. Call me when you get here."

"But is it good news?"

He paused for a moment, and through the bad earpiece she heard him breathe in and then exhale a controlled jet of air.

"It's not bad news," he said. "Come back to Madrid and I'll tell you."

"I'm coming."

Saying good-bye to Covadonga felt like leaving family. She felt like a teenager setting out on her own after a sheltered childhood in a small town where everybody doted on her. She thought she should leave something for Fulgencio—a token of some kind, something to remember her by—but Covadonga reassured her that it wasn't necessary. News, that was the only thing they wanted from Vicky. They would not forget her; she should not forget them. She promised her landlady she would call when there was news.

Driving back to Madrid was like rowing across an immense, bright lake. Leaving Sor Epi in Wyatt's green Opel, she headed toward Huelva and then picked up the highway east toward Sevilla. Andalusia was interminable. Even with sunglasses, the fierce sun gave her a headache, and her eyes stung. Horses and cattle moved sluggishly across the dry brown fields. Towns full of boxy white houses were frozen still in the heat, and the few people out on the streets looked out of place, as though coming out into the summer heat had been an accident, and now they were dazed.

On the steep slope of a hill covered with yellow brush, a huge black bull loomed larger than landscape in the middle of a pasture. As Vicky approached, the bull didn't get any smaller, and she realized it was a billboard for Osborne Sherry, an advertisement for a Spain even the Spaniards were nostalgic for, the Spain the tourists came for but couldn't seem to find.

She couldn't have the radio on. The story of the kidnapped American diplomats continued to dominate the airwaves. Sometimes they read the names of all the embassy people who had been abducted, making it sound as though they were dead.

Outside of Córdoba, along the Guadalquivir River, she hit the first police roadblock. A squad of Guardia Civil had made a barricade of their official vehicles and were stopping cars traveling in both directions. The thin policeman with a pinched white face who studied her driver's license and Wyatt's registration seemed nervous, as if he couldn't quite make sense of what he was seeing. When she offered to show him her diplomatic passport, her smile felt false, as though she were acting a part she was not temperamentally suited to play.

He took her documents and walked them over to a black SEAT sedan where his boss sat in the backseat, overseeing the operation out of the direct sunlight. When he returned her papers, he apologized stiffly. His reaction was as strained as hers. He had not expected to stop an American diplomat.

Traveling north and east toward Madrid, Vicky had the impression of driving across time. She was rowing against the current. No matter how fast she drove Wyatt's car, she wasn't going to be able to make up for what she had lost. She stopped at a convenience store and bought a packet of aspirin and a bottle of cold water. She drank a cup of coffee, but it was bitter and the acid burned her stomach. The tips of her fingers, she noticed, each ached separately.

In the afternoon, she hit two more roadblocks. They were part of the effort to control movement across the country and locate the kidnapped Americans. She was waved through the first one, as the policeman in her lane took note of the diplomatic license plate. At the second, she was stopped again, and the officer who inspected her papers recognized Wyatt's name on the registration.

They held her for twenty tense minutes until they satisfied themselves that she was in fact an American and an accredited diplomat and that she had permission to drive a car that belonged to one of the kidnap victims they were looking for. The effort it took to explain herself and the time she lost rattled her, and she left the highway thinking she might do better on back roads.

But north of Valdepeñas she was stopped at a fourth roadblock, and this time it took forty-five minutes for the police to be satisfied that she was not part of the problem they were trying to solve. They were apologetic, they were brisk and courteous, but they were extremely cautious. They did not want to be the unit that let a terrorist get away.

Following the Fourth of July incident with the Americans, there had been an upwelling of outrage across Spain. It was preposterous, it was unacceptable, that Colombian terrorists, aided by a Basque ETA cell, had been able to impersonate uniformed officers in downtown Madrid. The sense of shame was felt even more intensely among the police themselves.

By the time the police released Vicky it was getting late, and her nerves were shot. She stopped at the first place along the road she came to. In a ramshackle town called Manzana Pelada, located alongside a newly built industrial park, she rented a room and fell quickly asleep on a very hard mattress in a very small bed.

In the morning she woke at four-thirty but didn't want to get out of bed. She forced herself to get up, dressing in the dark as though she were hiding. Leaving her room, she thought, for some reason, about her father in Vietnam. She pictured him striding into an ambush to save Nelson Ruff from the Viet Cong. She thought about an American tourist, a matronly woman with unnatural orange hair and violet nail polish, who had once waited outside the embassy on Serrano until the consulate closed and Wyatt came out. After she was robbed, Wyatt had helped her recover her stolen documents. The moment he appeared on the street, the woman lunged to hug him, announcing in a loud voice to anyone who would listen that Wyatt Willis was a credit to the nation he served.

She also thought about the persistence with which Jack Baines had tried to lie to her, and how miserably he had failed.

Downstairs, there was no one at the desk. But in the lobby she found an old man, in a brown uniform with a security badge and polished boots, reading *ABC*. Without asking or explaining, he got up and served Vicky coffee and buttered toast, treating her with exactly the right mix of courtesy and reserve that she needed.

She drove fast as the day dawned, and it was still early when she reached Madrid. There wasn't much of a rush hour. It was still July, but the *madrileños* had gotten a jump on their traditional August vacations, and the traffic in the streets was manageable.

She drove to the garage on Almagro where Wyatt rented a space for the Opel and left the car there. Then she walked until she found a pay phone. On Calle Jenner, she heard birds twitter reassuringly in old trees. There was dew on an iron bench, and a small, steady breeze, and a transvestite prostitute in black fishnet stockings walking toward a bus stop, his blouse open, bra unhooked to reveal his perfect alabaster breasts. The sense of momentary peace that Vicky felt in the city she loved seemed like a trick.

Marc answered on the first ring. "I'm here," she told him.

"You haven't checked in at the embassy yet, have you?"

"I just got here."

"Good."

"Where do you want to meet?"

He thought for a moment; she thought she heard the tension in his voice. "Come to my apartment. I live in Lavapiés."

He gave her the address, and she flagged down a taxi. She knew it was absurd to suspect the driver. He was young, thin, and badly dressed. He might have been from anywhere: the Maghrib, or a dry village in Murcia, or someplace in Latin America. He punched the meter button but didn't say a word to her. He handled his gearshift poorly, but that was no reason to think he was a terrorist in disguise.

When he opened the door of his apartment, Marc Karulevich

looked as though he hadn't slept. Red lines tracked across the whites of his eyes. He needed a shave, and he hadn't combed his hair. He was wearing jeans and a dark green T-shirt, and his feet were bare.

"You want coffee?"

"Is it made?"

"It can be."

She followed him through his bachelor-spare apartment into the kitchen, where he turned the radio on and twisted the volume button to high. The fatuous babble of a talk-show host annoyed Vicky, and she willed herself to tune him out. He had nothing to say about American foreign policy that she was willing to listen to.

"I'm about to break every rule in the book," Marc told Vicky as he handed her a blue ceramic mug of coffee. He pointed her to a chair and shoved a container of milk and a glass sugar bowl across the table in her direction.

She understood that the radio was on to cover their conversation. She also understood that at some point Marc would be required to take a polygraph test, and that one of the questions would be whether he had ever passed on compartmented information to an uncleared person without specific authorization from his supervisor. The answers he gave would have a bearing on his career. Although she was walking away by choice from her own career, Vicky did not despise him for wanting to hang on to his.

He was visibly uneasy, not his normal cocky self. She liked him a little more, in that moment, than she had when he was in complete control of himself and his surroundings.

"It's about Wyatt, isn't it?" she prompted him.

He nodded. He was not reconsidering his decision to tell her what he knew, only choosing his words with care before he spoke. He squinted and rubbed his eyes like a man waking up who hadn't had enough sleep. He gulped half a mugful of coffee.

"We think we know where they're holding him."

"You think?"

He frowned, but not at her. "We're ninety-five percent sure."

"Where? Is he still in Spain?"

He shook his head. "Don't ask me questions I can't answer, please."

"Then tell me what you *can* tell me."

"We may have located Mara, too. The new guy in the political section. Do you know him?"

"I know him. He came from Chad."

"We're less sure about him than we are about Wyatt."

"Then go get them."

"It's not that simple."

"Yes, it is. Go get him." She felt the anger rising. Anger was much better than fear; it was safer and more productive.

"We're watching them, Vicky. If we're lucky, they'll lead us to some of the others."

"But you don't know that for sure."

"No," he agreed, "we don't know that for sure."

"And you do know for sure that Wyatt's alive, and you know where he is."

"As sure as we can be."

"Bastards," she said. She stood up, looked down on him with contempt. "You're risking Wyatt's life, and maybe Mara's, to take a chance on getting the others. The others may be dead, for all you know."

He looked even more uncomfortable than he had, and more worn out. "I figured I owed you the information, Vicky," he said quietly.

She was looking hard at him. He looked just as hard back at her.

"I'm sorry," she said. She struggled to back down. "I appreciate what you're doing."

"When the time comes," he said, "we'll make our move."

"Wyatt was leaving the foreign service to go with me. Did you know that?"

He shook his head again. "I've gone over the edge with you," he told her. "When there's more I can tell you, I'll be in touch. Are you going to the embassy?"

"I can't. Not today."

"When you do, heads up. Your favorite writer has been calling day and night asking for you. He even got through to Duffey. He demanded to know your number. He said something about it being his constitutional right."

"According to the *New York Times,* Jack Baines is a hero."

"I read the editorial. All about using his impeccable leftist credentials to try and broker a solution with the Colombians, and then being shot for his pains. I don't know where they got that crap. In my book, the guy is still scum. If he'd had the guts to talk to us in the beginning, maybe we could have stopped the whole thing before it went down."

"You weren't there," she said, meaning Marc Karulevich wasn't at El Refugio when a handful of Spanish police came down the road toward the hunting lodge with high-powered rifles and a bullhorn and the advantage of knowing the ground they were hunting on.

Jack and Vicky were in the kitchen with the two phony cops, who had untied the Americans so they could use the bathroom, drink something, feed themselves.

"Just so you understand," the hulking one explained as his partner untied Jack's hands. "You two aren't the only assets we have."

"What Raimundo means to say," the slight one clarified, "is that if you do something stupid like try to run away from us, or anything else that we don't like, then shooting you becomes an acceptable cost, since there are so many of you. We can afford a loss if we have to take one."

"Fuck your ugly mothers," Jack said to him in English then. His smile stretched the limits of his mouth and of his emotional constitution. "Up their hairy asses. Both of them."

"We understand what it is you're telling us," Vicky interpreted to the Colombians for him, "and we agree."

The driver came in from outside wiping grease from his hands on a white terry cloth towel. He was whistling another Mexican tune, a *ranchera* this time. He was sweating. His T-shirt clung to his thin, boyish chest.

"Is it ready?" Raimundo asked him, and Vicky realized they were going to change cars and keep moving. She wondered which was worse, staying put in the country in a place no one would think to look for them, or moving farther away from the capital in a second vehicle.

The driver took off his beret, fanned his face with it, and grinned. He had the teeth of a small shark, and the ragged beginnings of a goatee, and a light in his black eyes that signified the marriage of commitment to the cause and pleasure in the execution of the plan. Vicky had heard one of the other men call him Fredo.

So fast.

Because she never heard the name of the third Colombian, the slight one, Vicky gave him one. Osvaldo. It was Osvaldo who picked up the sound of the police car coming down the hill.

"You stay with them," Osvaldo ordered Fredo, who drew a stubby black pistol from his belt, behind his back, where he must have stuck it while he checked out the car in the barn.

Raimundo and Osvaldo went back through the living room toward the foyer.

Fast.

The sound Jack made as he lurched toward Fredo did not form itself into words. There was anger in it, and a brittle bleat of fear, and outrage. He stumbled, or else he pretended to stumble. He wanted to fall onto the driver and take him down, or he didn't. He wanted to give Vicky a break, or he didn't. He knew he was going to get shot in the chest. Or he didn't. Falling forward, he wrapped his arms around the driver's own skinny chest, and Fredo went down with him in a body tangle that gave Vicky the moment she needed to pick up a liter water bottle from the kitchen table. The bottle was glass. It was empty. It broke when it came into hard contact with Fredo's head. Because she was moving it was difficult to say whether the blood she saw came from Jack or from the Colombian she'd clobbered.

"What the hell is going on out there, Fredo?" Raimundo called from the foyer, but he didn't come looking; he had Spanish police on his mind.

There was firing from the foyer, and from outside the house. They were single shots, not a volley, like a small number of men taking careful aim, more like sport than fear or fury. She could distinguish the sounds made by the weapons belonging to the Spanish police from the Colombians' guns, but what difference did that make? There was a window in the kitchen. She went through it like an empty sack and fell onto the sun-baked dirt in the backyard. She got up and ran. There was a chance the police might mistake her for one of the Colombians, but waiting for Raimundo or Osvaldo to come at her from the other direction terrified her more than running did. They were in the country. There was nobody around. There was no reason Fredo would have removed the key from the ignition of the van. He hadn't. She drove blindly away from the sound of firing. She thought, as she drove, that Jack Baines was dead.

"The last Colombian, the big one, died yesterday in the hospital in Cuenca," Marc told her.

"Raimundo," she said. "That was his name."

She was walking toward the door. She didn't want to be around Marc Karulevich any longer.

"He was conscious, off and on, but he wasn't in any condition to answer any questions. The Guardia Civil in Cascadas Nebulosas are efficient with their firearms. Shooting straight is a point of honor for them. So is getting in position to have a clear shot."

"You'll get Wyatt out, won't you? It's just a question of deciding when."

"We'll get him," he promised. "But you have to be on your toes, Vicky. There's nothing to say the Justice Concept won't try something else."

"They couldn't. The whole world is watching, now."

"They've already pulled off one unbelievable operation. They must be feeling pretty goddamn good about that. I wouldn't put any money on them not trying again. They're on a roll."

She opened the door. "Good-bye, Marc."

He raised his hand as if he wanted to cradle her face in his palm, but then let it drop.

"How about I call you for dinner? Tomorrow. We can go some-place we won't run into anybody we know."

"I don't think that would be a good idea."

"You know something?" He shook his head, but then made up his mind to say more. "We could have been an item, you and me. You don't dislike me as much as you think you do. Me, I'm honest. I admitted to myself the first time we talked that I'd do anything to have a chance with you."

She shook her head. "You can't convince me if you don't convince yourself first. It sounds like something you wish were true. But it's not, and you know it."

"What about dinner?"

"Bad idea, Marc, let's leave it at that."

She kissed him. She didn't mind the taste of his lips. He smelled of coffee. Then she let herself be embraced for a moment.

He let her go. She was glad she wasn't having dinner with him.

Outside in the street, she stood in the morning shadow of his building for a few minutes to clear her head. She could not bring herself to go back to her apartment, not yet. Being there was too much like waiting for bad news in the emergency room of a hospital.

She went instead to the Plaza Hotel. Better to get it over with. At the front desk, she asked which room Mr. J. J. Baines was staying in. The receptionist, a tightly wound, middle-aged woman who seemed to disapprove of her, or else maybe she'd had contact with Jack and didn't like him, connected her on the house phone.

"Jack, it's Vicky Sorrell."

"Christ, Vicky, it's about time."

"Are you okay?"

"What do you mean, am I okay? Where the hell are you?"

"I'm downstairs in the lobby. I'll come up."

He was standing outside the door waiting for her. He was wearing blue silk pajama pants and a black, kimono-style robe. The robe was open in front so that she could see the bandages covering his chest and abdomen. There was a spot of dried brown blood on the bandages.

"You want some flowers, Victoria?"

There were bouquets everywhere in the room. He pointed them out to her.

"That's from my editor. Those are from my agent. This one is from my Spanish publisher. These are from the woman who translated *Mario Moving* into Spanish."

"The flowers are nice, Jack."

"Yeah, they're nice, aren't they?"

He looked older. When you were shot in the chest at fifty, it took time to heal, and it aged you. He had had time and motive to contemplate his own mortality.

"I thought you were dead, Jack. When Fredo shot you."

He laughed but cut it off when it came out like a bark. "You did the right thing, getting out. You're a resourceful woman, you know that?"

"When are you going home?"

"Not until I can stand the thought of sitting in an airplane for ten hours."

"They told me you called the embassy."

He flared. "Yeah, what the hell is that all about? They've been keeping the whereabouts of their cultural attaché a goddamn state secret."

"Why did you want to talk to me?"

"I wanted you to see the damage that was done to me."

His self-pity was too much to put up with. She pushed back.

"People have been shot before, Jack. You're alive, thank God. You're up and around. You'll get over it. Besides, you're a hero."

"For the record, I didn't ask the *Times* to do that editorial. As soon as I'm feeling up to it, I'll do a rebuttal. But I'm not talking about getting shot, I'm talking about what the whole lousy experience has done to me. I can't write anymore. I've tried. I can't write a word. I can't even write my name on a piece of paper."

"It's a temporary setback. Your system was shocked. You'll get past it."

"Easy for you to say. It doesn't feel temporary to me, Vicky. It feels like . . . It feels like I've been reamed out, and there's nothing left inside."

"And that's my fault?"

"You're part of it."

"Part of what?"

"The American world-domination machine that brings this bad shit on."

"Go to hell, Jack."

"Do I have to spell it out for you? I'm afraid."

"It's over," she said. "You don't have to be afraid anymore." She wasn't sure she believed that.

"But I *am*. I can't help it. I'm afraid they'll come at me again. Not my nephew this time. Me, Jack Baines. They could, you know. Can you guarantee me they won't?" His voice was pitched so high he almost whined.

"No," she told him, "I can't guarantee they won't. I can't guarantee anything at all."

"Well, then," he said.

He had made his case. He stood picking at the flowers in one of the larger bouquets, pulling the petals from daisies and tulips and letting them drop onto the floor.

"I can't write," he told her again. "I'm scared shitless. It's not temporary."

"You should go home, Jack. Your part in this nightmare is over."

"What about you?"

"I'm waiting. Until it's over. Until they get our people back."

He nodded as if she had finally said something that made sense, something he could understand. He pulled the belt of his beautiful black robe around his torso and cinched it.

"I just figured it out," he said as she moved toward the door. She wasn't sure he meant to be talking to her, except that he had raised his voice.

"Figured what out?"

"Why you're so goddamn appealing. It's because you're so clean. You're a very clean person, Vicky Sorrell."

He gave her a yellow rose from one of his bouquets but made sure his hand didn't touch hers when he did.

"You're going to be okay, Jack."

"You think so? Good-bye, Vicky."

"Good-bye."

Downstairs in the lobby, the severe woman at the reception desk adjusted her hair bun and glared at the good-looking black-haired girl who had arrived to take her place. Vicky looked for a wastebasket and tossed the rose into it.

She stepped outside onto the sidewalk. She could no longer avoid going back to her apartment. She was glad that the Prado was filling up with pedestrians. The city bustled.

Just north of the hotel, two Guardia Civil policemen were standing in dappled shade. Vicky tried not to look at them directly, but she couldn't help taking in the green uniforms, the guns, the black patent leather Bonaparte hats. They looked almost like twins. They were the same height, they had the same stance. Even their faces were similar, long in the jaw and with the same square cheekbones.

She didn't really believe that the Colombians would try the same trick twice. The Spanish authorities would be scrutinizing every policeman on the street, looking for fakes. That was how people reacted, how governments responded. They spent everything they had bracing for the last attack, because they couldn't imagine where the next one was coming from. There was no reason to think that the men on the corner were anything but what they looked like.

Unless they were watching the Palace to see when Jack Baines came out.

One of the twin policemen lit a cigarette. She tried to remember whether she had ever noticed a Guardia smoking on duty before. Was that allowed? How could she not remember?

She stood there for a minute feeling conspicuous and foolish. She looked at her watch, realized she wasn't wearing one.

This was the way it was going to be. For a while; maybe forever. But she couldn't call Marc Karulevich for help every time somebody on the street spooked her. She had to get used to it, just as she had told Jack.

The Guardia with the cigarette looked casually in Vicky's direction and said something to his partner, who stared openly at her.

It couldn't happen twice. Her nerves were bad, that was all.

Her apartment in Bilbao lay to the north. To go in that direction, she would have to pass the two Guardia. She didn't, she couldn't. Feeling a slow prickle in the back of her neck, Vicky walked south down the Prado. She was taking the long way home.

ABOUT THE AUTHOR

Mark Jacobs is a former foreign service officer who served as cultural attaché and information officer in Spain, Turkey, and several posts in Latin America. He has published three previous books and more than sixty short stories in a range of literary and commercial magazines.